An All Night Man

DON'T MISS THESE FABULOUS ANTHOLOGIES
FROM ST. MARTIN'S PRESS

•

Welcome to Leo's
Sistahood of Shopaholics
Rosie's Curl and Weave
Della's House of Style
Island Magic
Let's Get It On

An All Night Man

With stories from

Brenda Jackson

Joylynn Jossel

Kayla Perrin

Tamara Sneed

ST. MARTIN'S GRIFFIN
New York

AN ALL NIGHT MAN.
"The Hunter" copyright © 2005 by Brenda Streater Jackson
"Just Wanna Love Ya" copyright © 2005 by Joylynn Jossel
"Never Satisfied" copyright © 2005 by Kayla Perrin
"Fantasy Man" copyright © 2005 by Tamara Sneed

All rights reserved. Printed in the United States of America. No part of this book may be used or reproduced in any manner whatsoever without written permission except in the case of brief quotations embodied in critical articles or reviews. For information, address St. Martin's Press, 175 Fifth Avenue, New York, N.Y. 10010.

www.stmartins.com

Design by Kathryn Parise

ISBN 0-312-32877-X
EAN 978-0312-32877-1

First Edition: February 2005

10 9 8 7 6 5 4 3 2 1

CONTENTS

•

"The Hunter" by *Brenda Jackson*   1

"Just Wanna Love Ya" by *Joylynn Jossel*   89

"Never Satisfied" by *Kayla Perrin*   161

"Fantasy Man" by *Tamara Sneed*   263

THE HUNTER

Brenda Jackson

So teach us to number our days,
that we may apply our hearts unto wisdom.

—PSALMS 90:12

1.

Hunter Sloan wondered if a man could die from horniness, and if so, he was about to take his last breath.

His sexually intense affair with Mallory Standish had ended six months ago, but still, as he watched her pace back and forth in his office after arriving unexpectedly less than ten minutes ago, he couldn't help but admit the time he'd spent with her had been unforgettable, which was one of the main reasons for his present sexually deprived state. Since they had split he had not been attracted to any other female.

Mallory was everything a man could want in a woman. She was intelligent, sensitive, witty, and passionate with a capital P. The latter is what he remembered the most. It was hard to think about anything else while his gaze took in everything about her. She was too damn good-looking for her own good, not to mention his. Everything about her was a total turn-on, especially her walk... even when she was clearly agitated about something.

At thirty-four he was a man who avoided commitments and Mallory had decided during some point in their four-month affair, that she had wanted more. Unfortunately, more was the one thing he could not give her or any other woman. It had been a mutually agreed-upon decision, that since they wanted different things out of the relationship, the best thing to do was to go their separate ways. So they had, and this was the first time they had seen each other since that time.

And he was definitely seeing her.

His gaze scanned her from head to toe, taking in the dark chocolate coloring of her skin, her pert nose, high cheekbones, and bright red lips. Then there were the dark brown spiral curls that crowned her face and bathed her shoulders, giving her a radiant look. And he definitely liked the business suit she was wearing. It was chic, stylish, and fit the curves on her body as if it had been designed just for her.

There wasn't a time she didn't look good in anything she'd worn, even jeans... especially jeans. His favorite outfit had been tight jeans with a low-cut top. But he had to admit the outfit she was wearing now was running a close second. The skirt was short, stopping way above her knees and showing off long, gorgeous legs—legs he distinctively remembered having the ability to wrap tightly around him while he thrust in and out of her with quick and deep strokes. Then there were her breasts. He couldn't help but recall how it felt to caress them, cup their fullness in the palm of his hands, and tease her nipples with the tip of his tongue. There also were those times when he used to lick around her navel before his lips would nuzzle lower to give her an intimate kiss between her . . .

"Hunter! Are you listening to me?"

He quickly met her gaze. She was annoyed with his distraction, but he was glad she was clueless as to why his mind had shifted elsewhere. With tremendous mental as well as a physical effort, Hunter forced his attention back to what Mallory had been saying, and away from the enormous erection that was straining against his zipper. He shifted in the chair he was sitting in behind his desk, grateful that she had no idea as to the torture she was putting him through, and even more grateful that she didn't know that he hadn't slept with another woman since their breakup.

"Let me get this straight, Mallory," he said in a somewhat strained voice. "You are accusing your brother-in-law of being unfaithful?"

Hunter saw her uncertainty when she answered. "Yes and no. All I know is what I saw."

Hunter nodded. "How about telling me again what you saw." He hated admitting it but he hadn't heard a word she'd said. Instead he had been wondering how long it would take to strip her naked, like he had done once before when she'd come to his office unexpectedly. He would never forget how he had taken her on this very desk. "And maybe it will be better if you sit down," he added, not knowing how much longer he could handle seeing the sway of her hips while she paced back and forth wearing out his carpet, not to mention wearing on his libido.

Thankfully, she nodded and took the chair across from him. But then he almost groaned when she crossed her legs, which made the already short skirt inch a little higher, showing a better glimpse of her thighs. They were thighs he used to ride, from the front, from the back, right to left, any way and every way he could. Even now he could hear in his mind the sound of flesh slapping against flesh.

His attention was drawn to the gold ankle bracelet on her right ankle. He had given it to her after they had dated a couple of months. It had been a gift for her twenty-eighth birthday. He was surprised she was still wearing it and a part of him was glad that she was. He would never forget the night he had given it to her and how she hadn't wasted any time thanking him in some of the most provocative ways. It was definitely a pleasant memory.

He shifted in his chair again and decided it would be safer to concentrate on something that was not pleasant, like the thought of going to dinner at his aunt Judith's house that evening when she would relentlessly remind him that he needed to settle down, get married, and have a lot of babies for her and his mother to spoil. In fact it was his aunt's fault that he had met Mallory in the first place.

Aunt Judith had convinced him that he needed to hire an event planner for his parents' fortieth wedding anniversary party. He had delegated the task of finding someone to his aunt and would never forget the day she showed up at his office with Mallory in tow. The attraction between them had been quick and immediate and his life hadn't been the same since.

Hunter sighed as he brought his thoughts back to the present and his gut clenched when Mallory nervously swept her lips with the tip or her tongue. Boy, he used to thoroughly enjoy that tongue. Forcing his mind back to the business at hand, he again prompted her. "Now, what makes you think he's cheating?"

"Because I saw him yesterday at a hotel. I was there and I saw him."

Hunter raised a brow. The first question that immediately came to his mind was why was she at a hotel? And who had she been there with? His heart began beating like a jackhammer and he forced himself to calm down. He had no right to question what she did and with whom she did it. But still, the possibility that she'd been at a hotel with someone didn't sit too well with him. He, of all people, knew just how passionate she was. He'd had quite a few sizzling nights with her but it was either at her place or his . . . never a hotel. He hoped she hadn't gotten involved with a married man. A part of him refused to believe that. One thing Mallory possessed was a high sense of what was moral and, besides, her father had relentlessly cheated on her mother, so she would never do that to another woman or herself.

He cleared his throat. "You were at a hotel yesterday?" he asked as casually as he could.

She leaned back in her chair unaware of the chaos going on in his head. "Yes. I had an appointment at the Hilton on Monroe Street. I'm planning a client's daughter's wedding and we're holding the reception there. I needed to check the location to make sure the banquet room would be adequate."

He nodded his head. Relieved. "And while you were there, you saw your brother-in-law?" He had met her sister and brother-in-law only once during their four-month affair. From what he remembered, the man seemed to be a likable guy who was very devoted to Mallory's sister, Barbara. Barbara was two years older than Mallory and if he remembered correctly, she and her husband had been married for five years. He also recalled Mallory once sharing with him the couple's desire to have a child, but the last he'd heard Barbara hadn't gotten pregnant.

"Yes, I saw Lewis," Mallory answered, breaking into his thoughts. "I tried to get his attention, but he didn't see me. He was too busy trying to get on the elevator without being seen. I noted it had stopped on the fourth floor before coming back down. I caught it back up to the fourth floor thinking there was probably a conference room on that floor and Lewis was attending some sort of business meeting, but all I saw were rooms. Hotel rooms. That meant he was meeting someone in one of those rooms."

"Yes, but that doesn't necessary mean he was doing anything illicit, Mallory," Hunter pointed out. "People do hold business meetings in their suites at hotels."

He watched her nervously chew on her bottom lip before saying, "I know that, Hunter, but I have a funny feeling about this. A few weeks ago Barbara mentioned that she and Lewis were having marital problems. I think it has something to do with the both of them wanting so desperately to have a baby and not being able to have one."

He shook his head. There were a lot of things he desperately wanted, but a baby wasn't one of them. Over the years he had learned to turn a deaf ear to his aunt whenever she brought up the subject of babies. She was quick to remind him that he was the last of the Sloans unless he produced a child to carry on the family name.

When Mallory shifted positions in her seat, Hunter's gaze followed the hem of her skirt and saw even more thigh. "Have they consulted a doctor to see what the problem is?" he asked more because she seemed so concerned about it than of any real interest on his part.

"Yes, but according to all the tests results, there's nothing wrong with either of them."

"Then I'm sure things will happen when it's time."

"Yes, that's what I keep telling Barbara but she thinks the problem is with her."

Hunter picked up a paperclip off his desk and began fiddling with it. He didn't want to talk about people wanting babies any longer. "What do you want me to do, Mallory? Why are you here?"

She gave him an exasperated look like it should have been obvious. "I want to hire you, Hunter. I need to know for sure whether or not Lewis is having an affair."

"And if he is?"

"Then Barbara should know about it."

"And you're going to tell her?"

"Of course, she's my sister."

He sighed and knowing the Standish family history she had shared with him once, he could see her thinking that way. "But why me, Mallory? There are plenty of private investigators here in San Diego."

"Because I want to keep this private, Hunter. I'll feel a lot better if you're the investigator handling this for me. Will you do it?"

Hunter stared at her long and hard as he thought of the problems that could arise if he associated himself with Mallory again, even for a business reason. She would always remind him of sharing a bed, enjoying nights of passion and excitement that culminated in orgasms that came back-to-back for hours. No other woman had the ability to do that.

And no other woman had made him imagine going to bed with her every night and waking up beside her every morning on a permanent basis. When those thoughts had begun formulating in his mind he'd known it was time to cut out, and when she'd thrown out the words "a committed relationship," he hadn't wasted any time putting distance between them. He didn't do committed relationships. What she was asking him to do would bring them back in contact again and a part of him wasn't sure he could handle that.

He took a shaky breath. Hell, he was about to go bonkers just from the twenty minutes they had spent together already. "I don't know, Mallory Considering our history, maybe you should—"

"No, Hunter. There's no one else I'd trust. If Lewis is cheating on Barbara you're the only one I'd want to know about it. I really do need your help."

Hunter knew if he lived a whole lifetime, he would always be drawn in by Mallory's dark brown eyes that were pleading with him now. And for the life of him, he couldn't turn her down.

"Okay, Mallory, I'll do it."

Relief spread across her face. "Thanks, Hunter."

He glanced down at his watch. "There's some information I'll need to get from you before I can start, but I have another appointment in a few minutes. Is there any way we can meet again later today?"

He watched as she quickly pulled her palm-pilot out of her leather purse. Less than a minute later, she said, "My last appointment is at five. Do you want me to stop back by here before going home?"

He frowned. He had an appointment on the other side of town that would last until around five and then he was to join his aunt for dinner at seven, which didn't give them much time in between. The best solution, although he didn't want to suggest it, would be for him to drop by her place on the way to his aunt's house. Bad move if he wanted to keep things strictly business.

Then he thought of another idea. "How about if we met at Rowdy's at five-thirty? I have dinner plans for later and that way we can talk and I won't be late for my seven o'clock dinner date." She didn't have to know that his dinner date was with his aunt. It might be best for the both of them if she thought he was involved with someone.

The expression on her face indicated she didn't care one way or the other. He wasn't sure if he should be relieved or monumentally pissed. "All right, that's fine. I'll be at Rowdy's at five-thirty," she said, standing. "And I really do appreciate this."

He stood and came around his desk to walk her to the door. When they got to the door, he considered locking it and throwing away the key and having his way with her. He knew she liked wearing colorful undies and wondered just what color panties she had on. And he knew that whatever color they were, she was wearing a matching bra.

She reached out her hand to him. "Thanks again, Hunter."

He took her hand and immediately felt a sexual pull in his groin. For a moment he forgot to breathe. The intense attraction, the sensuous connection was still there and although she remained expressionless, he knew she had to have felt it as well.

"You're welcome and I'll see you later this evening, Mallory." The words sounded a lot more intimate than he had wanted them to.

She nodded, then opened the door and quickly slipped out. When the door closed behind her, he leaned against it and drew in a deep breath, then let it out slowly. It shouldn't take long to find out if Lewis Townsend was cheating on his wife. Once that was done Mallory would be out of his life again and he could regain the harmony he had worked so hard to achieve over the past six months, although the horniness was almost killing him. In his present state, if he hung around her too much there was no telling what would happen.

Engaging in another passionate and thrilling affair with Mallory Standish was definitely out of the question.

2

Mallory Standish stepped onto the elevator and was grateful it was empty. After the doors closed behind her, she pushed the button that would take her down to the first floor and expelled the breath she hadn't realized she'd been holding.

It had been hard seeing Hunter again and if it weren't for Barbara she would not have come. But her sister was all the family she had and she was determined to find out the truth one way or another, and like she had told Hunter, she trusted only him to find out.

Hunter.

He was still the tall, dark, and handsome predator. His name suited him well. That had been her first thought when they had first met. She had walked into his office with his aunt and the moment their gazes connected, she had discovered there was such a phenomena as instant attraction.

One of the first things she had noticed about him when they had first met was just how tall he was, way over six feet, with powerfully built shoulders, tapered thighs, and muscular legs. He had returned to the office after playing a game of tennis with a business associate and hadn't yet showered and changed back into his suit. He'd possessed a physique that left her inside tingling and she had quickly reached the conclusion that no man should have been blessed to have it good in both the looks and the body departments.

His dark brown hair was cut low and neatly trimmed, and his face, the color of semi-sweet chocolate, had the most arresting features of any man she had ever met. He was so startlingly handsome that it was both a sin and a shame. The eyes that had locked with hers were stark black, intense and predatory. Since he'd been intent on giving her the same thorough once-over she had given him, it had taken a full two minutes after his aunt had made the introductions before either of them spoke.

In just that span of time her emotions had gone from relatively calm to veering on the edge of turbulent. There was no way she could have ignored the electrifying attraction or the sizzle along her nerve endings when she'd seen him. And when he had taken her hand in his in the appropriate handshake, a tingling warm, pulsing heat had quickly settled between her legs.

She had never had such a physical reaction to a man and it had been the most bizarre thing she'd ever encountered, instant heat had been fueled by a sexual need that she hadn't known could exist. From that first blazing encounter, the die had been cast. It was a foregone conclusion that the two of them would eventually hook up.

And they had.

Although she had been determined to keep things strictly business while working on his parents' anniversary party, she'd been fully aware that he was a man waiting patiently, biding his time. However, as the time came closer to the date of the party, he had become impatient and more than once he had tried coming on to her and she'd known without a doubt that he'd been anxious to make his move.

And when the time had come, he had done so in a very smooth and suave manner the night of the anniversary party. He had not left the country club where the festivities had been held when the party was over. Instead he had hung around while she finalized the very last detail . . . waiting for her. And they left together, ending up at her place where he spent the night.

Yes, she had known all she needed to know about Hunter and his reputation. There were those who referred to him as the untamable Hunter and claimed he had a wild side when it came to women. His reputation was legendary. He was a ladies' man, although indiscriminately so. She'd also heard that he avoided commitments and had often said he didn't plan to settle down until he was well into his forties, and since he hadn't yet reached the age of thirty-five, he had a few more years to go.

But regardless of all that, she thought she could handle Hunter Sloan since she was too caught up in her own work to get serious about anyone. However, fate had dealt her a reality check when by their third date she'd found herself falling heads over heels in love with him. And by the fourth month of their affair she had gained enough courage to test the waters to see if he reciprocated her feelings and had voiced them aloud. Unfortunately, he made it clear what his position was on a serious relationship with any woman: he wasn't interested.

That was not good news for her since she was interested, extremely so. However, Olivia Standish hadn't raised either of her daughters to be fools and Mallory had known that the best thing to do was to walk away with her pride intact although her heart was in shambles.

Over the past six months she had managed to survive the pain and heartache, but now it seemed that fate had brought them back together, even if it was for business. Seeing Hunter again made her realize that she still loved him although she wished it were otherwise.

When the elevator reached her floor and the doors opened, she breathed in deeply as she stepped out. She knew that dealing with Hunter would not be easy, but she was determined to do it. Even if it killed her.

Hours later Hunter walked into Rowdy's and glanced around. He immediately saw Mallory sitting at a table by the window. She was so absorbed in the oceanic view that she hadn't noticed he had arrived. It was just as well since he needed to get his bearings.

For as long as he could remember, cars and women had been the only two things that had held his attention after he graduated from Grambling College. Then he had opened his company and it had become part of the mix. He enjoyed being footloose and fancy free, although he knew his parents and his aunt Judith were hoping he would settle down, get married, and have kids. For some reason they couldn't quite understand that he wasn't in a hurry. There were a lot of things yet for him to experience—places to go, women to do, and he definitely enjoyed doing women. At least he *had* enjoyed doing women but Mallory had even ruined that for him. He couldn't seem to think about sleeping with another woman for fear he would find her lacking. In his mind, no other woman could hold a candle to Mallory Standish in any way. And no matter how many times he had tried convincing himself to move beyond that assumption, he couldn't.

Sighing deeply, he began walking toward her and had just reached the table when she lifted a glass of water to her lips. Immediately, his guts clenched when he remembered all the naughty things he'd taught her to do with those lips.

Heated thoughts flooded his mind. Wicked thoughts. Sexually intense thoughts. He felt his erection beginning to rise and harden and thought it was best to sit down as soon as he could. "Mallory," he said.

She glanced up. Surprised. "Hunter. I wasn't expecting you for another ten minutes or so."

He nodded as he took the chair across from her. "I finished up with my last appointment early." His heart began beating as he glanced around, trying to look at anything but her. This was crazy. Absolutely nuts. Why in the hell was he feeling this way? The nervousness. The tension. She was just a woman. Someone he used to sleep with. The last woman he'd slept with. No big deal.

But when he finally brought his gaze back to her and met her eyes, he knew it was a big deal. There was something about her that he just couldn't shake. Even after six months.

He shook his head, determined to shake it anyway or at least try. "Is water the only thing you're drinking?" he decided to ask.

"Yes. I have a dinner engagement later, too."

Luckily for him, she shifted her gaze to look back out of the window. Otherwise she would have seen the jealousy that flared in his eyes. She would be meeting a man later? For dinner?

To keep his hands from hitting something, he grabbed the menu that sat in a rack on the table. He had to be realistic even if he didn't want to be. It had been six months. Had he really expected her to not get on with her life although for some reason he hadn't been able to get on with his?

He had thrown himself in his work, he had convinced himself that the only reason he hadn't gone back to women was because he'd been too busy. Six months was a long time for a man to go without, especially a man who'd been use to getting some on a pretty regular basis.

"How's your aunt?"

Her question interrupted his thoughts and he glanced up from the menu he was pretending to study and met her gaze. Her expression was cool and he wondered how she could sit so calmly across from him and appear so detached. Whenever he thought of her the one word that always came to mind was hot. That was followed by sexy, beautiful, and passionate.

He decided to answer her question. "Aunt Judith is doing well. She asks about you often."

She smiled as she began fiddling with her water glass and all he could do was sit there and stare at that smile while his need for her escalated another notch.

"I always liked your aunt," she said, before taking another sip of water.

He almost said, *and she likes you, too,* before deciding that wouldn't be a good idea. The last thing he wanted to do was to give her any ideas. Besides, although he loved his aunt dearly, what she liked or didn't like really didn't matter to him, although he had to admit that Mallory had been the first woman he'd gotten involved with that both his mother and aunt had approved of. That should have been the first warning sign and it would have been if he hadn't been so into getting Mallory into his bed. And once he had gotten her there, he hadn't been in any hurry to get her out.

Thank goodness a waiter came at that moment to take their order and the only thing the two of them wanted was coffee. He stared at her for a long moment when her mobile phone went off and she answered it. Moments later, he sat back, relieved. He had listened to enough of her conversation to know the person she would be meeting later for dinner was a girlfriend.

"So what do you want to know about Lewis that could possibly help the investigation?"

Hunter drew in a deep breath and let it out slowly. Although he had been watching her every move he hadn't realized she had ended her conversation and had placed the mobile phone back in her purse until she had spoken. "Does he still work for the IRS?" he asked.

"Yes."

Hunter nodded. That had been another reason he hadn't been overly eager to make friends with Mallory's brother-in-law. Although Hunter paid his fair share of taxes like the next guy, people who worked for the Internal Revenue Service made him nervous. "Do you know whether or not he's been going out a lot at night lately? More so than usual?"

He watched as a frown marred Mallory's forehead as she thought about his questions. "No," she said moments later. "Lewis is a homebody and I can't recall Barbara mentioning that he's started going out at night. In fact, Barbara and I usually talk every night and he's always home in bed already."

"Has he begun talking any business trips?"

"No."

Hunter nodded. "That means if he is involved with someone, he's doing it on his lunch hour."

Mallory brow raised. "His lunch hour? That wouldn't give him enough time, would it?"

His lips curled into a lazy smile. The reason she had probably asked was because whenever they'd made love they would stay in bed for hours and hours. Sixty minutes had not been enough time for them. "It might. Depending on what all he's doing."

He watched as she swallowed hard and saw her lips tremble when she said, "I hope for Barbara's sake that he's not doing anything."

"Well, that's what you've hired me to find out. Starting tomorrow I'll watch how he spends his lunch time."

Mallory nodded. "Anything else you need to know?"

There was something else he needed to know, and it was something that had nothing to do with business. But it was a question that had been gnawing at him every since he had seen her earlier that day and his mind just wouldn't let it go. It was as if he was driven beyond reason to know the answer, like his very life depended on it. "Yes, there is one other thing I need to know, Mallory."

He leaned forward across the table so his next words could not be heard by anyone else. It brought him so close to her, he could clearly see the darkness of her eyes and when she also leaned forward to hear what he had to ask, their mouths almost touched.

When he hesitated, she raised a brow and quietly breathed out her next words through water-damp lips. "What is it, Hunter? What else do you need to know?"

He swallowed and felt his sexual frustrations come to a head when he again remembered that sex with Mallory had been absolutely mind-blowing fantastic every single time. He felt a shiver of heated desire go up his spine and the erection straining against his zipper harden even more. And when she tilted her head slightly, which only inched her lips even closer to his, he couldn't hold back his question any longer.

"I need to know what color panties you're wearing," he whispered.

3

Mallory went still.

Her hand, which had been reaching for her coffee cup, dropped to the table as a small gasp escaped her lips. Of all the questions she had anticipated Hunter asking her, the color of her underwear was definitely not one of them.

She met his gaze, not sure she had heard him right and that she must have imagined his question. However, the heated look in his eyes indicated she had heard him correctly and that he was actually waiting on an answer.

Mallory's eyes went wide. Only the untamable Hunter Sloan thought he could ask such a thing. She sat back in her chair and straightened her spine. "Is there a reason you want to know?" she asked coolly, thinking that he really had a lot of nerve.

He shrugged. "Just curious."

Mallory frowned wondering why he was "just curious." It

wasn't like he would be getting into them so why the interest? He was the one who'd decided to end their relationship six months ago, so the way she saw it the color of her panties was no business of his.

When she saw the intensity of his gaze she couldn't help but remember a time when what she wore under her dress *had* been his business. She had vivid memories of how his dark gaze would sweep over her and his breathing would quicken whenever she would strip down to her panties and bra. And likewise, her body would flare in heat anticipating what was to come.

In the back of her mind she could actually hear the moans she would make when he would remove her bra and then kneel before her to remove the matching pair of colorful, scanty panties she'd worn. But before he would take them off, he would take his hand and stroke her through the material, making her panties soaked as the scent of aroused woman filled the room. He would ease the scrap of lace down her legs and continued to stroke her in such a way that would leave her quivering and gulping for air. Then he would look up at her and give her that damn untamable Hunter smile and proceed to show her just how much he loved that particular area of her body by cupping her hips into his hands and leaning forward, kissing her intimately, letting his tongue thrust deep. She would nearly pass out from his lusty enjoyment of her, eliciting her cry of release and giving her one hell of an orgasm even before they reached the bed.

Bringing her thoughts back to the present, Mallory breathed in deeply, inwardly admitting that she missed those times with him. Hunter was definitely a man who brought fantasies to life. Sex with him had always been incredible, devastatingly wild and bone-curling, desire-filling good.

He had found out rather early in their relationship—that first night to be exact—that he was her first lover. And he had set out to make sure he would be her only lover by raising the bar and raising her expectations high for anyone who followed. When it came to making love to her, his delivery had always been intense, overwhelming, and very gratifying.

Mallory knew that any woman who had an affair with Hunter would be getting the best. That thought reminded her that she was no longer that woman and in fact, in a few hours he would be meeting another woman for dinner. The thought that he wanted to know the color of her panties when he would be seeing someone else later didn't sit too well with her and she became downright angry. She placed her hand in her lap, fighting the impulse to lean over and slap him silly. But then she was too dignified to let any man bring out the worse in her, no matter how much she wanted to lash out in pain.

Deciding she didn't owe him an answer to his question and that they had finished the only business between them for now, Mallory picked up her purse and stood. "Enjoy your dinner date, Hunter, and I would think *she* would be the one whose panties you would be interested in."

Without saying another word Mallory walked out of the restaurant.

"You don't seem to be in a good mood tonight, Hunter."

Hunter glanced up from his meal to stare into the concerned face of his aunt. He knew if he didn't give her a reason for his surly mood she would only continue digging. "I had a rough day," he said, and then as he resumed eating his food, he realized it wasn't far from the truth. He had wanted Mallory to think he'd had dinner plans with another woman. No sooner had Mallory walked out of Rowdy's than he had felt the impact of his deception.

"So when was the last time you saw Mallory?"

Drawing in a slow breath, Hunter lifted his gaze and stared across the table at his aunt. Not for the first time in his life he wondered if she had ESP or something. "Why do you ask?"

She smiled at him. "Just curious."

He swallowed hard. Those had been the same words he'd given Mallory when she had asked why he wanted to know the color of her panties. Even now he couldn't believe he had actually asked her that and far worse was the fact that he still wanted to know. It was as if it was privileged information that he felt that he was entitled to. But he had to be realistic enough to know when it came to Mallory Standish he was no longer entitled to anything.

He placed his fork down, knowing his aunt was waiting on an answer. As casually as he could, he said, "I saw Mallory earlier today." There was no need to tell his aunt that he and Mallory had also shared coffee less then a few hours ago. He leaned back in his chair when he saw his aunt's eyes fill with speculation.

"Really?"

"Yes, and before you ask the answer is no. Mallory and I are not getting back together. It was strictly a business meeting. She thinks her brother-in-law may be messing around on her sister and has hired me to find out if he is or isn't."

"Oh."

He looked at his aunt uneasily. "And what does that mean?"

She smiled that same smile his mother would often give him. And not for the first time he thought that she should have been his mother's sister instead of his father's since the two women had similar mannerisms and thought so much alike. "I meant nothing by it, Hunter. You're a grown man and I think a fairly smart one. It's been six months and if you haven't realized by now that Mallory Standish was the best thing to happen to you then that's your loss." She pushed back her chair and stood. "Now, if you'll excuse me, I'll go into the kitchen to get our dessert. I tried out a new recipe. It's called the 'better than sex' cake and I want you to let me know what you think."

Hunter leaned back in his chair as he watched his aunt leave the room. He didn't have to eat a piece of cake to know there was nothing on this earth that was better than sex, especially if it was with Mallory. Just the thought of kissing her made him hot because locking lips with her always led to other things, intimate and erotic. The woman was so irresistibly sexy he couldn't think straight. And the thought that he had been her first lover still left him in awe. She had been an eager student, a quick learner, a woman who'd taken in everything he had taught her and had put it to good use.

Before he could dwell on his intimate encounters with Mallory any further, his aunt returned with a huge slice of cake on a plate. "Here you are, Hunter. I hope you like it."

He took the plate from his aunt. "I'm sure I will." He took his fork and after tasting the cake, he thought it was good. But not as good as Mallory, and by the time he had finished half of it he had concluded although it was delicious it wasn't better than sex.

"It's a shame about that lunatic on the loose isn't it?"

He looked up from eating his cake and met his aunt's concerned expression. "What lunatic?"

"That man who's going around calling himself The Mighty Charger and attacking all those women."

Hunter frowned. He had remembered reading something about it in the papers. "They haven't caught him yet?"

"No, and I'm concerned that most of the attacks have taken place not far from where Mallory lives. I hope she's taken every precaution to stay safe."

He finished off the last of his cake before responding. "I'm sure she has." He then remembered that she planned to go out with a girlfriend tonight. Had she returned home safely?

He stood quickly knowing he wouldn't rest until he knew for sure. "Look, Aunt Judith, I hate to rush off but I just remembered something that I need to do." He walked around the table and gave his aunt a kiss on the cheek. "Lock the door behind me."

And then he was gone.

So much for getting Mallory out of my life and keeping her there, Hunter thought, a half-hour later while parked in the yard of a vacant house that was directly across the street from where she lived. Her car was not in the driveway, which meant she hadn't come home yet.

If anyone would have told him that he would be spending a good portion of the night waiting for a woman to arrive back home just to make sure she got into her house safely, he wouldn't have believed them.

He eased his car seat back for better comfort and folded his hands across his chest. He had turned off the radio a while ago when nothing was playing that he wanted to hear. He glanced around thinking that he actually liked this older neighborhood of homes and knew that Mallory had bought the house a few years ago not long after her sister had gotten married. Up until that time, she and Barbara had lived together in an apartment while they had worked and attended college.

He straightened when he recognized her car as it pulled into the driveway of her yard. He exhaled a sigh of relief and watched as she got out and walked up to her door. Moments later she went inside and closed the door behind her.

He cursed softly when he felt an overwhelming urge to march up to that house and force her to answer the question he had asked her earlier. He'd never had a fetish for a woman's underwear until he'd made love to Mallory. She used to wear some of the sexiest and most colorful panties and he used to enjoy taking them off of her. For months after their breakup he would still fantasize about her. In fact he still did.

Hunter lost track of time as he just sat there in his car and stared at Mallory's house. Then he figured he had done the gentlemanly thing tonight by making sure she had gotten into her house safely. As he turned on the ignition to start up his car he decided that he would handle the case involving her brother-in-law as quickly as possible so that his life could return to normal.

But for some reason the prospect of that happening didn't seem real.

4

"Boy, don't you look serious."

Mallory glanced up from the huge calendar spread out on her desk and gazed into the smiling face of her sister Barbara. She couldn't help but smile back. Evidently her emotional state was so apparent that Barbara sensed that something was wrong.

As always her sister's appearance into her office always brought a ray of sunshine. At five foot eight in stocking feet with a petite build, which they had both inherited from their mother, Barbara took great pride in the way she looked and always had the ability to garner a lot of men's attention. In fact, they both had, only Barbara was always the one with the willingness to return that attention. She had been able to balance with ease getting her schoolwork done and dating.

Not only was Barbara her sibling but she was also her best

friend. With only a two-year difference in their ages, they had grown up as playmates and confidantes among the chaos that constantly seemed to go on in the Standish household.

Her father, a financial advisor with a major bank, went on numerous business trips and always returned home with sloppy evidence that the trips had been more pleasure than business. Instead of getting fed up with her husband's unfaithfulness, Olivia Standish was the dutiful wife, intent on making her marriage work and providing her daughters with a roof over their heads. However, their father finally took the decision out of their mother's hands when he arrived home one day and announced he wanted a divorce to marry his "young" assistant. Mallory would never forget that day for as long as she lived since it just happened to be on her twelfth birthday.

Although their mother had been devastated by her husband's departure, both Mallory and Barbara had thought, *Good riddance,* and had tried moving on with their lives. It didn't help matters when less than a year later their mother, still suffering from a broken heart, had gotten killed in a car accident.

For Mallory, the moral of the story had been to never grow up and fall in love with a man who had "playboy" tendencies. Yet she had done that very thing after meeting Hunter Sloan.

Barbara, on the other hand, had always looked at things through rose-colored glasses. Her take on the entire Standish family affair was that their father had been a class-ass jerk and that not all men were like him, and had been determined to fall in love with one who wasn't. She and Lewis had met four years ago after Barbara had completed college and gone to work for a huge marketing firm in San Diego. They had met one night at a nightclub and according to her sister it had been love at first sight.

Their courtship had been short and sweet and they had gotten married less than a year later.

Mallory had always liked her brother-in-law, although she did consider him somewhat too serious at times, the complete opposite of Barbara. But it always appeared that he loved Barbara immensely and went out of his way to make her happy. Other than their desperate desire to have a baby, she always considered Barbara and Lewis a happy couple and perfect for each other.

At least she had until that day she'd seen Lewis at the hotel. Like their mother, Barbara would be devastated if she ever discovered Lewis was cheating on her and Mallory hoped and prayed that was not the case.

Standing, Mallory quickly rounded her desk and crossed the room to give her sister a huge hug. "I'm always serious, Barb. You're the playful one. Besides, it's different when you run your own business." She glanced back at the calendar on her desk. "Although business is good for the remainder of the year, I often wonder how I'm going to pull things off. For instance, in two weeks I have three big parties planned on the same day. Luckily, they're at staggered times but still that's almost stretching me thin."

Barbara raised a concerned brow. "Then why did you do it, Mal?"

Mallory smiled. "To stay busy."

From the look on Barbara's face they both knew there was a lot more behind her response. Every since her breakup with Hunter she had been working extremely hard to keep him off her mind. Now it seemed her attempt to do so had been a waste of time since he was definitely back on her mind and had been there since she'd seen him on yesterday.

And then there was the question he'd asked her . . .

"You need a life, Mallory," Barbara said interrupting her thoughts. "Let me introduce you to this guy I was telling you about who works with Lewis. He moved to town recently from Atlanta and—"

"Forget it, Barbara. I'm not interested."

Barbara took Mallory's hand in hers. "I wish you would get interested. I think he would be perfect for you."

Mallory sighed. As far as she was concerned the only perfect guy in her book was Hunter. Although she knew their breakup was the smartest move for the both of them, she had to give him his due. There was an out-and-out sexiness that made any woman want to tumble between the sheets with him. Hunter Sloan was fabulous in and out of bed.

Deciding she needed to change the subject and quick, she asked. "And what brought you by today? Although I'm always glad to see you, I wasn't expecting you. When we talked last night you didn't mention that you would be stopping by."

Barbara folded her arms across her chest. "I took some time off from work today to do a few things and decided to visit. I was worried about you. I didn't like the way you sounded last night. It was as if you were keeping something from me."

If only you knew, Mallory thought, feeling somewhat guilty, and wondering what Barbara would think if she knew that Mallory was having her husband investigated. She sighed, not wanting to think about that since she felt that she was doing the right thing and that it was for Barbara's benefit and future happiness. She didn't want Barbara to become like their mother.

"I'm fine," Mallory tried to assure her. "Like I said a few moments ago, I've been busy a lot lately."

"There is more to what's going on with you than work, Mal,

so don't pretend otherwise and I know it's all because of Hunter Sloan. The way I see it, if you're going to be miserable without him in your life then you may as well be miserable with Hunter and go back to him."

Mallory's eyebrows lifted. "What are you talking about?"

Barbara grinned. "I'm talking about you being sexually deprived. I bet you haven't slept with a man since Hunter."

Mallory frowned. "There is more to a relationship than sex, Barbara."

Barbara's grin widened. "And I agree, but I also think a person shouldn't be alone and miserable. You were always the uptight one, not me. I know you aren't into casual relationships, and that's cool, but you loved Hunter. I can't believe he didn't have any feelings for you, no matter what he said."

Mallory shook her head as she gazed at Barbara. This was her sister who thought everyone should be in love and happy. "Well, he didn't have feelings for me and I've accepted it and moved on. I admit that even after six months it's hard, but I'll survive."

An hour or so after Barbara had left, Mallory was still thinking about the words she had said. Yes, she would survive and eventually she would get over Hunter. However, in the meantime, she would continued to be sexually deprived and was determined to get over that as well.

There was more to a relationship than sex, but at the moment it was a part she definitely missed.

Hunter sat in his parked car and watched as Lewis Townsend walked out of the Federal Building where he worked and strolled across the parking lot to his dark blue sedan.

Keeping at a comfortable distance, Hunter started his car to follow behind Lewis when he pulled into traffic. It was lunchtime and it seemed the man had a destination in mind and Hunter had a feeling it wasn't Burger King. Nor did it appear that he was headed for the same hotel Mallory had seen him at yesterday. He took the interstate and that led in an entirely different direction.

Hunter sighed. He wasn't crazy about getting involved in Mallory's family's affairs but then it was a job. He cursed softly knowing that when it came to Mallory there was nothing he considered as business, even this, as much as he wanted to. During the four months of their affair they had shared an intense physical desire for each other and he had begun getting petrified that it would lead to something more serious. The last thing he had wanted was to begin developing deep feelings for any woman and when he'd discovered he was doing just that, he had thought the best thing to do was to cut out, which is precisely what he'd done. But now, six months later, after seeing Mallory again, he was finding out that out of sight had not been out of mind. He had thought of her a lot, he had craved her a lot. And last night, like a number of other nights, the memories of her had filled his dreams.

His thoughts were momentarily interrupted when Lewis pulled into the parking lot of the Marriott Hotel. Making sure he wasn't seen, Hunter parked in a space across from where Lewis parked his car, then watched as the man got out of the vehicle and, after glancing around a few times, went inside.

It didn't take long for Hunter to get out of his car and follow, still maintaining a safe distance. He hated admitting it but the way Lewis was nervously glancing around and making sure he wasn't recognized by anyone would lead anyone to believe he was definitely doing something he shouldn't. You could tell the man was an amateur at being discreet. If he wasn't in the process of being unfaithful to his wife, he was certainly giving the appearance that he was. No wonder Mallory's suspicions had been raised.

Hunter pulled what appeared to be an ink pen from his top pocket. In truth, the instrument he held in his hand was a miniature digital camera that could pick up a subject as far away as a hundred feet. It had been costly but over the past year had proven to be highly effective. He decided to take a few shots of Lewis to show Mallory later.

Moments later Hunter stood behind a huge planter and watched as Lewis was given a passkey without signing in, which meant someone was already waiting for him in one of the rooms. Hunter folded the newspaper he was holding and watched further as the man crossed the lobby and entered the gift shop. Lewis emerged a few minutes later with a bouquet of flowers in his hand. He glanced around again before stepping into the elevator.

It would have been too risky to get on the elevator with the man since they had met once before. Hunter knew the only thing he could do for now was to sit and wait. All Mallory had asked for was evidence that the man was cheating on her sister, and so far in Hunter's book the man's actions were conducive of that, although he felt he needed more proof. The next step would be getting pictures of him and the woman together. Today, he would merely report back to Mallory on what he'd seen and let her decide if she needed for him to investigate things further.

Hunter went into the coffee shop to wait out his time. An hour or so later, a smiling Lewis Townsend stepped off the elevator. After glancing at his watch the man quickly made his way out of the hotel.

Some men have all the luck. What a way to spend your lunch hour, Hunter thought as he stood. There was no need to follow Lewis since chances were he would be returning to work. Knowing there was a strong possibility that Lewis had been involved in some sort of a sexual romp reminded Hunter of what he wasn't getting and hadn't gotten in over six months.

Automatically, his thoughts fell on Mallory.

Damn, he wanted her, and just thinking of how he wanted her made him go hard. He needed to call her to set up a meeting to discuss what he'd seen today. But he intended for their meeting to be more than that. He couldn't ignore his intense desire for her any longer. Fate had her stumbling back into his life and he wasn't exactly sure what to do about it. He shrugged, knowing that wasn't entirely true. The one thing he was sure of doing was making love to her again. His sanity depended on it.

Squinting his eyes against the sharpness of the midday sun, Hunter walked out of the hotel planning the seduction of Mallory Standish.

5

As Mallory brought her car to a stop in front of Hunter's home she thought she needed to have her head examined. Why on earth had she agreed to meet with him here instead of at his office or some other neutral place?

The thought of being alone with him in such close quarters didn't sit too well with her. But he had taken pictures of Lewis that he wanted her to see and since her last appointment had been with someone who lived within a mile of his home, his suggestion of meeting him here had sounded logical.

However, as she got out of her car she knew there was nothing logical when it came to Hunter Sloan or her love for him. Considering everything, she should have gotten over him months ago, but she hadn't and now he was back in her life, even if it was just on a temporary basis.

When she reached his door she felt heat sizzle down her spine.

Her body was remembering other times she had shown up here and what she'd always gotten once she crossed over the threshold. Trying to convince her anatomy of what not to expect was a job in itself and the way her breathing was quickening meant she wasn't being convincing enough. Taking a deep breath she rang his doorbell and listened while it echoed through his home.

He opened the door on the second ring. Mallory almost stopped breathing when her gaze met those of the strikingly handsome man standing less than a few feet in front of her. With his shirt unbuttoned and his belt hanging out of the loops, it was apparent he was just about to change clothes. But still he looked so smooth and suave that she felt her toes curl in her shoes.

She stared at him for a moment then released a long-suffering sigh. "I hope I'm not too early."

The corners of his eyes creased in a way she'd always found irresistibly sexy as he stood back to let her enter. "No, you're right on time," he said smiling, closing the door behind her. "I got home a few minutes ago and hadn't had time to set things up. I thought you could view the pictures from my computer."

She unconsciously slid her tongue over her lips. "All right."

"Do you mind if I shower first?"

She blinked at him. "Excuse me?"

"I said that I'd like to take a shower before showing you the pictures."

His statement nearly paralyzed her. There had never been a time when she had been in his home when he'd taken a shower and she hadn't joined him, whether she needed one or not. Vivid scenes of them in the shower stall began playing around in her head. Blood pounded through her body, especially the parts he had once touched, which meant she was tingling everywhere.

She knew the sensible thing to do was to tell him his shower needed to wait and that she wanted to see the pictures now so that she could leave. But there was a part of her that didn't want to be sensible, and it was reminding her that he had graciously taken this case on very short notice and she should be more appreciative. However, sexual need was replacing appreciation and she knew if she hung around she could get into trouble.

"Maybe I should come back later," she said and wondered if he could hear the frustration in her words.

"There's no need. My shower will only take a minute."

Mallory doubted that. Nothing Hunter did only took a minute. He could take the word slow to a whole other level and put the word anticipation right up there with it. No one had ever kissed her the way Hunter kissed her: slow and thorough. He would take his time like he had all day and all night. She cleared her throat. "Yes, but if you're busy then—"

"I'm not busy, Mallory, I'm just hot and sweaty. Come sit in the living room and make yourself comfortable. I'll be back before you know it."

A confusing mixture of emotions swept through her. "Okay, I'll wait for you to finish," she finally said.

He smiled. "Thanks."

He led the way and she followed appreciating how good he looked from behind. And if she remembered correctly . . . and she was sure that she did, she knew that his front wasn't so bad either. In fact it was the best although she hadn't had anything else to compare it with. But she couldn't imagine anyone being better than Hunter. From the first time they had made love he made her feel completely sexy and he could arouse every inch of her with just one heated look.

She blinked, noticed he had stopped to turn around and his mouth was moving. She blinked again. "I'm sorry, what did you say?"

He looked at her for a long moment and then he smiled again. "I said I want to clear the air about something else. About yesterday . . ."

She swallowed deeply before asking, "What about yesterday?"

"That question I asked you at Rowdy's that upset you."

Mallory stiffened, recalling exactly what he'd asked her. "Yes, what about it?"

"I need to apologize. I was out of line. I had no right asking you something like that and I knew it. I guess six months going without can make a person kind of crazy."

Mallory raised a brow. "What are you talking about?"

"Nothing more than the simple fact that I haven't slept with a woman since we broke up and I'm still going through withdrawal."

Mallory sucked in a breath. Hunter's words caught her off guard. She lifted her chin and narrowed her eyes at him. "Are you trying to tell me that you haven't slept with anyone in six months?"

"Yes, that's exactly what I'm telling you."

She shook her head, not believing a word he'd said. Hunter was too much of a passionate man to go without sex for that long. "And what about your dinner date the other night?"

"My date was my aunt Judith, Mallory. She had invited me to dinner and I accepted. Like I said, I haven't shared a bed with anyone since we split."

Mallory's skin began sizzling beneath the blouse she was wearing and fire began stirring in her stomach as she held his gaze. "B—but why?"

He leaned against the sofa and crossed his arms over his chest and stood in a pose that looked as serious as it could get. "I haven't gotten over you yet," he said as if those words explained everything.

Well they didn't. Her eyes widened. "You haven't gotten over me yet?"

"No."

Mallory stared across the room at him, not knowing what to say. The dark, brooding eyes holding hers were not happy and a part of her felt giddy at the thought that although he had been the one to make the decision to end their affair, memories of how good they'd been together plagued him.

"And I wouldn't get all that happy about it if I were you."

She tilted her head to the side and gazed at him. "Excuse me?"

"I said don't get all that happy about the fact that I haven't gotten over you yet because I have a very strong feeling you haven't gotten over me either."

With those final words he turned and walked out of the room.

Hunter walked into his bedroom, closed the door behind him, and squeezed his eyes shut for a moment. He hadn't meant to say those things to Mallory. He should have thought clearly before opening his mouth and telling her he still hadn't gotten over her. Now she would think he definitely had a thing for her.

He cursed softly when he had to inwardly admit that he did have a thing for her. He wanted her more than he had ever wanted any woman and since their breakup, he had literally lost his appetite for anyone other than her. His shoulders relaxed as he let his breath out. Maybe it wasn't so bad to let her know where he stood. That way she would know exactly where he was coming from and right where he intended to go. He began stripping off his clothes as he headed for the shower. He glanced at the bed before entering his bathroom and thought that would be a great place to start.

Like he had told her, he believed she wasn't over him yet either. It was there in her eyes whenever she looked at him. He had been her lover long enough to know deep longing and desire within her when he saw it. He hadn't paid any attention to it yesterday at Rowdy's but here in his house, in his domain where he had made love to her many times, he felt it and was attuned to it. There was no way he was overreacting to the situation. Mallory wanted him as much as he wanted her and as soon as he took his shower he intended to prove it. Oh yeah, he would show her those pictures, and then he would show her something else. He wanted her to see just what a bad state he was in. He needed to make love to her. She needed to make love to him.

They needed to make love to each other.

Mallory nervously paced around Hunter's living room. She paused for a moment and blew out a breath as she tried to steady her emotions. Hunter had been able to read her so clearly. He could tell that she had not gotten over him but what he didn't know was why. She loved him.

She couldn't help but wonder what was his reason for not getting over her. Oh sure, the sex between them had been good but he had dated plenty of other women before her and she hadn't been much of an expert in the bedroom. In fact he had taught her a lot of his preferred techniques. So what was the deal with him? She wasn't the one who had run away from a relationship that had started getting serious. He had.

Deciding Hunter was a puzzle she didn't want to figure out at the moment, she made a vain attempt to distract herself from the tingling that was going on throughout her body. She glanced around the room to see if he had changed anything since the last time she had visited.

Everything looked the same. She remembered the first time she had spent the night with him here. They had gone to a movie and he had invited her back to his home for ice cream. They never did eat the ice cream because the moment the door had closed behind them they had begun stripping naked.

"Sorry, if I took long."

She quickly glanced up when Hunter reentered the room. She studied him, accessed him. He had changed into a pair of cut-off jeans and a tank top and boy did he look good. He radiated, energy, vitality, and sensuality. She knew at that moment she needed to take care of what she'd come for and leave as quickly as possible.

"You weren't long at all. Can I see the pictures now?"

"Sure, let's go into my office."

Again, he led the way and she followed. He pulled out the chair to his desk. "Come on and sit down and I'll turn the computer on and get things started."

She nodded and took a seat at his desk. When he leaned over her to boot up the computer she took a deep breath. The aroma of his aftershave was doing crazy things to her body parts. Her heart began beating faster. He appeared big leaning down so close to her like he was. He was so close all she'd had to do was to stick out her tongue to lick the side of his face and she was tempted to do just that.

"That should do it," he said softly, close to her ear.

She blinked and noticed his computer was now on and several pictures were on the screen, all of Lewis. One showed him walking into the hotel, the other of him at the check-in desk with the receptionist handing him a passkey. Then there was the one of him walking out of the gift shop with a bouquet of flowers in his hand, and the last frame showed him getting out the elevator minus the flowers with a huge smile on his face.

Mallory frowned, disappointed, and leaned back in her chair. "So, what do you think?"

"Umm, what I think doesn't matter. What do *you* think?" Hunter asked her.

She glanced back at the pictures. "I would say it looks like he's involved in an affair."

Hunter raised his eyes to the ceiling. "You need more evidence then this, Mallory. There still may be a plausible reason behind what he's doing."

She rubbed her upper arms as if to ward off a chill when in essence the room felt hot, especially with Hunter's close proximity. And it didn't help matters that her heart was pumping hard. He hadn't moved an inch and was still standing next to the chair. "Come on, Hunter, the hotel, the flowers, the smile. What other proof do I need?" she asked, tipping her head back to look at him.

"The identity of the woman would be nice." He moved to sit down on the edge of the desk. "Look, Mallory, I know those photos may look pretty damn damaging, but until you actually see him and this alleged woman together you really don't have a case. If he's involved in an affair it's apparent this female is in a hotel room waiting when he arrives. And it seems he's not using the same hotel, maybe for fear of being seen or recognized. That will make it hard to set any kind of trap for him beforehand since I have no idea what hotel he may be using next or when he'll be using it."

Mallory nodded, knowing Hunter was right. She needed a female's face to go along with her accusations, otherwise it would continue to be sheer speculation on her part. "I want to be there when it's discovered who she is, Hunter."

He lifted a brow and looked surprised. "Why?"

"Because it might be someone Barbara knows—a neighbor, a coworker, a person she considers a friend."

Hunter wondered if her request had anything to do with what her father had done to her mother. She had shared with him one night that the woman her father had had an affair with had been a coworker, a person who had befriended her mother. "I'm not sure that's a good idea, Mallory."

She frowned. "Why?"

"Things could get messy."

Mallory's eyes narrowed. "The way I see it, things are going to get messy anyway when I tell Barbara what I've found out."

"Which at the moment is nothing," Hunter reminded her.

Anger fired through her. "I happen to think it's something."

He leaned toward her, so close their lips almost touched. "Are you willing to destroy your sister's happiness on these few pictures, Mallory? What if there's a good reason for what he's doing and it has nothing to do with being unfaithful to your sister? There're too many what-ifs until you have more proof," he said angling his mouth a little closer to hers. His hand fell to her nape and his fingers skimmed softly through her hair.

"I know how much finding out the truth means to you and you've hired me to find out what you need to know. I think doing things my way is the best way," he murmured softly.

Mallory inhaled deep and found herself saying. "All right, I will." His touch was electric and her mind was more on what he was doing than what he was saying. Her brain was becoming muddled as heat skittered up her spine. At that moment she became keenly aware of just how close their faces were. They were so close she could feel the tantalizing sweetness of his breath fan across her lips. He slowly inched a little closer and she couldn't help herself when her lips parted and he slipped his tongue inside her mouth.

He immediately went after her tongue, tasting it, gently sucking, taking control of it and sending desire all through her body. Hunter was an ace at doing wicked things with his tongue and he was doing them now. He was proving a point. He hadn't gotten over her yet. It was there in the way he was kissing her, making a combination of pleasure and heat rip into her. And when he stood and pulled her up from the chair, her eyes fluttered close and she wrapped her arms around his waist. He began exploring her body as his hands moved over the lower part of her back, her hips, and her behind. His arousal was huge and pressed hard against her middle and when she moved her hips against him and felt the heat continue to build to intensity level between her legs, she realized he was proving another point.

She hadn't gotten over him either.

The kiss was destined to last forever and when she began whimpering in need, he let go of her mouth and moved his lips to her ear. "I want you. I need you, Mallory," he whispered. His words, as well as his hot breath, made her shiver in his arms.

Mallory sighed deeply and tipped her head back to gaze into his eyes. She might regret her decision in the morning but at that moment, she needed him like she had never needed him before. She wanted to touch him, run her hands all over him, especially along the hard erection that was pressing against her belly. She wanted him on top of her, inside of her, thrusting in and out. She needed the degree of ecstasy she could find only with him. When his hips moved against her with deliberate attempt, letting her feel what she was doing to him, she knew she had to have him the same way he had to have her. Total and complete.

Her pulse quickened and she groaned inwardly. Tonight, for a few brief hours, she longed to be the woman to tame the untamable Hunter.

Deciding to be daring and handle him the same way she'd always done, which was to meet him on his turbulent and oftentimes naughty level, she reached up and cupped his face in her palms and began teasing at his lips with her tongue. She felt his erection get harder, bigger, and took some satisfaction in knowing she was driving him as crazy as he was driving her.

Her hands moved from his face and slowly grazed over his shoulders. As she continued licking his lips, she was surrounded by his scent. It was a scent she had missed, a scent that was pushing her off the edge by sending shivers through her and turning her on even more.

Then suddenly as if his restraint broke, he took things over and kissed her, putting an end to her teasing. He kissed her like doing so was his top priority, the only thing he wanted in life. The feeling was great, intoxicating and she began trembling with anticipation. When he suddenly pulled back, the deep chocolate-colored eyes that met hers made her shudder that much more.

"Stay with me tonight," he whispered in a voice so sexy, more heat began flowing around in her belly. "Please, say you'll stay."

She swallowed hard, her decision made. Leaning up on tiptoes she met his gaze and whispered. "Yes, Hunter, I'll stay."

6

Upon hearing Mallory's words, Hunter released a low, throaty groan and swept her off her feet and up into his arms, wasting no time carrying her to his bedroom. Not wanting to place her on the bed just yet, he placed her back on her feet, loving the feel of her body sliding down his.

He reached down and grabbed her thigh, pulling her body closer to him, wanting her to again feel his need for her. He had never wanted a woman with this much intensity in his life and a part of him wanted her to know that. He wanted to do more than just seduce her, or satisfy his desires with her, he wanted to take her, heart to heart, body to body, and soul to soul, and as mad as it sounded for him, Hunter Sloan, a man known to take what he wanted and not look back, it was a revelation he didn't understand. He was beginning to realize that when it came to Mallory

Standish he had a crazy streak. And the craziest thing at the moment was his need to see the color of her panties.

He leaned down and began kissing her, as his hand got busy raising her skirt up her hips. He then slid his hand underneath and pulled her backside to him as his hand touched her lacy panties.

A growl erupted in his throat when his fingers came into contact with the scrap of lace and when she began moving against him, heat began building at the tip of his erection and going all the way to the bottom of his feet. In a desperate need, his fingers tugged at the lace at her hip and when he dragged his mouth from hers he took a step back.

She was wearing a pair of mint-green panties.

His breath caught. "You are so beautiful," he said, barely able to breathe as he got down on his knees to remove her skirt and then her panties. He was aching to touch the skin hidden by her panties and had a desperate need to taste her. After she was completely bare below the waist, he leaned forward and rested his forehead against her stomach and inhaled deeply, needing the scent of her in his nostrils.

He heard the tiny sigh that slipped from her lips when he began dragging his mouth across her stomach, tasting her with the tip of his tongue. His mouth moved lower, to the very essence of her and he kissed her there as if the taste of her could somehow satisfy the hunger that was raging within him.

It seemed that his brain shut down to the sounds she was making—her groans, her whimpers. The only thing he could concentrate on was ravishing her over and over again as his hand, tight and firm on her legs, held her to him greedily devouring all of her. He wanted Mallory to feel everything he was feeling. By the time their bodies joined he wanted her to know how much he had missed this, had missed her.

When he heard her scream out her orgasm he tightened his hold on her, his kiss plunging deeper, harder, and more intense. Only when he felt she was too weak to stand did he pull back, taking his mouth away and tilting his head back to meet her gaze.

"Now I want to get inside of you," he whispered, slowly standing. "And I want to stay there all night. My body has been starving for you, Mallory, and it wants to get fed."

He reached down and touched the area between her legs where he had kissed. "You're still wet and hot and we haven't gotten started yet," he said as he began removing her blouse to reveal, not surprisingly, a mint-green lace bra. Without wasting any time he removed that as well and smiled when he saw how the tips of her breasts were firm and ready for him to devour as well. He leaned forward, opened his mouth and captured one nipple in his grasp, making provocative sounds of enjoyment while he did so, determined to get his fill.

"Hunter." The sound from her lips was soft; it trembled with a need he totally recognized and had definitely missed hearing.

He stopped his torment and met her gaze. "Let me make love to you all night long, Mallory. Let me give you pleasure by loving you in every way known to man and in ways man haven't discovered yet." He leaned down and whispered in her ear. "I want you bad, Mallory. Feel me."

He heard her soft gasp when he leaned forward and his erection pressed against her naked body as if seeking a way out of his jeans and inside of her. Satisfied she'd gotten a good idea of the degree of his desire, he stepped back and they stared at each other for a long moment.

"It's not fair," Mallory finally said, leaning closer to him, her bare breast brushing against his arm. "You have on clothes but I don't."

He smiled, giving her a slow once-over. "You look good naked."

She returned his smile. "If I remember correctly, so do you." She reached up and ran her hand beneath his T-shirt, letting her fingers skim across his hairy chest. He released a sharp intake of breath with her touch. Talk about not playing fair.

Deciding not to waste time he took a step back and whipped the shirt over his head. The only things left were his jeans and boxer shorts and he planned to dispense with both quickly. However, it seemed that Mallory had other ideas when she slowly unzipped his pants and eased her hand inside.

It took every ounce of self-restraint he possessed not to come right then and there the moment she touched him. It had been a long time since any woman had touched him and no woman could touch him the way Mallory could. Her fingers were soft on his hardness, and each time that she stroked him, she increased the risk of him being pushed over the edge. When he did he wanted to be inside of her.

Heat began simmering through his veins and he briefly closed his eyes when he felt her push back the opening to his jeans to pull his shaft out. He reopened his eyes, aware of the shallowness of his own breathing as Mallory's capable hands continued on the path of total destruction, unrequited pleasure, sliding her fingers over him, pulling on him, letting the tips of her fingernails gently scrape along his hypersensitive skin.

He tipped his head back and gloried in how her touch was making him feel, wanting to get inside of her with a force that had him nearly gasping for breath. He had to stop her since he was less than a heartbeat away from climaxing just where he stood. "Now who isn't playing fair?" he said in a throaty whisper, taking a step back out of her reach and quickly removing his jeans and boxer shorts.

He watched as she licked her bottom lip. "Umm, I feel extremely naughty."

He gazed into her beautiful face while standing before her stark naked. "And I feel extremely horny and I know of a way to take care of both."

He watched her eyes darken and knew she was dying to find out what he had in mind. The one thing he'd always liked and enjoyed about Mallory was her willingness to trust him on all levels when it came to giving her pleasure. Whenever they shared a bed, making love had always been an adventure and they had enjoyed the activity with wild abandonment each and every time. Just thinking about some of the things they'd done made his blood boil.

He reached out, picked her up in his arms, and walked over to the bed and placed her in the center of it. Desire, the likes he'd never experienced before, suddenly overwhelmed him and some unnamed emotion that was new to him took control. For a brief moment he thought of how good she looked in *his* bed, and he inwardly admitted that she had always looked like she belonged there.

Suddenly, a part of his brain hurled the question at him as to why he had ever let her leave in the first place and he knew the answer. Fear. He had gotten scared that she had begun getting under his skin. His heart thundered at the memory of how he had begun to get possessive with her and how the thought of seeing her each day would send shivers of excitement up his spine.

"Hunter."

The sound of her calling his name made his chest tightened and he marveled at how she could still affect him. Mallory Standish was the most fascinating woman he had ever met as well as the most sexy.

And he wanted her and was driven by a need to have her.

He made a small sound in his throat as he slowly joined her on the bed. And as he gently reached for her he realized that he had her back where she belonged, in his bed, and that he wouldn't ever let her go again. Hunter caught his breath at the depths of his thoughts. He wasn't exactly sure why that revelation had come to him at this particular time; all he knew was that it had, and he meant it.

Instead of teetering precariously on the edge, he had definitely fallen over.

Mallory's heart began pounding deep within her chest as Hunter's predatory gazed slammed into her, making her feel things she had never felt before. Her sexual appetite was high and from the look in the deep brown of his eyes, she knew so was his.

They had not made any promises to each other; the notion of anything beyond this night hadn't even been discussed, yet she was willing to go all the way with him, sleep with him again, in a way that made had her breathing ragged.

"You're hot, Mallory."

His observation brought a heated smile to her face. She was more than hot, she was burning to a sexual crisp.

"I can tell by your scent," Hunter said further, leaning over her and whispering the words in her ear. "You're hot for me, aren't you?" he asked, positioning his body over her in way that kept their middle parts from touching.

"Yes," was the only response she was able to give before he slanted his mouth over hers, tasting her with the skillful stroke of his tongue. He was kissing her in such a way that had flames racing through every part of her body, especially between her legs, making her wetter.

"Ahh," she whispered through her lips moments later when he finally released her mouth. She could actually hear the thumping of her heart as his tongue feasted on her breasts. Moments later he moved his mouth to the center of her chest to lick off the beads of moisture that had gathered there.

"Hunter . . ."

He then pressed his forehead against hers, holding her gaze hostage, demanding her full attention, which was hard to do when his fingers had made their way between her legs, intent on stroking her sensitive flesh.

"Are you still on the pill?" he whispered the question against her ear.

Mallory grasped his shoulders thinking if she didn't hold on to something she would surely pass out from the feelings he was evoking within her. "Yes." She could barely get the single word out.

"Good. And I meant what I said, Mallory, I haven't made love to another woman since so you don't have to worry about me not being safe, okay?"

"Okay." Again the word was forced from her lips. "And I haven't been with anyone else either."

Her words touched him, pleased him tremendously. "Then lead me home," he whispered, in what sounded like a strained voice. "Take me inside of you, Mallory. Please."

Mallory's breath caught as she squeezed her fingers around Hunter's hard arousal. His flesh felt hot to the touch and the moment the tip of him touched her opening, he threw his head back and released a deep-in-the-gut groan that could be heard throughout the room.

She tried ignoring the sound as she continued to take him into her, almost losing it the moment his shaft touched her womanly core. Her muscles greedily clenched him, tightened, while he pushed forward, filling her to the hilt. She reached up and wiped the sweat from his brow as she fought to catch her own breath.

"This is what I've been wanting the past six months, so much that I haven't been able to think straight," he whispered through clenched teeth as he slowly began thrusting in and out, withdrawing then surging back inside of her again as if he could not get enough, at least not in this lifetime.

Mallory lifted her hips to his, meeting him stroke for stroke, glorying in the feel of his length and thickness as it slid in and out of her, pushing her out of control at the sensations that were ramming through her body. Whether they had another encounter after tonight or not didn't matter to her at the moment. What mattered was that her body was getting satisfied and her wants fulfilled.

She wrapped her legs around him, feeling incredibly dizzy with desire as he continued to thrust into her. And when he threw his head back and let out a torturous groan at the same moment that her body tightened when a climax roared through her, he tightened his grip on her hips and pushed deep into her as he, too, was consumed within the throes of passion.

She felt his release inside of her as he furiously bucked into her while aftershocks quaked through her and went directly to him, toppling them both over the edge. She tightened her legs around him, wanting everything he was giving and then some.

For long moments, after the explosion was subsided, they lay there, unable to move, their breathing labored, their bodies still connected. Then slowly Hunter leaned up and kissed her, deeply, passionately. She felt him getting hard inside of her again and her feminine muscles reacted, tightening, clenching, and cradling his hard growing erection.

"Ready for another round?" he whispered huskily, nipping at a sensitive area of her neck.

The room had the aroma of sex, intoxicating and potent. Mallory wondered just how many more rounds they could go and knew that the sky was the limit. Tonight he would be her all night man and she would be his all night woman. And tomorrow she would not have any regrets, just more memories to add to all the others.

"Yes, I'm ready," she murmured, barely able to speak.

"Good." And he began thrusting into her all over again.

1

Hunter slowly opened his eyes when he felt Mallory stirring beside him. He groaned heavily and wondered if he'd ever be able to get his body into anything other than a bucking position again.

They had made love all through the night, nearly nonstop and if the truth were told he would gladly, without much thought, make love to her again. He gazed over at her body that was uncovered above the waist. Passion marks were everywhere and the nipples of her breasts were perked, as if ready to be licked and sucked.

He closed his eyes against his renewed desire, as if that would help yet knowing that it wouldn't. He reopened his eyes and gazed at Mallory. As he continued to watch her, another kind of sensation began taking over him and it had nothing to do with sex.

He shifted positions as he tried to rationalize what he was feeling and the one question that had haunted him all last night returned. Each and every time he had made love to Mallory he inwardly questioned why he would settle for a commitment-free life when he could have this every night. It was clearly obvious that he cared about her, and it was also pretty damn blatant that he felt a connection to her that he hadn't felt to another woman.

Mental images of what they had done over the past ten hours flitted through his mind. Every aspect of their night had been incredible, not just the physical releases they had shared but also the emotional release as well. He had to be completely honest and admit that he'd been dealing with more than the desires of the flesh. He had to finally admit that he'd also been dealing with the desires of the heart.

His heart.

It was the heart he could now admit that Mallory possessed. The mere thought of not being able to share another night like this with her was too difficult to imagine.

He loved her.

His breath caught at the thought that Hunter Sloan could love any woman, but he knew he loved Mallory. What other reason could there for him not wanting another woman since their breakup? What other reason could there be for him desiring her with a desperation that bordered on obsession?

Reaching out, he gathered her close while she continued sleeping. His lips tilted into a smile. Mallory Standish had conquered the untamable Hunter Sloan and his body felt a satisfying warmth at the thought.

As he closed his eyes and snuggled her closer into his arms, he knew that the mighty Hunter had fallen and he had fallen hard.

· · ·

Mallory opened her eyes and groaned softly into the hairy chest that cushioned her face, loving the manly scent of the man holding her in his arms.

She shifted her body and felt an ache everywhere, especially between her legs. She didn't think she would ever be able to walk again and was glad it was Saturday; otherwise, she would not have made any of her appointments today.

Hunter had definitely proven to be an all night man. He had the stamina of a bull and had literally driven her wild over and over again. At some point she had stopped counting how many orgasms she'd had and enjoyed each and every one he'd given her. She had wanted a night of passion and had gotten more than she'd bargained for.

She wondered what category last night would fall in. Since they had made love numerous times before, it probably wouldn't be considered a one-night stand, especially since they weren't really involved anymore. The first time they had made love, the night of his parents' anniversary party, it had started out as a one-night stand and had ended up lasting for four months.

Mallory closed her eyes knowing that would not be the case this time around. Hunter had made it pretty clear that he was not interested in anything beyond sex with any woman. She reopened her eyes and released a mental sigh when she thought of what had brought her and Hunter back together—even for a short while—which was her brother-in-law's unfaithfulness. She didn't care what Hunter said, those photographs he had taken of Lewis spoke volumes and she had to deal with how she would break the news to Barbara.

She wondered why serious relationships, especially those between married people, always ended in pain. Maybe breaking up with Hunter had been the right thing to do six months ago. At the time she had been willing to take a chance and give her heart to a man but now she realized that would have been an ultimate mistake, considering how the men the Standish women had a tendency to fall for seemed to let them down. First it had been her father and now Lewis.

She was intent on putting any thoughts of ever indulging in a serious involvement with a man out of her mind. Although she hated admitting it, it appeared that Hunter had the right attitude involving relationships—get physical but stay emotion-free. She hadn't understood his attitude six months ago but she understood it now.

"Good morning, sweetheart."

She glanced over at him and saw that he was awake. Without allowing her a chance to return his greeting, he leaned over and kissed her hard and deep. Moments later he pulled back and smiled at her. "How do you feel?"

How she was feeling could be summed up in one word. "Sore."

He nodded. "Then it's time for me to take care of you. I'll be back in a second."

She watched as he threw off the covers, got out of the bed, and walked naked into the adjoining bathroom. She slowly shifted her body when she heard the sound of water running and knew he was filling up the bathtub for her to soak in. He had done that very same thing the first time they had made love and he'd discovered she'd been a virgin. If the truth were known she would readily admit she had fallen in love with him that very night. There had been something about the tender and delicate way he had treated her both before and after their sexual encounter that had endeared him to her for life. Although she knew she still loved him, she would be satisfied with things not moving beyond this—the bedroom.

She should have listened to her coworker, Gail Turner, who used to brag about her sexual exploits and say you should take a man to bed but never let him go to your head.

She glanced up when she heard Hunter return. "Ready for a soak?" he asked coming over to the bed.

"Yes."

Effortlessly, he brushed the covers aside, picked her up in his arms, and carried her into the bathroom. After placing her in the warm, sudsy water he knelt down and using skillful hands and expert fingers, he began massaging the soreness from her body.

Mallory closed her eyes and leaned back against the tub when he freed one hand to brush his fingers through the thickness of her hair, actually making her moan.

"How about if we get dressed and go somewhere for breakfast?" he asked, leaning down close to her ear.

Without opening her eyes, she smiled. "That would be wonderful if I had more clothes to put on, but all I have to wear is what I wore over here yesterday afternoon."

He nodded. "Then how about if I go out and grab us something and bring it back?"

She opened her eyes and met his gaze. "Or I could fix you something here," she said softly.

Like a little kid, Hunter's dark eyes widened. "Some of your mouth-watering pancakes?"

Mallory chuckled, glad he remembered the breakfast meals they'd shared. "Umm, yes, there is that possibility. In fact, I—"

She never finished the rest of her sentence when he leaned over and captured her mouth in one hell of a mind-blowing kiss.

* * *

Hunter anxiously tapped his fingers on the kitchen table to a beat buried deep in his head while watching Mallory stack pancakes onto the platter. Merely watching her was turning him on big time and it wasn't helping matters that she was wearing was one of his T-shirts that hit her mid thigh, and he knew for a fact she didn't have a stitch of underwear on underneath.

Sexual hunger was riding him with the need to rid her once again. He was having anticipation attacks right and left, especially during those times when she would bend over to look into the oven to check on the sweet rolls she had decided to bake. Her behind was definitely a real nice piece to look at.

His heart was hammering in his chest at the thought of just how much he loved her and how he had finally admitted that fact to himself. She was exquisite, gorgeous, and everything he wanted in a woman. His aunt had been right. Mallory was the best thing to ever happen to him and he couldn't wait until she brought up the subject of where they would go from here now that they had gotten back together. When she did, he would not waste any time telling her of his feelings for her and that he wanted them to move into a committed relationship.

"I hope you have an appetite, Hunter."

Her comment recaptured his attention and he flashed her a quick grin. "Oh, you wouldn't believe the appetite I have, sweetheart," he said huskily, watching as she walked over to the table carrying the tray filled with pancakes in one hand and the container of syrup in the other.

She placed everything on the table and tipped her head back to look at him. "Why do I have a feeling that these pancakes aren't the only thing on your mind?"

His gaze drifted over her body, then he stared intently into her eyes as he reached out and took hold of her hand. "Because they aren't. But since I plan to give your body a rest, you're safe for a while."

She smiled as she leaned down and placed a feather-light kiss on his lips. "Thanks for being considerate."

"For you, always."

When she tried pulling her hand from his, he didn't release her. Instead he pushed his chair back and pulled her down into his lap. "But that doesn't mean I won't taste my fill," he murmured, threading his fingers through her hair and then capturing her lips with his. He kissed her long and hard, doing what he'd wanted to do every since she had joined him in the kitchen.

Incredible, he thought moments later, releasing her mouth. The taste of her was incredible and would remain with him for quite some time. It was amazing just how she affected him, how much she suddenly made him think of marriage and babies.

Marriage! Babies!

He swallowed hard. He'd never been able to formulate thoughts of either before but now he did. And only with her. "I could kiss you all day," he whispered against her moist lips.

"And I can kiss you all day as well," she whispered softly. "But that won't get rid of the sound of our stomachs growling. We need food."

He chuckled as she slid out of his lap. "That's true." He watched as she walked across the room to open the refrigerator to pull out a carton of orange juice, wondering when she would bring up the subject of them getting back together and decided to be patient.

A few moments later after she sat across from him while enjoying breakfast he decided that he couldn't wait any longer. Patience had never been one of his strong points. He leaned back in his chair looking at her after wolfing down all four of his pancakes and drinking a tall, cold glass of juice. "My mother and my aunt will be ecstatic to know we're back together, Mallory."

He watched as the fork she'd been using slipped from her fingers. She met his gaze. "We aren't back together, Hunter," she said softly.

He lifted a gaze wondering why she would think such a thing. "Sure we are. Last night we—"

"Had sex. Plenty of times but still it was sex. How many times have you said that you have sex with women, you do not make love?"

He frowned. "But that was before."

Now it was her time to lift a brow. "Before what?"

"Before last night."

Mallory slowly shook her head, confused. "What was so special about last night?"

Smiling, Hunter reached out and tenderly stroked her cheek. "I discovered that I've missed you and want you back in my life."

Mallory shook her head again. "No, you want me back in your bed."

"Yeah, that, too, but I want you in my life more than anything. I don't want a woman who'll just be available for me to sleep with. I want to have a committed relationship with you."

Mallory's eyes widened, clearly shocked. "A committed relationship? Since when? Have you forgotten why we broke up in the first place? I mentioned the word commitment and you hauled ass so fast it left my head spinning."

He shifted uneasily in his chair, remembering that night. "I've changed."

"Yeah, right. And you want me to believe that all it took was several romps in bed for you to change your way of thinking? I'm not buying it, Hunter."

He crossed his arms over his chest. This was clearly not going the way he had figured it would. Six months ago she was the one who was pushing for a committed relationship and now that he was ready it seemed she was no longer interested. "And what will it take for you to buy it?"

"Nothing since I doubt that I will, especially with what's going on with Lewis."

Confusion settled in Hunter's features. "What does Lewis have to do with us?"

Mallory stood and began gathering up the dishes. "He reminded me that relationships hurt, especially the committed kind. Men are all alike. They can't be trusted."

Her statement angered Hunter and he quickly stood. "Now wait just a damn minute. I don't appreciate being grouped with other men that way. I make it clear with any woman I date what the score is. But with you things have always been different. Not once did I see other women while we dated, Mallory." He rubbed a hand over his face. "Hell, I wouldn't have had energy to bed anyone other than you anyway. You were all the woman I needed. How can you even think that I was unfaithful to you while we were together?"

Mallory released a deep sigh. "I'm not accusing you of that,

Hunter. All I'm staying is that at some point in a relationship things can happen, no matter how much the two people loved each other in the beginning. Loss of interest sets in. It happened with my parents and now it's happening with Barbara and Lewis."

He glared at her. "You don't know that. You're making assumptions and jumping to conclusions."

She glared right back. "Maybe so, but that doesn't explain why you've had a change of heart all of a sudden, Hunter. Six months ago a committed relationship was the last thing you wanted and now I understand why and I'm buying into what you believe."

"But I don't want you to buy into it because I don't think that way anymore. Like I said, I've changed." He could tell from her expression that she didn't believe him. He also knew at that moment there was no point in telling her that he loved her since she probably wouldn't believe that either. He sighed deeply, deciding to use another approach. "If you don't want a serious relationship with me, then what is it that you do want?"

Mallory shrugged as she thought about his question. "What we had before and what we shared last night. I don't want anything serious. I want to be your bed partner on occasion."

Bed partner? His heart thudded in disappointment. What he'd shared with her last night had been more than that but he decided to hold back from telling her that. He would have to operate under the theory that action spoke louder than words. "Exclusive bed partners?" he asked, crossing his arms over his chest once more.

"Yes, that'll work."

Maybe it would work for her but it certainly wouldn't work for him. "All right, we can go that route if that's the way you want things to be."

"It is."

He nodded. He planned to change her thinking on a lot of things. Given even the slightest opportunity, he intended to show her that no matter what her father or Lewis did, it had no bearing on their relationship. He had to prove that he loved her and she was a woman worth loving and worth being faithful to.

"How about if we go to your place for you to pack a bag," he said, taking the dishes out of her hands to place them back on the table and then pulling her into his arms.

She tilted her head back to look at him. "Why?"

"I'd like for you to spend the rest of the weekend with me. Say you'll do it."

His lips came down on hers with a hunger that he knew she felt. Her body began shivering from the thrust of his tongue into her mouth as it swept her breath away. And he knew the feel of his hands squeezing her backside wasn't helping matters. He had Seduction 101 down pat.

"Say you'll stay," he whispered against her moist lips after breaking off the kiss.

Mallory momentarily closed her eyes as she remembered what they had shared last night. He would give her body possibly a brief reprieve but then he planned to make love to her again.

She reopened her eyes thinking she didn't have a problem with that. Hunter Sloan was a man created for sex and she was overjoyed that she was the woman he wanted in his bed. She might be planning to avoid serious relationships but like she'd told him, she had nothing against being his bed partner since concentrating on the physical and not the emotional was safer.

"Mallory?"

She glanced up at him, knowing he was waiting on her answer. She moved her hand down his chest and then purposely stepped closer. She met his gaze. "Yes, Hunter, I'll spend the rest of the weekend with you."

8

A week later Hunter was sitting in his car in the parking lot of the Federal Building. It was Friday and so far he had shown up here for the last four days and the only thing Lewis Townsend had done for lunch over those days was to go to McDonald's or run errands. Either he had ended his supposed fling or this was an off week for him.

Hunter sighed as he rested his head against the seat. He still wasn't as convinced as Mallory that the man was engaging in an affair although his actions that other day had hinted otherwise. For some reason there was something that Hunter felt he was missing, something vital.

He tapped his fingers on the steering wheel, anticipating seeing Mallory again. They had spent time together three times that week and as much as it almost killed him, he hadn't made love to her again. He wanted to prove to her that there was more to their relationship than sex. He had taken her to the movies, to dinner, and they had even gone to a concert. And he was glad he hadn't had anything new to report to her about Lewis. She had had dinner with her sister and brother-in-law two nights ago and according to Mallory, the two appeared to be more in love than ever.

Hunter glanced at his watch. It was way past the noon hour and it appeared that Lewis wouldn't be doing lunch today, which was fine and dandy with Hunter. He had other things on his mind like doing Mallory. His body was hot and aroused which clearly meant that he had reached his limit.

He picked up his cell phone, clicked it on and punched in her phone number. She answered it on the second ring. "Standish Event Planning. I aim to please."

He smiled, liking her greeting. "So do I," he whispered huskily. "How about meeting me at my place in half an hour?"

Without waiting for her to respond he clicked off the phone.

Mallory raised a brow when Hunter opened his front door. "What's that smile for?" she asked when he moved aside for her to come in. Her body was tingling from head to toe and had been ever since his call. Her nipples felt tight and sensitive against her blouse and the deep throb between her legs was enough to make her scream.

She hoped that he had invited her over for a little afternoon delight, which she badly needed. This had been the week from hell. One of her clients, a high society dame, had called on Monday to inform her that her daughter and her fiancé had had a huge argument over the weekend and for the moment the wedding was off. Then she had received a call on Wednesday informing her that it was on again. Then she'd received a call that morning saying it was off again. That meant all her plans were on hold until the couple got things together.

"You seemed frustrated about something," Hunter said, interrupting her thoughts.

She smiled and walked over to him when he closed the door behind them. The sound of the lock clicking in place sent sensuous chills up her body. She had a feeling they were about to get naughty and naughtiness was something she definitely needed today.

"I was frustrated before I got here," she said, raking her hands down his chest, toying with the buttons on his shirt with her fingertips. "But I'm depending on you to make sure I'm frustration-free when I leave. And you never did answer my question about what the smile is for."

"It's for you and the good news I have for you."

"Which is?"

"I have nothing new to report."

Mallory nodded. In a way it was good news but it didn't mean just because there was nothing new to report that Lewis hadn't been unfaithful. Hunter must have read her thought because he then said, "The man is innocent until proven guilty."

She frowned. "And what if he's never proven guilty, Hunter? It'll be hard for me to completely trust him until I know for sure."

He nodded as he pulled her into his arms. "I didn't invite you here for us to argue, Mallory."

She had figured as much and had hoped as much as well. She tipped her head back and met his gaze. "And why did you invite me over here?"

"I'm horny."

A huge smile touched the corners of Mallory's lips. "I like a man who's straight and to the point, Hunter."

"That's not all I am," he said, pulling her body closer and letting her feel the hardness of his erection.

"I'm just as bad off as you are," she whispered, easing her legs apart so the firmness of him could settle comfortably in her middle.

"You're wet?" he asked softly against her lips.

"Practically drenched."

He smiled. "Exactly the way I want you."

"And you're exactly the way I want you," she said, as her hands moved down to his belt, unbuckled it, snapped open his pants and then eased his zipper down. "You've been holding out on me for the last three times we were together, so if you're horny it's your own fault."

"I was trying to be nice."

Her smile widened. "Don't you know by now that I prefer naughty to nice?" Her hands slipped into the opening of his pants and his briefs and began stroking him.

"Umm, I'm getting the picture," he said, barely able to get the words out.

"And I'm getting something else," she said as her thumb flicked over the hot tip of his shaft and liking the feel of him getting harder in her hands.

"No fair," Hunter said moments later, almost losing the little bit of control he had, especially when he began inhaling her intimate fragrance. There was nothing like the scent of an aroused woman. A woman ready to spread her legs and mate with her man. And he was definitely ready for that to happen. He had issued the invitation. It was his bash and he intended to provide the party treats, the fun, and all the excitement.

He took a step back, which meant she had to release him, and he immediately felt the loss of her hands on him. He also felt somewhat lightheaded and unmistakingly aroused. He smiled, wanting to see her naked. "Undress for me, Mallory."

"Are you sure that's what you want me to do?"

"I'm positive."

She reached under her skirt to tug her panties down her legs and shimmied out of them. They were black lace. He watched as she kicked them aside. Then she removed her short skirt, which left her completely bare below the waist. He licked his lips when his tongue tingled, wanting the taste of her but deciding his aroused body needed something else right now.

He watched as she removed her blouse to reveal a matching black lace bra. The moment she took it off he felt a mirage of heat swirl around in his belly. She stood in the middle of his living room stark naked, looking sexy and feminine; provocative. The urge to have her clogged his throat and he quickly began removing his own clothes.

"Come here, baby." His voice was low and unsteady but it couldn't be helped. He loved this woman to distraction and wanted her equally as much. And his libido kicked up a notch when she didn't waste any time crossing the room to him.

When she came to a stop in front of him, she placed her hands on his shoulders. "What do you want, Hunter?" she asked, moving her hand slowly back and forth across his shoulder blades.

He leaned down, taking his fingers and stroking between her legs. She was right. She was drenched. "I want this," he said as he gently moved his fingers inside of her when she eased her legs farther apart to accommodate him. He felt her hold on his shoulders tighten and knew she was enjoying the feel of him stroking her. "For starters, I want to take you in my kitchen, on the counter."

Of all the places they had done it before, his kitchen counter hadn't been one of them. Swallowing hard, she whispered. "The kitchen counter?"

"Yes. I've been fantisizing about getting you on the kitchen counter all week."

Consuming desire was taking over every part of her body. "And what's stopping you?"

He smiled before swooping her up into his arms. Crossing the room to the kitchen, he didn't stop until he had placed her naked bottom on the edge of the counter. Then he separated her knees, parting her legs and stepping between them, readying things by placing the tip of his erection against her entrance.

Every nerve ending, every sensation in Mallory's body was prepared for what was about to happen. She looked deep into Hunter's eyes, and for this one time, she wanted him to know just how much she cared for him. For a moment it seemed that everything got silent, even the sound of their breathing appeared to have stopped as their gazes locked. The very air between them seemed to sizzle with fierce sexual need as well as with something else. Love. Neither of them blinked and she knew the exact moment he saw love and not lust in her eyes.

"Why didn't you tell me?" he asked in a whisper.

"Would it have mattered, Hunter?"

A deep sigh escaped his breath when he realized that at the time, no it probably would not have and would have made him put distance between them that much sooner. Realizing what he had almost lost completely, he leaned down and began nibbling the corners of her mouth while he ran his hands along her thighs, making a flood of intense love and desire course through her body. Then his tongue began licking the lining of her lips with a slow, deliberate pace.

"I love you, too, Mallory," he murmured, moving his hands from her thighs to her belly. "I recently realized just how much. I didn't think you would believe me if I told you, but now that I know how you feel about me, I believe in my heart that things will work out."

She shook her head, needing to make him see that things couldn't work out for them. A committed relationship wasn't what they needed no matter how they felt about each other. But all thoughts of debating the issue with him escaped her mind when she felt his shaft pressing against her womanly core, eager to get inside. She shuddered with need when he parted her legs a little more.

And then he stopped teasing her mouth and took it with a voracious fierce hunger than had her moaning. The feel of his tongue tangling with hers sent shock waves all through her body. The sensation of him tasting her mouth with such torrid intensity made a deep groan escape her throat.

The sensations intensified when she felt him pushing himself into her, overwhelming her, possessing her. What little control she had snapped like a rubber band when she felt the hard and thick length of him delving deeper inside of her, stretching her, finding her wet and hot, her womanly muscles straining for release.

Her breath came out in short gasps and her sensitive breasts were pressed against his bare chest. She clutched his shoulders, her fingers bit deep into his blades as he continued to push forward, taking his hand and pulling her hips as close as he could. Automatically, she wrapped her legs around his waist as the intensity of their kiss continued.

"I could die inside you this way," he said softly, beginning to thrust in and out while holding her hips tight in his hands. Each stroke he made gripped her, sent her closer to the edge, and her entire body quivered from the pending orgasm. And when it happened, when a climax ripped through her with the force of a volcano, she pulled her mouth from his and screamed.

It seemed her climax gave him renewed urgency and he began pumping into her, over and over, picking up the tempo of their mating, almost bringing her off the counter as a fierce, deep growl erupted from deep in his throat. He threw his head back and hollered out her name as he spilled inside of her, saturating her already drenched body, filling the kitchen with the scent of sex.

He began kissing her again with light, passionate kisses. She was crying, unable to help herself and he kissed away her tears. When the explosion inside of them subsided, he placed his hands under her hips and keeping their bodies locked, he carried her to a straight-backed chair and sat down with her legs dangling off the sides.

He pressed her face against his chest, holding her while she continued to cry.

"I love you," she sobbed, wetting his chest. "And you love me, but it doesn't matter now."

He tightened his arms around her. "Shh, it's okay and yes it does matter, sweetheart."

"But, I don't want to love you. I don't want us to get together. I don't want a serious relationship with you. Not anymore."

He heard her words but refused to buy them. He refused to

believe that she would base what they felt for each other on the actions of others.

"But I do want you to love me," he whispered back. "I do want us to get together. And I want a serious relationship with you more than anything. I was a fool for giving you up. Don't expect me to do it a second time, Mallory."

"But—"

"No buts." He kissed her and groaned heavily when he felt his body starting to get hard again. He stood and her legs automatically locked around his waist. "I'm going to take you into the bedroom and make love to you all afternoon and all through the night. I hope you don't have any more appointments scheduled for today."

"I don't," she said, liking the feel of him growing long and hard inside of her again. She tightened her arms around his neck as he maneuvered his way from the kitchen, through the living room, and into the bedroom.

He smiled down at her. "Good. I want you to spend the night with me again. And in the morning, I want you to wake up knowing I've made love to you all night along. And every time my body stroked into yours, I want you to know I was reaffirming my love for you."

Hours later, Mallory sighed deeply as a worn-out Hunter slept, holding her close. One of his muscled legs was thrown over hers as if holding her hostage. Letting Hunter know that she loved him had been a big mistake but at the moment she didn't want to think about it.

She would have time to regret what she'd done in the morning. At the moment, the only thing she wanted to think about was the man resting next to her who was beautiful even when he slept.

Her all night man.

It would be merely minutes before he woke up again with the fierce sexual appetite he was known for. She leaned over and placed a gentle kiss on his cheek, wishing the night would never end and that they could love each other this way forever.

9

For the following two weeks Hunter and Mallory's relationship continued to blossom, although she made a point not to use words such as serious or committed to describe what they were sharing. As far as he was concerned, they never had to because their actions spoke louder than words. They did things together and his parents as well as his aunt knew his feelings for her ran deep.

Also, during that time Hunter continued to keep tabs on Lewis only to report nothing new to Mallory. Then when it appeared Mallory was about ready for him to close the case, Lewis left for lunch one Friday and it didn't take long for Hunter to realize he was headed to a hotel again.

After pulling into the hotel's parking lot behind Lewis, Hunter parked the car and watched as Lewis got out and walked into the Sheraton Hotel, whistling as if he definitely looked forward to getting with whomever he was supposed to meet there.

Hunter followed a safe distance behind and saw Lewis as he quickly crossed the lobby and walked straight over to the woman who was walking out of the gift shop with a huge shopping bag.

Hunter watched as the couple kissed passionately before holding hands to catch the elevator. He shook his head. Lewis was definitely having an affair.

Mallory checked her watch as she walked into the Sheraton Hotel. She had received a call on her mobile phone from Hunter asking that she meet him here and to catch the elevator up to room 560 where he would be waiting. The only other thing he'd said before quickly ending the call was that the meeting involved Lewis.

It didn't take her long to reach the room and Hunter opened the door on the first knock. "You didn't waste any time getting here," he said, stepping aside to let her in.

She glanced around. It was a beautiful suite with teakwood-colored furnishings. "You said it was about Lewis. Is he here at this hotel?"

Hunter closed the door and locked it before turning around to answer her "Yes, he's in the room next door. These are connecting rooms."

Her eyes widened. "You mean he's actually in the room next door to us in bed with someone?"

Hunter shrugged. "I have no idea if he's in bed with anyone or not, Mallory, but I figured you would want to know what I found out. And I figured you would want to take a look at the woman as well as letting your brother-in-law know he'd been found out. I normally don't do things this way but the least I can do is to serve as a witness in case one is needed."

Mallory nodded. Hunter's suggestion wasn't a bad idea. She shook her head not wanting to believe any of this. How was she supposed to act knowing her brother-in-law was probably in the connecting room being unfaithful to her sister? "How long have they been here?"

"Less than thirty minutes and it's been pretty quiet over there."

Mallory thought of all the times she and Hunter had made love and all the noise they made and decided on a hopeful note that maybe, just maybe, her brother-in-law was involved in some sort of business meeting after all. She glanced over at Hunter. He had loosened his tie and was in the process of taking it off. "Did you see him with a woman, Hunter?"

He nodded. "Yes."

Disappointment set in and her next question was cut off by a knock at the door. She arched a questioning brow at Hunter.

"I ordered lunch. I figure you had probably missed it and would be hungry."

Mallory nodded, appreciating his thoughtfulness. She was hungry but she doubted if she could eat anything for the anger that began replacing the hunger in her stomach. Didn't Lewis care how much Barbara loved him and that she would be deeply hurt by what he was doing?

The waiter who wheeled in the cart was efficient and didn't waste any time setting things up and leaving. Mallory took in a deep breath and let it out slowly, watching as Hunter uncovered the food. "I don't think I'm going to be able to eat anything."

He glanced up at her. "Why not?"

"I've lost my appetite."

He nodded as he recovered the dishes. She then watched as he began removing his shirt and it was then that she noticed just how huge the bed was. Colossal was a better name for it.

Confused, she watched as Hunter proceeded to take off his pants then climbed on the bed to lay in the center with his hands underneath his neck wearing nothing but his briefs. "What do you think you're doing?" she asked, barely able to get the words out.

He smiled. "Waiting for you."

She looked appalled. "Waiting for me?" At his nod she placed her hands on her hips as a frown covered her face. "Do you think there's any way I can think of making love with you with what's going on in the room next door?"

Hunter lifted a brow. "Sounds pretty quiet over there. I suggest we make some noise."

"This isn't funny, Hunter."

"And you don't see me laughing. Now relax and come here for a minute. You're all tense. Let me rub your back."

Mallory sighed. He was right. She was tensed and agitated and when it came to giving body massages, Hunter was the best. Besides, it wasn't fair for her to take the anger she had for Lewis out on him. She slowly moved to the bed but didn't sit down.

"You're going to have to sit down for me to help you, Mallory."

She slowly eased down on the edge of the bed and when she heard him move when he got on his knees behind her, she felt her breath catch. "Why did you take off your clothes?" she asked, barely able to get the words out when he pulled her blouse over her head to massage her back.

"The room comes with the job and since I'm billing you for it I thought we might as well use it."

"I can't, Hunter. I can't make love to you in here knowing Lewis could be next door cheating on my sister."

He leaned over and kissed the side of her face. "Forget about what's going on next door, Mallory, since there is nothing you can do about it. But there is something you can do about this," he said, straightening and letting his erection press against the center of her back.

"Hunter..."

The name was breathed from her lips when he reached around front and unsnapped her bra and then began massaging her breasts. Too weak to resist him, she let him pull her back on the bed with him and he immediately went after her bare breasts as his entire body shifted in place over hers.

Her brain was torn in two. One part wanted to concentrate on what was going on in the room next door and another part wanted this, another chance to be with Hunter. And when he pulled her skirt up to her waist and began removing her panty hose then fumbling with her panties, the latter part of her won out. Especially when he reached down and parted her with his fingers and began stroking her.

"I love you, Mallory," he said, while simultaneously nibbling at her lips. "And you love me. No matter what your father did to your mother, and no matter what Lewis is or is not doing to your sister, it doesn't take away from the fact that we love each other, right?"

Mallory shuddered. It wasn't fair for him to ask her a question like that while doing this to her.

"Right?" he repeated.

When he sank his fingers deeper, she whispered breathlessly. "Right."

"And we're going to have a committed relationship, aren't we? One that ends with marriage and babies, right?" His mouth skimmed over hers slowly, provocatively as his fingers continued stroking her mindlessly. Her belly was quivering and her nipples felt tender to the feel of his chest rubbing against them.

"Right," she responded again, squirming beneath his hand as delicious sensations flooded her.

"And no matter who stays together and who don't stay together won't concern us. We may sympathize but we won't assume it will happen to us. Our love is solid and it will be stronger than that, won't it?" he asked, growling his words in a whisper.

She lifted her hips toward his hand and moaned, "Yes! Yes, it will."

Hunter smiled. "I'm glad we're in agreement on all things." He then scooted his body downward. "And now I want the taste of my future bride, the woman who will be the mother of my children, in my mouth."

She came the moment his tongue replaced his fingers and the orgasm that tore through her almost ripped her in two, and she began trembling uncontrollably. And the more she shivered the more he locked his mouth to her taking the quakes that rocked her body.

"That was nice," he said, moments later as he gathered her sated body in his arms. He held her tight like he never wanted to let her go. "How would you like to be the person to plan my wedding?" he asked, lovingly stroking her cheek.

"I won't have a problem with it as long as I'm the bride," she said, finally accepting her love for him and his love for her. In doing so all the insecurities she felt suddenly faded away. Hunter was right. Although she had to deal with the issues of her father and Lewis, it didn't mean what they felt for each meant less. If anything it meant more because they were determined to love in spite of.

She was about to open her mouth to say something else when a woman let out a loud scream in the connecting room. She stilled, recognizing just what kind of scream it was. Then she was off the bed in a flash, trying to put back on her clothes. The more she tried putting them off the quicker Hunter was trying to take them off her.

"Hunter, stop it! I need to get dressed. I'm going to demand that Lewis open that door. I intend to catch him red-handed."

"Then put on one of the hotel robes from the closet because I intend to keep you in here naked for a while."

Mallory looked at him like he had gone mad. How could he think of sex at a time like this? "Get up and have your camera ready, Hunter. I want pictures. Barbara will need them when she files for a divorce."

Hunter shook his head as he slowly got out of the bed. "I'm charging you overtime for this. This job is going past Lewis's lunch hour."

Mallory raised her eyes to the ceiling, not believing Hunter's attitude but decided she couldn't worry about it now as she raced to the closet to get a robe and tossed the other one over to him. She quickly crossed the room to the connecting door. "Okay, open it."

Hunter didn't move. In fact to Mallory's way of thinking he stood in the middle of the room looking somewhat bored. "We can only unlock it from this side," he said. "In order to get inside the other room, they will have to unlock it from their side as well."

Mallory nodded. "All right then, I'll make him open it and just in case the woman he's with tries to split and run, I want you to be in the hallway to snap pictures."

He crossed his arms over his chest. "I doubt if she's going anywhere."

Mallory frowned, wondering how he figured that, but didn't waste time asking him as she began taking the lock off the connecting door. Then she raised her hand and gave two sharp knocks on the door and yelled at the top of her voice. "Lewis Townsend, I know you're in there so open this door immediately!"

Mallory heard people scrambling about in the other room and glanced over at Hunter before turning to raise her hand to beat on the door again. Hunter quickly crossed the room and caught her hand in his. "The least you can do is to give them time to put their clothes back on or at least time to grab a robe, Mallory."

She glared at him. "Why should I?"

Before he could answer, the connecting door was snatched open and a half-dressed Lewis Townsend stood in the doorway looking furious, as if he was pissed off at being interrupted. He was bare-chested and only wearing his pants. "Mallory? What the hell are you doing here?"

Mallory didn't answer right away. It was apparent that Lewis' question had thrown her for a loop but she recovered quickly. "How dare you ask me that! I should be asking that question of you. You're a married man. I don't know the identity of the woman you've been screwing around with for the past month, but need I remind you that you're married to my sister and I don't appreciate you being unfaithful to her and—"

"Hi, Mallory."

Mallory stopped talking and stared at the woman who was standing behind Lewis and peeping over his shoulder at her and smiling. "Barbara? But—but what are you doing here?"

Barbara chuckled as she came to stand beside her husband

wearing the hotel's thick velour robe. "I'm the woman Lewis been screwing around with for the past month."

"Come to bed, Mallory."

Mallory shifted her gaze from looking out of the window to glare across the room at Hunter. "You think this whole thing is funny, don't you?"

Hunter grinned. "Yes. You should have seen the look on your face when you discovered Lewis had been having an affair with his own wife. And you should have seen the look on Lewis's face when he discovered you had paid me to nail him for adultery."

Mallory winced when she remembered Lewis's brief period of anger. She was thankful that Barbara had made light of the whole thing and made Lewis see how such a wrong assumption could have been made. It seemed their doctor had suggested that to take their mind off making love mainly to create a baby, they should get back into the routine of making love just for the enjoyment and pleasure of it. He figured with the stress eliminated, pregnancy would come easy.

It had been Barbara's idea for them to role-play and engage in lunchtime romantic romps at different hotels just for the sheer fun of it. The idea had worked. Today they had met at the hotel to celebrate the news that Barbara was pregnant.

"I'm so happy for them," Mallory said softly, thinking of how radiant her sister looked.

"Me, too," Hunter said. "Now come back to bed."

Mallory smiled as she walked back over to the bed. They had decided to spend the night at the hotel since they had paid the price for a full night anyway. She tossed back the covers and slipped between the sheets and right into Hunter's arms. He had explained that he'd known who the woman was that Lewis was having an affair with the moment he'd seen her that day in the lobby, which was the only reason he had summoned Mallory to the hotel. He had been determined to make her face her insecurities about them no matter what was going on in the room next door. And she had.

She snuggled in Hunter's arms and smiled proudly. "I'm going to be an aunt, Hunter."

He raked his hand through her hair. "You're also going to be a bride, and I want you a bride before you become an aunt. Let's set a date."

She glanced up at him. "Are you serious?"

"Yes. I want you in my life permanently. Your all night man wants to become a forever man with you. Make it happen."

Mallory's smile widened through her tears. She would make it happen and she knew she would spend the rest of her life loving him.

The untamable Hunter had been tamed.

JUST WANNA LOVE YA

•

Joylynn Jossel

Jai stood in the entrance of Club Cream and scanned the place in hopes of spotting her best friend, Rissa. Every Friday evening after work, Jai and Rissa met at Cream, a downtown Cincinnati, Ohio, singles bar/bistro. Jai always made it a point to run at least ten minutes behind their meeting time of 6:00 P.M. because she hated arriving first and alone. This way Rissa was sure to arrive first and be forced to sit at the bar alone looking desperate instead of Jai. Perhaps on this particular Friday Rissa had finally caught on.

Feeling uneasy, as if all eyes were on her, Jai continued to scan the room. She tugged the bottom of her white Liz Claiborne sweater, pulling it over the slight swell of her stomach. Even though Jai wore a size ten, she had this little gut that she couldn't seem to get rid of no matter how many crunches she did. Other than her kangaroo pouch, she adored every other part of her body. Thirty years old, standing almost six feet tall, Jai had perfectly toned medium brown legs and long slender arms. She had the breasts of a sixteen-year-old—nice, round, and perky—something she was sure to miss after nursing the baby she dreamed of having some day.

After leaving a light brown thumbprint on the bottom of her sweater, compliments of her Mary Kay bronze cream to powder foundation, Jai then ran her manicured, natural nails through her shoulder-length multilayered hair.

Where in the hell is she? Jai said to herself as she tapped her black Nine West strappy to the beat of the music.

"Boo!" Rissa said, coming up behind Jai and tickling her waist.

"There you are," Jai smiled as she turned around and hugged Rissa.

"I got stuck on a call," Rissa explained. "It was my mom bugging me again about who I'm dating and when I'm going to marry him."

"You don't have to tell me how that is." Jai sighed. "I get stuck on calls all of the time. Don't let one of my client's foodstamp cards not be working. They'll have me on the phone for hours."

Rissa rolled her eyes up into her head and began walking toward the two empty stools at the bar. How is it that Jai always managed to fuck up a perfectly decent Friday evening with talk about work? Rissa knew Jai well enough to know that once she said one little thing about work, more was sure to follow.

"I mean some of those women are just lazy," Jai continued, following behind Rissa. "They would be content staying on welfare their entire lives if they could. And what really pisses me off is when they bring their kids to their redetermination appointments and all the little crumb snatchers are wearing Tommy Hilfiger.

Can you believe that? That shit ain't cute, a welfare recipient wearing designer clothes. That's idiotic."

"Two Coronas with lemon please," Rissa said to the bartender as she sat down, flinging her permed blonde hair that just reached the small of her back. Rissa was one of those ideal white girls that all women envied. She was five feet eight inches with beautiful blonde hair. Her eyes were as blue as the sky with fluttering, thick lashes. Her lips were luscious and she had a body like Britney Spears. Rissa wasn't your typical dime, she was a roll of dimes. Three years ago she had won the Bud Girl contest at Cream and traveled all over representing Budweiser. Jai even tagged along to a couple of the events. Rissa posed in a calendar and everything. It was almost like she was a celebrity.

"Is something wrong?" Jai asked, sensing some tension with Rissa.

"No, nothing's wrong," Rissa replied. "You know how much I love hearing you talk about your job all night long. Please, by all means, continue."

"I'm sorry, Riss," Jai apologized. "I promise, not one more word about the County Human Service Department."

The bartender placed the girls' drinks in front of them and complimented Rissa's ocean blue eyes. Rissa thanked him with a huge grin and an eyewink like she did every Friday. This innocent flirting routine always guaranteed that the first round of drinks would be on the house.

Rissa pushed her lemon down into her Corona bottle and with beer in hand, she turned around in her stool to check out the scene.

"Oh my God," Rissa said in a soft tone, as if she were talking to herself. "I swear the most beautiful man in the world is sitting right over there."

Rissa pointed to a table that was blessed with the company of three gorgeous males. One guy in particular stood out like a rose in a garden of weeds. He was a tall, white male. His eyes were deep brown. His lips were pouty, in a manly sort of way, and his black shiny hair waved back from his forehead and curled up at the ends. And that dimple—it was a sexy ass dimple—in the middle of his chin that had probably persuaded countless number of women to drop their panties on their first date with him. Hell, one couldn't blame them either. His dimples in his cheeks damn near swallowed up his face when he put on that million-dollar smile.

"I think it's safe for you to say that he is, indeed, the most beautiful man in the world," Jai agreed. "He looks like a CK underwear model, for crying out loud. Not bad at all for a white guy."

"Not bad at all for a guy period," Rissa said dazed, as if she were hypnotized by his presence.

"You got a little dribble on your lip," Jai said jokingly as she took her napkin and began wiping Rissa's bottom lip.

"Dribble my ass," Rissa said, still in a daze. "I think my mouth just had an orgasm."

Jai laughed.

"Oh shit," Rissa said, quickly turning around on her stool to the bar.

"What?" Jai said, looking over at the table with the three men, being anything but discreet.

"No, don't look over there!" Rissa said, nudging Jai's leg with her own. "He keeps looking over here. I think he checked out the fact that we are checking him out. I don't want to look desperate."

"Too late for that," Jai said, calmly turning around on her barstool.

"I'm serious," Rissa said in a serious tone. "That's the man I'm going to marry."

"Well, don't piss your pants," Jai said, looking over her shoulder. "But it looks like the most beautiful man in the world is heading this way."

Rissa quickly pulled out a tube of Wet 'n' Wild clear lip gloss and began to smooth some on to her pink full lips.

"Wet 'n' Wild?" Jai questioned, watching Rissa polish her lips. "You have on an $85-a-bottle perfume and you're painting your lips with $1.67 lip gloss?"

"Yeah, but check out the shine," Rissa said, puckering her lips while Jai nodded in agreement.

"Hello, ladies," the most beautiful man in the world spoke with an accent.

"Hi," Jai said nonchalantly.

"Hello to you, too," Rissa said in a sensual tone as she turned on her barstool to face him. "I love that sweater."

Rissa took her thumb and index finger and began to molest the neck of the black ribbed turtleneck sweater he was wearing.

"Thank you. It was a birthday gift from my mom," he replied.

"Oh, how sweet," Rissa flirted. "Do you live with your mom?"

"No," the gentleman said, smiling. "My parents live in Columbus, Ohio. I live alone here in Cincy."

"Oh," Rissa said, relieved as she uncrossed her fingers from behind her back. Jai smiled at Rissa and turned her attention to her half-empty bottle of Corona.

"Can I get you something?" the jealous bartender interrupted, directing his query to the unwelcomed stranger.

"Actually you can," the gentleman replied. "I'll take a rum and coke and bring the ladies another round of Coronas please."

"Thank you," Rissa said with a wink and a smile. "By the way, I'm Clarissa, but my friends call me Rissa, and this is my best friend, Jai."

"I'm Sloan," he said, extending his hand to Jai and Rissa.

Jai turned in her barstool to face Sloan, giving him a stern handshake. Rissa, on the other hand, extended her hand as if she was a princess expecting her prince charming to kneel and kiss her hand. Sloan politely shook Rissa's hand.

The bartender rolled his eyes and went to fill the order. Just then the disc jockey put on "Beautiful" by Snoop Doggy Dog.

"I like this song," Sloan said, nodding his head to the beat. "Do you want to dance?"

"Ooohhh, I like this song, too," Rissa said.

"That's nice," Sloan replied. "So, Jai, what do you say? Come on, let's dance."

Sloan grabbed Jai by the hand and pulled her towards him, eliminating any possibility of refusal. Stunned, Jai stared at Rissa in shock as Sloan dragged her onto the dance floor.

Once Sloan finally got Jai to the center of the dance floor he began to do this cool, smooth ass dance around her, checking out every inch of her frame. Not knowing whether to blush or feel guilty that she was on the dance floor with the man her best friend had smothered her lips in cheap lip gloss for, Jai just stood there. She stood there feeling sexy as hell. She felt like a juicy piece of meat smothered in gravy and Sloan was a biscuit about to sop her up.

"Move something," Sloan said, snapping his fingers and bobbing his head to he beat.

"Excuse me?" Jai replied, uncertain of his request.

"Let me see you move something. Come on, dance." Sloan

closed his eyes and snapped his fingers as he began singing the hook of the song, "Beautiful, I just want you to know that you're my favorite girl."

"You have a wonderful voice," Jai said, shocked at Sloan's soulful timbre.

"Thank you," Sloan said, grabbing hold of Jai's hands.

Jai loosened up as she began to sway a little bit. She freed her hands from Sloan's, tugged her sweater down over her stomach, and began to swing her hips from side to side, like they do in the Midwest.

This is a sexy motherfucker, Jai thought, watching Sloan croon on the dance floor. She had no conversation what so ever. She couldn't tear her eyes off of Sloan's sultry movements. She would smile on the occasions when he caught her trying to peek at what he was packing down below, but other than that, Jai just tried to concentrate on her nerves.

The song was over much too soon. It was now Christina Aguilera's turn to have her say on beauty as her song, "Beautiful," floated throughout the room. Jai already knew she had some "splainin'" to do with Rissa. She had broken girlfriend rule number one. When your friend places dibs on a guy, he's off-limits. To now slow dance with Sloan would have been to commit an atrocity.

"Thanks for the dance," Jai said as she backed up and prepared to go back over to the bar with Rissa.

"You're not going to just leave me on this dance floor butt naked are you?" Sloan asked, smiling.

"Excuse me?" Jai asked, confused.

"You just undressed me with your eyes throughout the entire song and now you're going to just leave me out here alone, and naked?"

Jai swallowed as Sloan held out his hand to her. Jai stared at him for a moment before softly placing her hand inside of his and rejoining him in the center of the dance floor. Sloan placed Jai's hands around his waist and his around the nape of her neck. He left a few inches of room in between them. This was Jai's space to do with whatever she pleased.

The scent of Sloan's musky cologne was like a drug and Jai was getting high. If this was what it felt like to be a bird flying high in the sky, hell, Jai didn't want her feet to ever touch the ground again. It was only a matter of seconds before Jai moved in close and pressed her body against Sloan's.

"You know my girlfriend had been checking you out," Jai whispered in Sloan's ear.

"I hadn't noticed," Sloan replied, closing his eyes as he tightened his hold on Jai. "I was too busy checking you out."

"I shouldn't have even danced with you, especially not a slow dance," Jai said, breathing a sigh of guilt. "She's going to kill me."

"I don't want to be the cause of any discord between you and your girlfriend," Sloan said, staring down at her. "Do you want to stop?"

How in the hell did Sloan expect Jai to say no while staring down at her with those bedroom eyes, gleaming with that "fuck me" look?

"No," Jai replied. "I don't wanna stop."

Sloan pulled Jai up against him even tighter and began massaging her neck. Jai tensed up a little bit and glanced over at Rissa. Rissa sat at the bar watching them like a hawk while throwing down shots of gin and juice. Jai quickly looked away.

"I've never seen you in here before," Jai said with an expression on her face as if trying to recollect ever seeing him before. "Rissa and I come every Friday and I'm sure I've never seen you in here before."

"How can you be so certain I've never been here before?" Sloan asked.

"I would have remembered you," Jai was quick to say in an appealing tone.

Sloan smiled. "You're right," he gave in. "I've never been here before. This is my first time."

"Well, what brought you here tonight?" Jai asked.

"I know those guys from the gym," Sloan said, nodding to the two gentlemen he had been sitting with. "One of them has been here before and suggested we come here for drinks."

Jai nodded and smiled. "Just hanging out with a couple guys from the gym, hey?"

"Yep," Sloan confirmed, as he spun Jai around and pulled her back close to him. "You smell good. What's that you're wearing?"

"I honestly can't remember what I put on this morning. I can't believe you can still smell it," Jai said, smiling at him.

"Mmm," he said, inhaling, and Jai's heartbeat began to pick up pace. "It must be your natural scent. Usually things that smell good taste good, also."

Jai felt heat pool between her legs. She laughed. "Is one of your friends holding up cue cards for you or something, because you are feeding me some lines."

"Then I hope you're hungry, because there are more where those came from. I could feed you all night long."

"And you're quick on your feet, too."

"Yeah, us Italian guys are," Sloan replied as he dipped Jai, staring deeply into her eyes.

"You're Italian?" Jai asked as Sloan pulled her up close to him.

"Yeah. My parents moved to the states from Italy when I was ten."

"And of all the places on the map to relocate they chose Ohio?"

"Nah, we started off in New York. That was a little too fast for the Mama Mia. So we pitched a tent in *Slowlumbus,* otherwise known as Columbus. I got a scholarship at the University of Cincinnati and my internship at LaVater Insurance turned into a permanent position. I'm now an adjuster there."

"Interesting," Jai said, very interested in hearing more about Sloan.

"You from the Nasty Natti?" Sloan said, turning the table to find out information about Jai.

"Born and raised," Jai sighed.

"This city has the most beautiful skyline."

"And you have the most beautiful eyes," Jai couldn't resist saying, then blushed.

"You're beautiful," Sloan said, staring into Jai's eyes.

"These song titles must be getting to us." Jai laughed.

"Yeah," Sloan said with a smile as the song faded out. "I really enjoyed dancing with you, Jai."

Jai blushed. "Me too."

"I hope your girlfriend doesn't give you too much hell."

"Ahhh, she'll get over it."

"Do you think maybe you could give me your phone number? I could call you sometime and maybe we could go dancing again . . . all night long this time."

Jai looked over at Rissa, who was still staring them down. The bartender was effortlessly whispering game in Rissa's ear, trying to hook up with her for the night. Jai knew that Rissa would have a fit if she saw her giving Sloan her phone number. Jai looked back at Sloan and decided to risk it.

"867-5309," she quickly rambled off.

"Excuse me?" Sloan said.

"My number . . . it's 867-5309," Jai repeated. "Can you remember that?"

"I'll never forget it. Those are my lucky numbers." Sloan winked, then turned and joined his friends at their table.

Jai took a deep breath before rejoining Rissa back at the bar.

"Hey, girl," Jai said nonchalantly as she sat back down at her barstool.

Rissa forced out a "Hey."

"It's hot in here," Jai said, fanning herself.

"If I had been all hugged up and sweaty on a man, I would be hot, too," Rissa said, signaling for the bartender, who dropped everything to respond to her.

"Yeah, baby?" the bartender said to Rissa.

"I thought about it," Rissa said, taking a pen out of her purse and grabbing a napkin. "The answer is yes. I'd love to hook up with you tonight. Here's my address."

Rissa wrote down her home address on the napkin and slid it to the bartender who snatched it up before she could change her mind.

"I'll be there as soon as I get off," the bartender said, walking away, planting a kiss on the napkin before sticking it into his pants pocket.

"You're kidding right?" Jai said, her mouth dropping open.

"What?" Rissa replied as if daring Jai to say something about it.

"Look, Rissa. I know what you're doing and I'm sorry. I had no idea the most beautiful man in the world was going to come over and ask me to dance," Jai said sincerely. "Besides, he's Italian. You said you'd never date another Italian after Tony."

"That was different," Rissa snapped. "Tony was an asshole. He had this obsession with John Travolta and *Saturday Night Fever*. His real name wasn't even Tony. It was Farco. And he really wasn't Italian after all. He was Irish."

"No, kidding?" Jai said, amazed that Rissa hadn't mentioned this before. But it was just like Rissa to hold out on something that might embarrass her. "Well, look at the bright side." She smiled. "He could have been gay. I mean his real name could have been Shaquan."

Rissa didn't smile back.

"Come on, Rissa," Jai begged. "You didn't know he was coming over here to ask me to dance."

"And I had no idea that if he did you would say yes," Rissa said, disappointed in her friend.

"Rissa, you saw him pull me out there. He didn't even give me a chance to decline."

"What about the second dance, the slow one?" Rissa said, rolling her eyes.

Jai sighed and buried her face in her hands. "Rissa, we are not about to let a man come between us. We never have and we won't start now."

"I agree," Rissa said, picking up her drink and gulping down the last swallow. "Hell, it was just a dance. We'll probably never see him again. It's not like you gave him your phone number or anything."

Jai's silence told Rissa everything she needed to know. Rissa slammed down her drink and grabbed her purse.

"See you tonight," Rissa said to the bartender, then stormed off.

"Rissa, wait!" Jai called to her.

"Oh, no," Rissa said. "You stay here and dance the night away with the Italian Stallion over there."

"Rissa!" Jai called as Rissa stomped her way out of the club. Jai sat at the bar, shaking her head. She couldn't believe Rissa had actually made such a scene. On top of that she was about to have a one-night stand with the slimy bartender. The guy's gut was so bulgy that it looked as though his water was going to break any day now. He had a bushy black mustache with matching greasy brunette hair. When a woman's ego was bruised there was no telling how low she would go to restore it.

Rissa could get any man she wanted, and was used to doing just that. Sloan being interested in Jai and not her was the ultimate low blow. Using the bartender to repair her ego for the night would be one of those mistakes women sometimes made.

Jai couldn't wait to get home and relax in a long hot bath with some soothing bath salts. Rissa had purchased Jai an African American greeting card for her birthday. Inside the card was a bag of bath salts. The aroma was unlike any that Jai had purchased in a bath and body store. Jai used them sparingly for those days she was in overdrive. Today was one of those days.

Showers were Jai's norm, but Mondays always called for long hot baths. Jai threw an armful of case files onto her big cushioned sofa she had gotten from Aaron's Sales and Leasing. On her salary, she couldn't afford to go out and buy the leather sectionals that most of her welfare clients somehow seemed to decorate their Section 8 homes with.

Jai picked up the phone and entered the code to check her voice-mail messages. Her sister, Joi, who Jai nicknamed Sissy, called wanting to borrow fifty dollars until next week. Her dad called wanting to know if she ever got her bathtub knob fixed or if she was still using pliers to turn the water on and off, and one of her credit card company's called to offer her two months free of her favorite three magazines. Jai, with disappointment, hung up the phone. There was not one message from Rissa, who still hadn't returned any of Jai's calls.

Not since their college days, when the two met, had they gone this long without speaking to one another. Jai and Rissa had always been inseparable. Back in college if you saw one, you saw the other. When the two eventually dropped out of college together to start their own so-called door-to-door cosmetic business (that they never saw through), they were even roommates for a couple of years. Never had they gone this long without communicating.

Jai had already called Rissa three times. Jai could picture Rissa staring at her phone number on the caller ID box and letting the call go to her voice mail. Rissa was just that simple to do something that silly. Jai shook her head. She didn't have time to fool with Rissa's nonsense, mad at her over a guy she spotted first . . . it's not like he was her ex or something (which would have been a violation of girlfriend rule number two: no dating one another's ex). Besides, if Sloan had really been interested in Jai, he would have called her by now. Hell, he probably just approached Jai on a dare from his friends. If Rissa wanted to act irrational over a man neither of them would ever see again, then it was her waste of energy.

Jai lit her melon, triple-wick candle and sank her body down into the steaming hot water, slowly, letting her body adjust to the heat. Times like this made her feel like Farah, a character she had read about in one of her favorite books, *Use Me or Lose Me*. She loved reading about women who had some of the same issues she did: no kids and no man to help produce any and if she did luck up on a halfway decent guy, nine times out of ten, he was somebody else's.

This was one of the reasons why Jai hadn't been in a serious relationship in the past few years. Along with men came drama and she had enough drama with work. She didn't need any in her personal life. She had dated a fella here in there, but she never allowed herself to get too involved. And she made damn sure she didn't put herself in a position to send any mixed signals that she wanted to get too involved either. There was no spending the night at his house or him at hers. A courtesy phone call here and there to keep in touch, dinner, and a movie was pretty much the extent of any relationship Jai had had. But she hadn't even engaged in those minor activities with a man in over a year.

After her bath, Jai cut up some lettuce to make herself a salad. She added some shredded cheddar cheese and bacon bits, drowning everything in Italian dressing, and headed into her living room. Jai turned on a court TV show and flopped down on the couch next to the pile of files. Times like this she didn't mind her own company.

About forty-five minutes later Jai was torn away from a case file she had started to work on by the ringing of her phone.

"Hello?"

"May I speak with Jai?" the caller asked.

"This is she," Jai said as her heart began to beat one hundred miles per hour. It was a man, which meant only one thing. It was Sloan. No other man, besides her father, would be calling Jai.

"This is Sloan," he confirmed Jai's hopes.

"Yes, I know," Jai said, smiling.

"What are you up to?" Sloan asked.

"Umm, nothing much. Just sitting here watching the game," Jai said quickly, thinking he would find that more interesting than court TV.

"Oh yeah?" Sloan said. "Who's winning?"

Caught off guard, Jai's mind raced frantically.

"Uh, can you hold on a second? That's my other line beeping."

"Sure," Sloan replied.

Jai hit the mute button and burst out laughing. She felt like a silly high school girl trying to get the captain of the basketball team to notice her. She shook her head with a smile, took a few seconds to compose herself, and then hit the mute button again.

"Sorry about that," Jai said.

"It's okay. So you're watching the game, huh? I wish I was there watching it with you," Sloan said, his voice low and seductive.

"Is that so?"

"Yes, it is."

"Are you beating around the bush for an invite?"

"It was that obvious, huh?"

"Most obvious."

"I'm sorry. I'm just not used to beating around the bush."

"Then don't," Jai replied.

"Can I come over?"

Once again Sloan had caught Jai off guard.

"Hold on a sec," Jai said, putting down the phone and hitting the mute button again. She then proceeded to scream.

She didn't mind her own company, but throwing a man into the equation never hurt either. Jai had to stop and think to herself for a minute, *If that fine ass man comes over here, I know I'm going to have sex with him. I can't even go out like that.* Jai hit the mute button again.

"I'm back," Jai said.

"And do you have an answer for me?" Sloan asked.

Jai wanted to say "no" as the word "yes" forced its way out of her mouth. Before Jai knew it she was spitting out her address, giving blow-by-blow directions to her house, and changing out of her cow printed pajama shirt and into a white button-up blouse and some Baby Phat jeans. She just hoped she knew what she was getting herself into.

Jai prepared some microwave popcorn and dumped it into a bowl. She placed it on the octagon-shaped glass table along with a bottle of hot sauce. After doing so she stopped and thought to herself, *Italians probably don't eat hot sauce on their popcorn, I'm sure.* Jai picked the hot sauce back up with the intent of returning it to the cupboard. *Fuck it . . . I'm black and I eat hot sauce on my popcorn,* she thought as she put it right back down on the table.

Initially Jai had set out two wineglasses for the bottle of wine she had chilling in the fridge to make the setting a bit romantic. She decided that the more romantic she set the scene, the more the chances were of her finding herself butt naked riding Mr. Italian like a stallion so she decided against the wine. Jai convinced herself that a man and a woman could enjoy a couple hours of television without jumping each other's bones and that every evening phone call wasn't deemed a booty call.

Headlights shone through Jai's living room window announcing Sloan's arrival. Jai took a quick survey of the house, quickly turned the television channel to a game of basketball, and took a deep breath.

"Just a minute," Jai called, when her doorbell rang. She took a second to straighten herself up, pulling her blouse down over her stomach, and opened the door.

"Well, hello," Sloan said, smiling. He had a six-pack of Corona in hand. "I brought you a little something to enjoy with the game."

"Thank you," Jai smiled from ear to ear. "Please, come in."

Jai moved aside and allowed Sloan to enter. He looked like he belonged on a runway as he walked in with his crisp creased jeans and Polo golf shirt . . . and umm, there was that scent that drove her crazy. Yes sir, Jai was sure in definite danger of giving up the panties tonight.

"Nice house you've got here," Sloan said, looking around.

"Thank you. Do you have a house?" Jai asked.

"An apartment. I'm not much into maintenance and yard work so if we ever get married, I hope you'd be happy with a condo," Sloan said with a grin.

Jai's heart began to pound. A man as fine as him did not need to be making marriage jokes.

"Is everything okay?" Sloan asked and Jai realized that she had been just standing there staring at him.

"Oh sure, I'm sorry. Please have a seat," Jai said, pointing to the sofa.

"Do you mind if I sit on the floor? That's more comfortable to me."

"I don't mind at all."

"What about my shoes? I want to be as comfortable as you," Sloan said, referring to Jai's bare feet. "By the way, nice toes."

"Thank you," Jai said, wiggling her piggies. "Feel free to kick your shoes off, relax."

Sloan smiled as he removed his shoes and the jacket he was wearing.

Jai flopped down on the sofa.

"I know you're not going to have me sitting down here by myself. You're not one of them stuck-up chicks are you, too good for the floor?" Sloan smiled again. "Let me guess, not afraid of getting a lil' ole rug burn are you?"

Up for the challenge, Jai slowly slid down next to Sloan on the floor, grabbing a fistful of popcorn on her way down. Sloan grabbed a handful after her, tossed it in his mouth, and then cracked open two bottles of Corona.

"I shouldn't have assumed this, but I take it you don't have any kids," Sloan said.

"Nah," Jai said, though she longed for them.

"Yeah, me either. Someday though, with the right woman," Sloan said, even though he had convinced himself that there was no right woman. Most of the females he had dated were more concerned about what was already at the table than with what they could bring to the table. So lately he had pretty much stayed focused on climbing the corporate ladder, without a woman weighing him down. Doing so enabled him to skip a few steps. Besides that, two of the head honchos at the insurance company where he works are women in their late thirties (a little older than he is)—one who would love to have a *thing* with Sloan and the other actually had a *thing* with Sloan back when he first started working for the company. Seeing that Sloan wasn't a womanizer, showing up with a different lady friend at every company function, always made them feel like Sloan was genuinely dedicated to the company, and that they had a chance with him, even though they didn't have a chance in the world. But, of course, Sloan didn't lead them on to believe otherwise. Although they were hardworking, educated women, he saw neither of them as women he could settle down and have children with.

Jai smiled. "Yeah, me too. I'd love to have children someday."

"Have you ever dated an Italian guy or white guy before?" Sloan asked suddenly and Jai damn near spit her mouthful of Corona out.

"Uhh, no," Jai said, wiping her bottom lip. "Have you? Ever dated a black girl?"

"No."

Jai bit her lip. "Then why me?"

Sloan turned to face her, looking directly into her eyes.

"I didn't see a black girl. I saw a beautiful woman I wanted to get to know."

By this time Jai's panties were getting a little moist.

"So I guess it's my turn to ask 'why me'?"

"I don't know. You were just this guy who forced me onto the dance floor and who I found myself deeply attracted to."

"Oh, I forced you onto the dance floor, huh?" He smiled. "Next you'll be saying I forced you into a relationship and then marriage. You know how you chicks do it."

He had said it again. He said the "M" word and nothing happened. Jai was certain that this time his face would swell up and his eyes would become puffy and watery, but nothing happened. Sloan just sat there eating popcorn, sipping on his brew, and watching the game.

"You're doing it again," Sloan said.

"What?"

"Staring at me like I'm transforming into a little blue Martian or something."

Jai laughed. "I'm sorry."

"That's okay. I could sit here and stare at you all night, too. I'm just a little bit more discreet than you are."

Sloan continued to speak but Jai only saw his lips move and his dimples flash. Her heart fluttered as she visualized ripping off her blouse, buttons shooting across the room, and climbing on top of Sloan to ram her tongue down his throat. Okay, now her panties were soaked.

"Excuse me," Jai said, interrupting him. "I'm going to go put the rest of these Coronas in the fridge."

Jai grabbed the remaining beers and carried them into the kitchen, setting them on the countertop. She placed her forehead against the refrigerator and took a deep breath. She had to relax and stay focused.

"Lemon," Sloan said, startling Jai. She whirled around to see him standing behind her. "I'm sorry, I didn't mean to scare you. Is everything okay? Are you not feeling well?"

Sloan put his hand on Jai's forehead to check for a temperature. His being that close to her made them both feverish.

"You were saying something about lemon," Jai said breathlessly.

"Oh, yeah. I forgot I had brought a lemon for the Coronas. It was in my jacket pocket," Sloan said, handing Jai the lemon.

Starring into Sloan's eyes Jai slowly removed the lemon from his hand. He couldn't resist pulling her close to him and planting a luscious kiss on Jai's lips.

"I don't know if your coming over here was such a good idea," Jai replied, unable to control her heavy breathing.

"Come on. I'm diggin' you, girl. I know you're diggin' me, too," Sloan said, licking his bottom lip.

The lemon slipped from the palm of Jai's hand and rolled across the floor as Sloan's hands slid down her body.

"Seriously," Jai said. "You need to go before something happens that I don't want to happen, not on the first date anyway. If that's what we can even call this."

"I'm not going to force you to do anything you don't want to do," he said seriously. "Like the way I forced you onto the dance floor." Then he smiled.

Jai caressed his shoulders. "That's the problem, I want to do it."

"Do what?"

"It."

"What's it?"

"Stop playing," Jai said, pushing Sloan playfully.

Sloan tilted his head to the side and licked his lips. "You really want me to go?" Sloan asked.

"My body doesn't, but I do," Jai told him.

"Okay, it's cool. I'll go. But I'll be back," Sloan said as he winked and headed back into the living room.

Girlfriend, don't you let that fine hunk of a man walk out of that door, Jai's alter ego scolded her.

Good girls don't go to bed with a guy that they just met. The longer you make him wait the more he'll respect you, Jai's conscience preached.

What do we look like here? Aretha Franklin? Damn respect, we want some hot steamy sex, Jai's alter ego reminded her.

Jai shook her head and reassured herself that she was doing the right thing by sending Sloan home. She pulled her shirt down over her stomach and headed back toward the living room where Sloan was sliding on his shoes.

Sloan didn't speak to Jai. He just looked up at her with a puppy-dog expression on his face and grabbed his jacket.

"I had a cool forty-five minutes with you," Sloan said, looking at his watch.

"I'm sorry," Jai said, walking slowly toward Sloan. She tried to be sexy with her steps but ruined it when she kicked the coffee table and stubbed her toe. "Ouch!"

"Are you okay?" Sloan asked, walking over to her. He picked her up and laid her across the couch. Sloan sat down and placed Jai's feet on his lap.

"Is it this one?" Sloan said, rubbing Jai's big toe.

Jai flinched. "Yeah, right there."

Sloan rubbed more gently. Jai was in heaven. Sloan took his index finger and traced it down the center of Jai's foot, from the big toe all the way to the heel, then back up again. Jai squirmed. Foot action had always been her downfall.

"It feels better now," Jai said, trying to pull her foot away from him.

"Uh uhh," Sloan said, raising her foot slowly to his lips. He glazed his tongue across the tip of her toes, then in between them.

Fuck it! Jai thought as she fell limp to Sloan's toe-licking technique.

Sloan teased Jai's toes with his tongue a little while longer with a lick here and a lick there before sucking them one by one. He watched her, her eyes closed, as she squirmed and wiggled. When Sloan put pressure on the meaty part under Jai's big toe, Jai went insane and knew it was time for Sloan to leave, for real this time.

"Yep, all better now," Jai said, tugging her foot from Sloan's hands. Sloan smiled, then stood up with jacket in hand and walked over to the door.

"I had a nice time with you, Jai," Sloan said. "I hope we can do it again sometime."

"Me, too," Jai said as she looked up at him shyly.

"Before I go I was wondering if we could do something?"

"What?" Jai said, shrugging her shoulders.

"Let's give thanks," Sloan said softly.

"Give thanks?" Jai asked with a perplexed look on her face.

He smiled again. "That's what I said."

"Okay," Jai said, unsure as she closed her eyes and bowed her head.

"I have several things I would like to give thanks for," Sloan said as he began to unbutton Jai's blouse. "Thank you for these big beautiful coconuts."

"You are so silly," Jai giggled as Sloan caressed her breast with his hands, pulled them from under her white satin bra, and kissed on them. He then moved downward, kissing every inch along the way.

"Thank you for this pit, deep like the pit of a peach," Sloan said flushing his tongue in and out of Jai's deep belly button.

"Umm, that feels good," Jai said, rubbing her hands through Sloan's hair as he unbuttoned her jeans, facing the fact that she had lost the battle.

"Thank you for sweet cherries," Sloan said as he rubbed his face across Jai's black lace panties. She was so sure that she wasn't going to sleep with Sloan that she didn't bother putting on a matching panty and bra set. Sloan didn't seem to mind as he inhaled her scent.

"Do you have anything for protection?" Jai asked in a soft whisper.

Sloan pulled out a string of three condoms in hot pink packaging from his pants pocket. He tore off one and handed it to Jai, placing the others back in his pocket.

"Lay down," Jai ordered.

"Right here?" he asked.

"What's the matter? You're not afraid of a lil' ole rug burn are you?" Jai smiled and licked her lips.

Sloan kicked his shoes off and laid down on the floor.

"Take your clothes off, and slowly. I want to watch and I don't want to miss a thing."

Sloan peeled off his clothes and once he was fully undressed Jai sat down beside him. She slowly rolled the condom down his stiff penis. The size of his cock defied the myth. Jai was pleased.

Jai climbed over Sloan on all fours, feeling like a panther stalking her prey. Sloan slid his hand behind her neck, pulled Jai's head down and thrust his tongue in her mouth. Jai moaned feeling as if she were being eaten alive. Sloan pulled Jai's head down so that he could give her some tongue. The two slurped and slopped like hungry kittens feeding from their mother's tits. Jai was so wet that she was afraid she would start dripping her juices on Sloan. So she reached down and began stroking Sloan's manhood. She pressed it against her clit and began to move it back and forth.

"Put it in," Sloan groaned.

Jai had only gotten the tip in when Sloan began to moan. Even more of her juices came down and he slid home, filling her. Slowly Sloan began to thrust. With each stroke he was deeper and deeper inside of her.

Up and down slowly was the tempo. The room filled with the sound of Sloan's dick moving in and out of Jai's wet pussy. Sloan held on to Jai's hips for dear life. Faster and harder he began to pump in and out of her. Faster and harder she began to bounce. Jai stared down at Sloan and knew he was about to cum by the intense pleasurable look on his face. She sat up and began to roll her hips like a belly dancer.

"Oooh shit," Sloan said, opening his eyes. "Wait, Jai. Stop!"

"What?" Jai asked, immediately ceasing her horizontal dance.

"I don't want to cum yet," Sloan whispered, his voice deep and intense. He lifted Jai up off of him and flipped her onto her belly. "I want to take you from the back."

"Okay," Jai said skeptically. She had never been a big fan of being fucked from the back. She never got as much out of it as the man did. But she was willing to try it with Sloan, but she wasn't going to expect much.

Sloan slid his hand beneath Jai's hips and lifted her up to him so that her ass was in the air and her face pressed to the floor. She was reminded of how vulnerable she felt in this position. Then he entered her in one hard thrust and Jai gasped. She arched her back and dug her nails into the carpet as he began to pump in and out of her. The man was definitely hitting all her spots just right.

Sloan pounded into her harder and harder. He pumped Jai until the condom filled with hot sticky cream. Jai moaned. She could feel Sloan cuming inside of her as his cock flexed uncontrollably.

"Ohhhhh, I'm about to cum. I'm about to cum," Jai gasped.

"Fuck that dick, baby," Sloan said, smoothing his hands down her hips until Jai's back arched up off the ground and she made that ooohh ahhh sound. She screamed as her orgasm slammed into her and knew that they both had been pleased.

Sloan pulled out of Jai then lay across her sweaty body, each of them breathing heavily. They lay there for what seemed like eternity before Sloan headed home.

"Who is it?" Rissa replied to the knock on her door.

"It's me," Jai said. "Open up, Rissa."

Rissa looked through the peephole to confirm that it was Jai. She took a deep breath, then paused. How could she not open the door at this point? She should have looked out of the peephole first and then left Jai standing out there knocking.

"What are you doing here?" Rissa said, opening the door, leaving Jai standing in the doorway as she walked, with attitude, back over to her computer station that was situated in the corner of her living room.

"Working on an article?" Jai said, closing the door behind her.

"More like brainstorming," Rissa said very short.

Jai followed Rissa over to the computer station and helped herself to a box of Cheeze-Its that was sitting next to her computer.

"Help yourself," Rissa said sarcastically. This was becoming a bit too much for Jai. These two had shared everything as roommates: clothes, shoes, groceries, hell, even boxes of tampons and now she was tripping over a Cheeze-It. Jai knew for certain now that it was time to nip the situation in the bud.

"Can we go over to the couch and sit down and talk?" Jai asked.

"Wait a minute. Some ideas just got to flowing. I need to type them before I lose them," Rissa said as she began typing away on her computer. She had been doing research and gathering data for a column she was producing and wanted to shop to major newspapers and magazines titled "He Said–She Said." It was her dream to be Carrie from the HBO hit, *Sex and the City*. Rissa took her writing very seriously so Jai didn't mind grabbing the entire box of Cheeze-Its and walking over to the couch to wait on her. It would only be a couple of minutes before Rissa was ready to talk.

"So, what's on your mind," Rissa said, turning her chair around at the computer table.

"You and the silent treatment you've been giving me," Jai replied.

"What silent treatment?" Rissa said, shrugging her shoulders as if she didn't have a clue.

"What silent treatment? You've been ignoring my calls all week long and I've left you a ton of messages, of which you haven't returned one of them. Hell, I'm surprised you answered the door when you found out it was me."

Rissa got up and walked over to Jai. She sat down next to her, stared at her, and just burst out laughing.

"What's so fucking funny?" Jai said, trying not to catch the contagious bug of laughter. Rissa continued laughing. "What? This isn't funny. You been playing me to the left and won't even give me a chance to explain things to you."

"I'm sorry, Jai," Rissa said, calming her laughter. "I guess I really have been acting stupid. I should have just told you how I felt and got it over with instead of acting like a three-year-old."

"Yeah, you should have," Jai agreed as she flung a Cheeze-It in her mouth. "So, how do you feel, Rissa?"

"Played," Rissa said, snatching the box from Jai and eating a couple herself. "I mean, you knew I was interested in Sloan. At the time I just felt like if you were any type of friend, then you would have told him, hey, my girl likes you, and left it alone. But watching you tango with him on the dance floor . . ."

"We weren't doing the tango," Jai interrupted.

"Figure of speech, Jai."

"Look, Rissa, I'm sorry. It's just that we've never had to deal with this type of situation in all of our years of friendship. We've never been attracted to the same guy before. It's just a given. I go for the black man and you go for the white man."

"Hold up, did you say you were attracted to him?"

Jai couldn't believe she let that one slip out. *Busted!*

"This is just unbelievable," Rissa said as she stood up from the couch in anger. "First you dance with him, then you give him your number. Oh let me guess, you came over to tell me that you've just happened to have slept with him, too."

Once again, *busted!* A puppy-dog look came across Jai's face and she put her head down in silence.

"Oh, I'm going to be sick to my stomach," Rissa said, standing up, holding her belly.

"I'm sorry, Rissa. I really am, but my God, you're overreacting. It's not that serious. It's not like he was ever interested in you in the first place. He came over to talk to me, so quit acting like I stole your husband from you at the altar."

"You just don't get it, do you?" Rissa asked.

"I guess I don't," Jai replied.

"Just forget it. It's always about Jai."

"No, I don't want to forget it. I love you, Rissa. You're my best friend and we need to rectify this situation. I can't have you mad at me. You're my best frie . . ." Jai said as she found herself choking back tears. "You're my only friend."

Rissa, with tears strolling down her face, sat back down next to Jai and put her arm around her.

"You're right, it's not that serious. What are we doing, arguing over a man?" Rissa said. "I can get any man. Hell, I'm sure the runner-up to the most beautiful man in the world is somewhere. What do you think the odds are that he's in Cincinnati, Ohio, too?"

Jai grinned. "I'm not going to lose my best friend of nine years over a man I haven't even known a week."

"So you're not going to ever see him again, right?"

"What?" Jai said, shocked.

"Just kidding." Rissa smiled. "I do want you to be happy, Jai. I know that's probably hard for you to believe with the way I've been acting. But you deserve to be with a man who makes you happy. Hell, you deserve to be with a man period."

"Hey," Jai said, play-punching Rissa in the arm.

"But seriously. If Sloan is the one who's going to pull you out of your drought, then go for it!"

"Thanks, Rissa," Jai said. "Now are you positive you're cool with this?"

"Yes, yes, yes," Rissa said. "Now stop asking me before I start hating on you again. Maybe now that you've finally been laid you'll be less bitchy."

"Me bitchy. Please, girl. You put the itch in bitch," Jai laughed.

"Truce," Rissa said, sticking her hand out to shake on it.

"Truce," Jai said, shaking her hand.

"Well, I need to get back to my brainstorming," Rissa said.

"Oh, yeah, of course," Jai said, standing up and heading toward the door. "Cream this Friday?"

"You know it. Oh and, Jai, don't think you don't owe me an earful of details about you and the Italian Stallion's little encounter."

"Oh, it wasn't little." Jai winked as she headed out of the door.

As Jai walked to her car she felt good. She could breathe again. She hated when there was tension between her and Rissa. One time Rissa didn't talk to Jai for a full week because of a dissension over a term paper.

In college, Rissa was the party animal of the two. She had been raised Catholic and was on lockdown for pretty much of her life. She was never allowed to date. As a matter of fact she took her cousin, Franklin, to her high school senior prom. When her parent's little angel was let loose off to college, she turned into the devil himself.

College schoolwork was foreign to Rissa, but frat parties were one of her favorite subjects. How she even made it through her freshman year was a miracle. All those tears and Hail Marys come final exam time must have paid off.

Jai was always on top of her game when it came to college. She hated school, but since she was on a full scholarship she figured she might as well do her best. Even in high school Jai was a dedicated and scholarly pupil. She was proud of it, too. She had kept in a trunk every paper she had ever written in high school. Rissa found out that Jai had an old term paper that she had written on Phineas, a priest who had murdered an interracial couple, as such marriages were an abomination to his religion. Rissa just presupposed Jai would allow her to use it for a final term paper that she had to write for her civilization course. Besides, Jai had written the paper in her senior year of high school. With a minor touch-up and the use of a thesaurus, Rissa could surely make the paper appear as though a college sophomore had written it. There was no way the college instructor would ever find out.

Jai, on the other hand, was just your typical by-the-book kind of girl. Her father had raised Jai, along with her twin sister. When they were only seven years old their parents divorced and Jai's mother moved away to Philadelphia. Jai always felt as though she was competing with her sister for their father's love and attention, so she always tried especially hard to excel at everything she attempted. But no matter how hard she tried it seemed that her sister was always right there to surpass her. If Jai got an A on a paper, her sister got an A+. If Jai found a dollar while walking down the street, her sister found two dollars. If Jai made the cheerleading squad, then her sister was sure to be named captain, and so on. Jai always tried to find her own shine, but there her sister would be, a cumulous cloud, following her everywhere she went. Even when Jai received notification of her full scholarship, the celebration only lasted so long before her sister received notification of a full scholarship, room and board, and a position on the volleyball team. So Jai had always taken pride in everything she did as she felt as though she was always in constant competition with the world.

When Rissa asked Jai to use her paper, it was like asking Iraq to turn over their deadly chemical warfare. Jai refused. Rissa thought that eventually Jai would see the light and realize that allowing her to plagiarize the paper was no harm done. It was a high school paper, for Pete's sake. But Jai had tons of excuses. "What if I want to use it in college? I won't be able to if I let you. How can you prosper on your own by using my work? The next thing you know you'll be wanting me to take your final exams for you. My allowing you to use my paper will only hinder you, not help you, etcetera..."

Rissa ended up getting a D- on something she contrived herself. The D- hurt Rissa's GPA and she solely blamed Jai. Rissa went an entire week ignoring Jai, even though they lived in the same apartment. Rissa made sure when Jai was around that she wasn't. If Jai did happen to be home when Rissa was, Rissa always made sure she had a cluster of friends over to sustain her attention so that she wouldn't have to pay any mind to Jai.

On the seventh day Rissa came home and found Jai's suitcases at the front door and it hit her that she was about to lose her best friend. She cried and pleaded with Jai to stay. Jai allowed her to plead her case for over an hour before deciding to stay. When Rissa went to help Jai carry her suitcases back in her bedroom, it was then when she realized that the suitcases were as light as a feather, empty. Jai had never planned on going anywhere. Jai knew that Rissa would be incensed about the situation with Sloan, but just like back in their college days, she'd eventually get over it sooner or later.

Jai was glad that it was sooner than later. She didn't want to worry about mending her and Rissa's friendship. She was completely wrapped up in the idea of having a good man in her life and allowing him to stay. It was too early to determine the direction her and Sloan's relationship was heading, but Jai was having fun and it had been a long time since she had had any fun. And it had been since forever and a day since a man cooked for her.

Sloan had called Jai up and invited her out to dinner. She was to meet him at his apartment and then they would go to the restaurant from there. Jai found her way to Sloan's apartment with ease. Once she pulled into his apartment grounds, she couldn't remember if she was supposed to go left at the rental office or right. She turned left when she should have gone right, which made her a couple minutes late.

The apartment complex Sloan lived in was nice. Jai passed a huge party house with an Olympic-sized pool behind it. She also passed a fairly large pond with a waterfall in the middle of it that shot water straight up into the air. The blue neon light that lit it up made it appear as though the water was as blue as that of the water on a beach in the Bahamas. There were no playgrounds of any sort, which made her think this was more of an adult community.

In order to get to Sloan's apartment door Jai had to go up a flight of stairs and down a hallway. When Jai got to his door she could hear music playing. It was Pink's new album. Jai recognized it from hearing Rissa play it over and over. Jai pulled her leather jacket down over her waist and knocked on the door.

"Well, hello. You're looking lovely," Sloan said, opening the door.

"Hello," Jai replied shyly.

"Do come in."

When Jai entered the apartment she was shocked to see a dimly lit setting at Sloan's living room table. There was a china setting for two. On each plate was a burgundy linen napkin shaped into a little hat. Next to each plate was a pair of chopsticks and a wineglass. The centerpiece was a Bonsai tree.

To Jai's surprise, Sloan had prepared some shrimp egg foo young over steamed rice. The sauce was divine and created a hot steam when Sloan poured it from the china gravy dish onto Jai's plate.

"I hope you don't mind that we didn't go out to dinner," Sloan said. "But I wanted to surprise you."

"Well, you did," Jai said. "And I love it."

Sloan softly bit into his bottom lip as he watched Jai enjoy her last forkful of food. She hadn't mastered the chopsticks well enough to eat her entire meal with them. Sloan had fed her a few bites from his, though.

"The bathroom is through my bedroom if you want to freshen up," Sloan said as he took their plates to the kitchen sink.

"Thank you," Jai said as she got up from the floor, where they had been sitting Indian style, and headed toward the bathroom. The light in Sloan's bedroom wasn't on but the light in the bathroom was. The bedroom was huge. It appeared to only have a bed, a chest, and a nightstand in it. Perhaps it was less that made the room look more. He had a canopy bed swimming with sheer drapery. It sat in the middle of the bedroom, which was a bit unusual, but it worked for this setup. There was a balcony that faced the bed. Jai could see the moon peeking in through the drapes.

The bathroom was gray marble. A couple of *Rolling Stone* magazines lay on the counter.

Jai used the bathroom, washed her hands, and dried them on one of the throwaway guest hand towels Sloan had sitting in a small wire basket. When she came out of the bathroom Sloan was standing in the doorway with nothing on but his pants, unintentionally showing off his cut physique.

Jai jumped and placed her hand over her heart. "You scared the shit out of me."

"Shh," Sloan said, putting his index finger over Jai's lips. "Follow me."

Jai let Sloan lead her over toward his bed. He had turned out the lights and the sheets were bathed in the soft, pale light of the moon.

"Take your clothes off and lay down on the bed," Sloan ordered.

"Wh—," Jai tried to speak before Sloan placed a finger over her lips again. "Shh. Just take your clothes off."

Jai slowly stripped. Sloan lay on the bed watching her. When she dropped her panties at her feet, Sloan rose from the bed, grabbing a cloth from the nightstand, and came to stand behind her. He slipped the cloth over her eyes.

"Sloan," Jai said nervously.

"Shh," he whispered, and finished tying it. He then took her hand and walked Jai over to his bed and made her lay across the bed on her stomach. Jai could hear him fumbling around and then she heard something wet as he rubbed his hands together. At first she thought Sloan might have been jacking off until he touched her with his hands slick with warm oil. He pressed the ball of his hands into Jai's back and began to massage her. He buried his fingers in her shoulders and kneaded his way down her back to her ass. He worked his way down the backs of her legs down to her feet. Jai had never felt so good. He then turned Jai over and cupped handfuls of her breast and fondled her nipples with his fingers. Jai arched into his hands. Once again he began a slow, luxurious descent, that left her loose limbed and languid. Jai sighed and let the feeling take over.

When Jai woke up, the first thing she did was remove the blindfold. That's when she realized that the moon had been replaced by the sun. She stretched and ran her fingers through her hair. She felt brand new, rejuvenated. She looked around and saw that Sloan was nowhere in sight.

Jai got out of the bed and peeked into the bathroom. No Sloan. She wondered if he were in the kitchen.

Jai walked into the living room where she found Sloan sound asleep on the sofa, snoring. He obviously didn't want to wake her when she fell asleep across his bed while being massaged, so he opted to bunk on the couch for the evening. He looked so beautiful just lying there and so at peace that Jai didn't even bother waking him before she got dressed and left.

Sloan couldn't believe he woke to find Jai missing. He couldn't believe she had left without even saying good-bye. Sloan figured that she would at least call once she made it home safely so he decided to hop in the shower and wait for her call. He even took the cordless phone in the bathroom with him.

However, when he walked out of the bathroom Jai was standing there with a box in her hand.

He stared at her with a stunned look on his face.

"Sorry. I hope you didn't mind that I left the door unlocked, but I wanted to go out and grab breakfast," Jai said, referring to the box of Krispy Kreme donuts in her hands. "You were such the sleeping beauty that I didn't want to wake you, and I didn't have a key to get back in."

Sloan smiled, walked over to her, took a glazed donut out of the box, and bit into it.

"Thanks for breakfast, babe," he said, polishing it off. Then he walked over to his dresser and slipped on some underwear and a T-shirt.

"Thanks for last night," Jai said. "I needed that."

"Anytime," Sloan said with a smile. "Aren't you going to have some breakfast?"

"Yeah, I think I will," Jai said softly. She put the box on the bed and slowly approached Sloan. "But not donuts. I was thinking of something with a little more protein."

Jai knelt down on her knees and slid Sloan's underwear down his hips until they settled around his ankles. She leaned forward and began flicking his shaft with the tip of her tongue. Then she took him fully in her hand and sucked the tip hard. Sloan groaned and put his hands on her head.

"Take it all, baby," he said, and Jai was more than happy to oblige.

Sloan cursed, grabbed her head, and began gently thrusting into her mouth. "Oh, oh, oh," Sloan moaned.

Jai's head bobbed faster and faster. Just knowing how much she was turning Sloan on made her clit throb. She began to moan in sync with Sloan and she knew he was about to cum.

Jai pulled back, gripped Sloan's dick in her hand and squeezed it while he ejaculated into the palm of her hand. When he finished she went into the bathroom and cleaned up.

"I've got to head out," Jai said to Sloan when she came out of the bathroom. "I've got tons of housework to do."

"Make sure you call me when you get home so that I know you made it safe and sound," Sloan said as he walked Jai over to the door. "I had a good time."

Sloan kissed Jai softly on her lips.

"Yeah, me too," she said with a smile.

"Don't forget to call me," Sloan said as he opened the door.

"I won't," Jai said, still smiling.

"And thanks again for breakfast." Sloan winked at Jai.

"Well, you know what they say?" Jai said as she headed down the hall. "Breakfast is the most important meal of the day."

"Human Services, Jai Bosly speaking."

"Jai Bosly, Sloan Devaroe here."

"Sloan," Jai said, excited. This was the first time he had ever phoned her on her job. "Is everything okay?"

"Yes," Sloan replied. "I know I don't call you at your job, but I was missing you like crazy today. I just wanted to know if you wanted to meet me over at Starbucks on Walnut for a quick cappuccino."

"I can't go to lunch for another hour," Jai said, regret lacing her tone.

"So do you want to meet at around 12:45?"

"Sure. I'll see you then."

"Bye now."

"Bye," Jai said, hanging up the phone and staring dreamily at it. Sloan was so different from the men she had encountered in the past. There was no baby mama drama to look forward to and no more having a man borrow money from her or, better yet, her car. No wondering whether or not when he invited her out to eat if she would have to pay or not. Sloan was a thirty-something-year-old college educated, financially and physically fit man who gave her pleasure instead of drama.

Sloan was already seated when Jai arrived at Starbucks, sipping on a cup of coffee. He had been watching for her. Jai was looking casually fine in Old Navy khaki drawstrings with a cream-colored V-neck body suit. She had on a nice pair of brown loafers.

When Jai spotted Sloan, a smile crept across her face. As Jai breezed through the little coffeehouse she passed a table of three handsome black men. One smiled a mischievous smile at her and they all spoke a hello. Jai smiled back and returned their salutations.

Jai reached Sloan's table and was greeted with a warm hug.

"Seeing you is just what I need to break the monotony of the day," Sloan told her.

"Having a rough one I take it," Jai said, sitting down.

"Being yelled at by claimants who want obscene amounts of money isn't what I would consider an easy day," Sloan replied. "But I don't want to talk about work. Come on, let's go to the counter and get you something."

Sloan pulled her chair out for her and they walked over to the counter.

"Can I help you?" the girl behind the counter asked Jai.

"I'll just have a regular coffee," Jai replied.

"You don't want a muffin or anything?" Sloan asked.

"No, just a regular coffee will do." Jai had packed her lunch and had a sandwich waiting for her back at work, but didn't want to tell Sloan that when he had called and ruin her chance of seeing him.

"I'll take another coffee, also," Sloan said to the girl behind the counter.

"Just black coffee?" the girl behind the counter asked.

"I take cream in mine," Jai said.

"And I take mine black," Sloan added with a smile and a wink.

It seemed as though the clerk took forever to retrieve their coffees, but they didn't mind the wait as long as they were with each other.

Sloan and Jai talked about everything under the sun in such a small allotment of time. Jai was amazed at how easy it was to talk to him. It seemed as though every time they talked, they discovered more and more of just how much they had in common.

If Jai and Sloan weren't spending the night together, then they were on the phone talking for hours. They talked mostly about their careers, whenever they weren't talking dirty that is. And every now and then they'd enjoy a game of twenty-one questions in which they inquired about different traits and characteristics of each of their races. For example, Sloan inquired as to whether the majority of black women really didn't go down on men. Jai inquired as to whether his people, which she just considered white, really didn't get cold when they wore shorts in fifty-five degrees weather. Sloan wanted to know if black people really got offended by the "N" word considering they used it more than anybody did. Jai wanted to know if white people used the word just as much amongst themselves. Sloan inquired as to how often black women washed their hair and Jai inquired as to how often white people wondered about the habits of black people.

Jai felt comfortable asking Sloan questions that Rissa might have taken offense to. Most of the questions were never things Jai normally thought or cared about. Being friends with a person of the opposite race was much different than dating one. If Jai was walking down the street with Rissa and people stared, she knew it was because they were beautiful, not because she was black and Rissa was white. She knew if minimum-wage clerks treated them funny it was because they were hating on their beauty, not because Jai was black and Rissa was white. Jai was in a whole new world, one she never imagined that she'd ever have to concern herself with. The same went for Sloan.

Jai was always in competition with herself that she never stopped to take notice of what the world thought about her. Her biggest critic had always been herself. On the other hand, Sloan was starting to take notice, and find a degree of concern, in what the world was thinking. This was natural for him, as he had always worried about what the people around him, namely his coworkers, thought about him.

Jai never really noticed how lunch in the park turned into lunch in a parked car. Jai never really noticed how dinner and movie nights out turned into DVDs and takeout food. She just simply enjoyed being with Sloan, no matter where they were.

Of course she was still sure to block out time for Rissa. Friday nights at Cream were still a given.

"You hooking up with Sloan later on tonight?" Rissa asked as she sipped on her Corona.

"Yeah," Jai said as she giggled and wiggled in her chair like a little flutter bug. "We're going to spend the evening with me running some of my family history down to him. We're having dinner at Dad's Sunday."

"Must be nice," Rissa said as she downed the last swallow of her drink. Rissa finishing her drink was always the bartender's cue to bring her another, but he had been ignoring her ever since she stood him up the night she and Jai met Sloan.

"You used to have another drink waiting for you before you finished your last," Jai said. "Bartender man been slippin' ever since you invited him over and didn't answer your door."

"Don't remind me," Rissa said as the two laughed. "I don't need another one anyway. I'm going to call it a night."

"What?" Jai said surprised. "We just got here."

"Yeah, well I'm sure you probably want to hurry up and get to Sloan so I'm going to let you off the hook. You two kids have a blast," Rissa said with a sarcastic tone.

"There it goes again," Jai said, throwing her hands up.

"There goes what?" Rissa asked, stopping in her tracks.

"That subtle streak of sarcasm," Jai said, rolling her eyes. "That same bit of sarcasm that continually has me questioning whether or not you are really cool with Sloan's and my relationship. One minute it's *Oh, Jai, I'm so happy you're happy* and the next minute it's *You stole the guy I was going to marry.* I mean get over it already. We can't be the first girlfriends this has happened to. Hell, in college we knew girls who used to share men."

"Well, we're not in college anymore," Rissa hesitated. "Besides, it's not that."

"Then please enlighten me. I'm sick of this sometimey shit," Jai said, raising her voice.

"Look, just forget about it. Have a good time with Sloan," Rissa said sincerely as she kissed Jai on the cheek and exited the club. Jai was close behind her. She wasn't letting Rissa off that easy.

"Rissa, wait!" Jai called, catching up with her.

"Jai, let's not do this. I said I'm cool with you and Sloan being together so just leave it alone, please! I thought we already agreed on this. Why do you keep beating a dead horse to the ground?"

"Let's not do what, Rissa? What is it? If you're over that fact that you initially liked Sloan and I'm seeing him now, then what else could it be?"

"Gosh, Jai, why is it that the rest of the world sees it and you don't?" Rissa said, getting in Jai's face. "Don't you see how people look at you two? I mean, don't you notice the stir you two cause?"

"No, Rissa, I haven't noticed and you know what? I don't care," Jai said, throwing her hands up and lifting her head proud.

"Well, maybe you don't care, but I'm sure Sloan does," Rissa said, pouting her lips and folding her arms. "How many of his friends have you met?"

Jai was silent. Come to think of it, she hadn't met any. They had never double-dated or gone over to a friend's house or anything like that. Not even one of his associates from the gym. But on the same token, Jai had never invited him out on a double date with Rissa, for obvious reasons.

"Sloan doesn't really have any friends," Jai said in defense. "He's mostly working all the time. When he's not working, he's with me."

"Is that what he tells you, that he doesn't really have any friends? And you were just so quick to believe him. Little ol' Jai, walking through life with blinders on. Is it that he doesn't really have any friends or is it that he doesn't bring them around you?"

"You're my only friend," Jai said, closing that matter. "I don't bring him around you."

"That's different. You don't bring him around me because of . . . well, you know."

"Rissa, this is crazy. You're talking crazy."

"Okay, let's say you guys do get serious. Well, have you thought about if you two have babies or something? Imagine how the world will treat your child. It's not fair to put a child through such unnecessary discrimination. I mean I'd never have a child with a black guy."

"Oh, you can be friends with a black person, but that's it?" Jai said, twisting her neck and bobbing her head. "Do you mean to tell me I've been friends with a bigot for the past nine years?"

"Think about it, Jai. If I had a baby by a black man, what if we break up? What white man is going to want me and my black child? That's something you should think about too. Say you have a baby with this Italian Stallion and it doesn't work out and you meet this rich good-looking black guy. Are you going to blame him for not wanting to play daddy to a child that biologically isn't his, let alone a white kid? And imagine how the white woman, Italian woman, whoever Sloan would probably end up dating, would treat your black child."

"The one person who I thought would be genuinely happy for me is the one person making me feel fickle about my relationship with Sloan. I can't believe the words I just heard coming out of the mouth of my best friend."

"And I'm only telling you this because I am your best friend. You two are still pretty much in La La Land right now, but what happens when you two have your first argument? What do you think is going to be the first word out of his mouth? Jai, I'm just giving it to you like it is."

Jai was shocked at Rissa's words. She just stood there looking at her friend like she was crazy. Jai's silence made Rissa think it was an open invitation to continue her lecture.

"You're taking Sloan to meet your parents on Sunday," Rissa said. "Well, when is he taking you to meet his? You have to step back and look at this thing for what it is. I'm not trying to be mean, Jai. I'm just being honest."

"Well, thanks for being so honest. Now allow me to be honest with you. No matter how you dish it out your remarks were very prejudiced."

"Oh, cut the crap. You people kill me, always ready to have a pity party having prejudice and discrimination as your guest of honor," Rissa said, rolling her eyes and shaking her head.

"Rissa, I'm walking away right now because it's the white thing to do," Jai said, maintaining her composure. "The black thing to do would be to sweep the streets with your white ass. This is just one of the advantages, as a black person, that I have over you. I know how to do the white thing when I need to and how to do the black thing when I need to. And *you people* are clueless of my advantage." Jai stomped away so hard that she was sure she had ruined the bottoms of her shoes. Thank God she wore the Payless imitation Gators instead of her real ones she lucked up on at TJ Maxx.

Rissa must have thought about everything she said to Jai because she phoned Jai's house back to back all weekend long, trying to apologize. Jai finally had to turn her ringer off, but Rissa left apologetic messages. Jai knew that most of what Rissa had said, had been said out of jealousy. No matter what Rissa said or how much she tried to hide it, Jai could see right through her and knew that she was still a little taken by the fact that Sloan had chosen to get with her and not Rissa. Nonetheless, her words did hurt. Jai felt that maybe she and Rissa needed some time apart until Rissa could get used to the fact that she was going to be with the Italian Stallion whether she liked it or not. Besides, Jai didn't need Rissa putting doubts in her mind about how Sloan felt about her.

When Sunday rolled around and it was time for Jai to take Sloan to dinner at her father's house, she was worried sick. She hadn't told her family that Sloan was Italian, which meant a white man in their eyes. She had only told them that she had a man in her life that she wanted them to meet. That morning Jai even went to the 9:00 A.M. service at her church, which she hadn't been to in a couple of months. She had to pray heavy on this one.

On her way home from church Jai stopped off at Media Play and picked up another Flowetry CD. She had let a girl at work borrow the one she had originally purchased so that the girl could record it onto a cassette. That was over a month ago and the girl still had not returned it. Jai was sure to save the receipt so that she could collect her $15.73 replacement cost.

Jai loved Flowetry's CD, *Flowetic*. She had met the two women who made up the duo at a club in Philly one Thanksgiving Eve when she and her sister were there visiting their mother. The CD hadn't dropped yet, but Jai had promised the women that when it did, she would support them. Jai bought the CD the day it came out and fell in love with it. Seeing Flowetry perform poetry on BET's *Lyrical Cafe* the night before reminded Jai that she needed to replace the CD.

When Jai returned home Sloan was parked in her driveway waiting for her.

"Hey, how long you been waiting?" Jai said to Sloan, getting out of her car.

"About fifteen minutes," Sloan said, walking over to Jai and kissing her on the lips. "I thought you would have been home by now. Did church run over?"

"No, I stopped off at Media Play to get a CD. I'm sorry for having you sit out here waiting on me."

"That's okay. You're worth the wait." Sloan smiled. "Are you about ready to head to your dad's house?" Sloan asked anxiously.

"Sure, let me run in and use the bathroom first," Jai said as they went inside her house. Jai's stomach was all knotted up from anxiety.

"You alright in there?" Sloan said, knocking on the bathroom door after Jai had been in there for several minutes.

"Yeah, I'm just brushing my teeth," Jai replied before joining Sloan. "All set. Let's go."

The drive to Jai's father's house was like the boat ride through that tunnel on *Willy Wonka & the Chocolate Factory.* Jai's head was spinning. Maybe not telling her family that her new guy friend was of another race was a major faux pas. But what could she do about it now? Call them up on her cell phone in the car and say, "Oh, and by the way, that guy friend of mine that I'm bringing to dinner, he's Italian"?

Jai directed Sloan to their destination and had him park in front of the house.

"That's a pretty house," Sloan said, a little taken by the fact that the house was a flamingo pink. You could tell by the lawn that Jai's father was retired and spent most of his time playing in it. There were bushes decorated with mulch trimming. There were trees decorated with white rocks plus bricks around the rocks. There was a little pond and some windmill flowers in a flower box that stretched the length of the porch. It was a very busy yard, but neat.

Sloan was just as excited as ever. He had no idea he was about to find himself in the new millennium version of *Guess Who's Coming to Dinner?*

"Sissy," Jai said as her twin sister greeted her at the door.

"Jai," Sissy said, giving her sister a long hug. "How are you?"

"You know me," Sissy replied. "Busy working on my masters, living like the struggling student I am. But it will all be worth it in the end."

Sissy was one of those people who used school as a reason not to enter the workforce. Once she got her masters, Jai was certain she would spend a few more years unemployed while she went for her doctorate.

"Where's this Darryl you've been talking about?" Jai asked her sister. Of course, once she found out that Jai was bringing her new guy friend, Sissy had to show off hers.

"He's running a little late," Sissy replied. "He'll be here shortly. Speaking of guy friends, where's your new honey?"

"Sissy, this is Sloan. Sloan, this is my sissy, Joi," Jai said as she pulled Sloan through the front door.

"Pleased to meet you, Joi," Sloan said, holding out his hand.

"Sissy, you can call me Sissy," Sissy said with her mouth open as she put her hand out literally in slow motion. "You're uh, uhh. You're uh . . ."

"Italian," Sloan interrupted. "People ask me all the time what I am. Some people think I'm English when they first see me."

"Yeah, that's what I was going to say, English," Joi lied. "So uh, Sloan, why don't you come into the dining room and meet the rest of the family."

"I'd like that," Sloan said.

The three walked through the living room and into the dining room where Jai's father and his wife, Emma, were sitting.

"Jai, baby," Emma said when she saw Jai enter the dining room.

"And this is Jai's friend, Sloan," Sissy couldn't wait to say.

Sloan felt like he was in an episode of *The Twilight Zone,* the one where the man had a watch that could stop time. The room was dead silent. No one moved. They just all sat there staring at him. Finally Emma broke the silence.

"Well, uhh, it's nice to meet you, Sloan," she said, offering Sloan a big hug.

Emma's hug could melt an igloo. She was a short, round, and pudgy woman. She always had her hair done up in a bun with a string of pearls around her neck. Day or night, she was always wearing an apron as she whipped up something in the kitchen. And she always smelled of old lady perfume, which was that scent of a terribly strong, sweet gardenia. Whether you had a splinter in your finger or a sore on your knee, a hug from Emma made it feel better right away.

"It's nice to meet you, too," Sloan said, squeezing Emma tight and not wanting to let go.

"Well, uh, Sloan, sir," Jai's father said. "Jai here didn't tell us that you were uh, well, uh, you know . . ."

"Yeah, I know, Italian," Sloan said, shaking Jai's father's hand.

"Yeah, uh, that's right," Jai's father said, wiping his hand down his pants leg. "Italian."

Sloan must have accidentally hit that button on the stopwatch because the room was dead still and silent, *again*. The ringing of the doorbell broke the awkwardness this time.

"I'll get it," Sissy said. "It's probably Darryl."

"Well, I guess we should sit down for dinner," Emma said as Sissy ran off to get the door.

"I like what you've done with the yard, Daddy," Jai said, but her father ignored the compliment. Instead he simply gave her the evil eye, the *Sanford & Son* Aunt Esther fish-eyed-fool look.

"Yes, I agree," Sloan said. "The yard looks lovely."

"Everybody, this is Darryl," Sissy said, reentering the room with a tall, bald, dark-complected, handsome man by her side. One by one she introduced Darryl to everybody as they took their seats at the dinner table.

"Daddy, Darryl is working on his engineering degree. He's already working over at Epstein's Electric," Sissy bragged.

"Is that so?" Jai's father asked with a proud smile.

"Yes, sir," Darryl replied. "This is my last year before I've earned my degree."

"Darryl also volunteers over at the boys' shelter. He heads the reading and writing program," Sissy added.

"You sound like a busy young man," Emma said.

"So, Sloan, what is it that you do?" Sissy asked with a fake smile on her face.

"I'm a claims adjuster," Sloan said, taking in a spoonful of black-eyed peas.

"Yes," Jai said. "He handles the large difficult claims."

Everyone just looked at Jai, completely uninterested.

"And Sloan can sing like a hummingbird," Jai said like a proud mama bragging on her son.

"Oh, really?" Sissy asked, eyes wide open. "Why don't you sing something for us, Sloan?"

"Oh, I couldn't," Sloan said modestly.

"Come on, Sloan. Blow for us," Sissy said.

"Well, okay," Sloan said as he swallowed and chased it with a sip of iced tea. "The very first time that I saw your brown eyes . . . ," Sloan said as he managed to put goose bumps on everyone's arms with his a cappella rendition of "If I Ever Fall In Love" by O-Town.

"Wow," Sissy said, surprised. "You have a lovely voice."

"Thank you," Sloan said. "I love music, rock 'n' roll, R&B, alternative, pop, jazz, opera, you name it."

"So, Darryl," Jai asked sarcastically. "Do you sing?"

"These greens are delicious," Sloan said quickly to Emma before Darryl had a chance to respond.

"Well, thank you, son," Emma said with a big grin.

"I didn't know white folks ate greens," Jai's father couldn't resist saying. "I mean Italian folks."

"Yeah, Daddy," Jai replied. "And they even eat watermelon, too. How about that?"

"I put a little secret ingredient in them greens," Emma jumped in.

"Well, ma'am, I do say they are the best I've ever had. You're one fine cook."

"Yeah, my baby can cook," Jai's father said proudly. "I done put on thirty pounds since I married her. Jai's mamma couldn't boil water. No man in his right mind could stand that woman's cooking. No black man anyway. You people don't care too much about seasonings though, huh? I s'pose that's why she run off to Philadelphia and married that white man. Or maybe he's Italian, too. Hell, Italian, white. It's the same difference to me. It ain't black."

"Really?" Sloan asked. "So Jai's mother is married to a white guy, huh?"

"Oh, yes, indeedy. Didn't Jai tell you?" her father said.

"Uh, Miss Emma, what you got for dessert?" Jai said, quickly changing the subject. "I know you whipped up something fine."

"Indeed I did. When your daddy told me you girls were joining us for Sunday dinner I made your favorite, Jello cake. Jai, I made you one with extra whip cream topping just like you like it."

"Yep," Sissy added. "Jai always did like lots of cream."

"I'm gonna have to give you the recipe, Jai, so that some day you'll be whipping it up for your kids," Emma said, clearly throwing a hint. "Hopefully one of y'all give us some grandbabies before we too old to do anything with them."

"Well, maybe Sloan here will be your great white hope," Sissy said with a straight face.

"Will y'all excuse me?" Jai said as she stood up and walked out of the dining room, unable to deal with the comedic comments. She was feeling suffocated and at the same time, like such a fool for putting Sloan, her family, and herself in such an uncomfortable situation. She hated leaving Sloan in there with them alone, but she had to get some air quick. She couldn't get back outside onto the front porch soon enough. She ran onto the porch and raced over to the railing where she took in a few deep breaths. For a moment there she thought she was going to puke right down into the flower bed.

"You okay?" Sloan said, walking up behind her.

"Sloan, I'm so sorry," Jai said as she turned around to face him.

"It's okay," Sloan said in a forgiving manner as he put his arms around her. "But not telling your people that I was Italian . . . not cool, Jai."

"I know. But, what was I supposed to say? It doesn't matter now. I know I messed up."

"Yeah, you messed up big time. This could have been ugly."

"Could have been?" Jai said as she dropped her head onto Sloan's chest.

"Baby, why didn't you tell me your mom was married to a white man?"

"I don't know. It wasn't a big deal. I mean what is it with people? So every time I talk about someone I'm supposed to define his or her race. This is Rissa, my white friend. This is Jenny, my Latino coworker. This is Iosif, my Russian mailman . . ."

"Okay, okay. I get the point. But, baby, you knew not telling them ahead of time was a big mistake. You were worried sick about it. I could tell something was up by the way you staked out the bathroom before we left. You were stalling."

"You mean you knew that I probably hadn't told my family?" Jai said surprised.

"I guess I did kind of sorta know," Sloan said with a mischievous grin on his face. "But I figured it would be more fun to watch you sweat."

Jai giggled and punched Sloan in the arm.

"Thank you, Sloan," Jai said, becoming serious. "Thank you for understanding me even when I don't understand myself sometimes."

"It's cool, but from now on if you plan on introducing me to any more of your people, could you please tell them ahead of time that I'm uh, well, uh . . ."

"I know, I know . . . Italian," Jai smiled.

Jai loved the feeling of waking up in Sloan's bed. He had an elegant feather-filled mattress and pillows. His bedding was a bright ivory and sinfully fluffy. Jai imagined that she was sleeping on clouds. It was heavenly.

Sloan's bed sat about twelve feet straight across from the bedroom window. On this particular morning the sun tapped Jai softly on her shoulder and kissed her on the forehead as she woke up. There was no better greeting. Jai raised up and stretched out. She yawned, looked around the room, and smiled. She could hear Sloan's voice chattering about in the kitchen. Jai got up out of bed and followed his voice.

She walked, bare naked into the kitchen. With any other man she would have worn a robe or something. A T-shirt at least. But with Sloan, nothing like that mattered anymore. He made her comfortable in the skin she was in.

When Sloan saw Jai coming he immediately began to end his conversation.

Jai lipped the words "good morning" as Sloan stayed on the phone wearing nothing but a pair of boxer shorts. He winked at her.

"Yes. Yes, next weekend. Yes, I'll be there. Um hm. Love you, too, Ma," Sloan said as he hung up the phone and walked over to Jai. "Good morning to you, beautiful."

"Hey," Jai said with a curious look on her face. "Talking to your mom on the phone, huh?"

"Yep," Sloan said, without making eye contact with Jai.

"Going to visit your mom and dad next weekend, huh?" Jai asked.

"Yep," Sloan said, running his index finger down her nose.

"A drive to Columbus. That sounds fun," Jai said, obviously hinting around.

"You want some juice?" Sloan asked, quickly changing the subject.

"Sure. So exactly how long does it take you to drive to Columbus?" Jai said, taking the conversation right back where she wanted it.

"Not long. A couple of hours or so." Sloan hurried with the juice and handed Jai a juice-sized glassful. "Do you want breakfast?"

"Nah, I'm gonna head out, go home, and get cleaned up. Rissa and I are going to catch a matinee down at the theater this afternoon." Jai wanted to stay, but she and Rissa had just made up. She didn't want to bail on Rissa to be with Sloan.

"Well, I'm going to be very busy for the rest of the day and evening cleaning up some claim files that I brought home from work. I have a huge box I need to go through. I was hoping we could spend the entire morning together. Have breakfast together at least since I'll be out of commission for the rest of the day," Sloan said, taking the glass of juice out of Jai's hand and setting it down on the counter. "I'm hungry."

"Umm, so you're hungry, are you?" Jai said as she accepted the kisses Sloan was putting on her neck. His lips were fire, burning through her soul. Her nipples stiffened and her clit began to tingle. She closed her eyes, now hoping that Sloan could put out the fire he had ignited in her. "I might have time to whip you up something real quick."

Sloan smiled mischievously and seductively as he grabbed a handful of Jai's jungle love. He slowly began to play with her with his fingers. Jai, with her eyes still closed, let her head fall back and enjoyed the feeling.

Softly, Sloan began to enter his finger inside of Jai.

"Ohh," Jai moaned, opening her eyes for a second only to be staring up at the ceiling.

"You like that?" Sloan whispered in her ear, nibbling on her lobe at the same time.

"Hell, yes," Jai replied, letting out another moan.

After each of his fingers had been kissed by Jai's wet pussy lips, Sloan put his mouth where his hands were. His tongue thrust in and out and around Jai's pussy. Soon, Sloan's fingers wanted another piece of the action. His tongue and his fingers battled for a position in her warmth. The tempo picked up as Sloan's fingers and tongue took turns dipping inside of her.

"Oh, oh, Sloan. Oh," Jai moaned unashamed.

Jai could hardly contain herself. The pleasure was becoming

unbearable. Jai grabbed fistfuls of Sloan's black locks and tried to pull him away. She was going to explode. At the same time she threw her hips, thrusting her pussy against Sloan's tongue and tightening her walls around his fingers.

"Sloan, oh, Sloan!" Jai screamed. Tears welled up in her eyes. Never had something felt so good in her entire life. She didn't feel worthy of such ecstasy.

"Umm umm," Sloan groaned as he buried his tongue in her. He gripped Jai's ass with his fingertips, pressing into her flesh as he held her as close as he could get her.

He knew he had been the first to ever give her pleasure like this. He carried the torch proudly and would accept his gold medal with conceit.

Sloan licked Jai's clit hard as if he were anxious for her creamy treat. Sloan felt Jai's trembles and knew that she was about to erupt. She began to grind herself harder against Sloan's tongue.

Sloan moaned hard. His baritone growl vibrated through Jai as he sucked up every drop of her juices. Jai screamed. Jai screamed and writhed.

Sloan stood up and massaged Jai's clit as he watched her come down off of her high.

"Wait right here," Sloan said to Jai as he kissed her on the cheek and exited the room.

A few seconds later Sloan returned to the kitchen with his cock standing at full attention protected by a condom. Sloan quickly bent Jai over the countertop and pushed himself inside of her. He pumped hard and the sound of his balls slapping on her thighs encouraged him to pump even faster.

Sloan moaned as he plunged in and out of Jai. When Jai

reached back and opened herself up for him even more, Sloan thought he was going to have a heart attack.

"Fuck me, baby," Jai whispered. "Fuck me just like I like it."

Jai's filthy talk was all it took to push Sloan to his climax. Right when Sloan was about to rupture inside of Jai, he pulled out his rock-hard cock, pulled the condom off, slapped it on her ass cheeks, and watched it ejaculate. He then grabbed his meat and began jacking off, cum squirting all over Jai's ass and back. Once he had squeezed every last drop out, he slumped over, his body covering Jai's.

All day Jai kept remembering her morning treat with Sloan and a smile would cross her lips. She could hardly pay attention to the movie she and Rissa had gone to see. Every time the memory would surface she would cross her legs to squeeze her clit. The memory was so intense. She had made herself cum three times during the movie (hands free). It's amazing what a girl's imagination and the strategic positioning of her legs can do. And she had managed it without drawing attention to herself.

Jai couldn't wait to wrap up her girlfriend time with Rissa and make her way back to Sloan's for seconds. She knew that he was knee high in work, but she didn't plan on staying long, just long enough to cum.

After the movies Rissa insisted she and Jai go grab something to eat and it was all Jai could do not to scream at Rissa. But her girlfriend didn't know she was jonesing bad.

After Jai and Rissa left Chedders Restaurant, Jai had every intention of heading straight to Sloan's place. Her body was calling for him. On her way, she stopped to fill up her car with gas for the upcoming workweek and while she was there she grabbed a bouquet of flowers for Sloan and a six-pack of Corona. While at the counter she admired a banana cream scented candle and imagined how delicious the melted wax would smell running down her belly.

When Jai pulled up to Sloan's apartment building a group of four people, who appeared to be just a little bit tipsy, were exiting the building. They were laughing and singing. Jai got out of her car and entered the apartment building and headed upstairs. On her way up the stairs she passed a blonde lady in a black sequin dress and knew that someone in the building must have been having a party. As Jai walked down the long hallway to Sloan's apartment she could see a woman standing outside of his door. It was a woman who looked to be maybe a few years older than Sloan was. She was wearing a sharp red suit that complemented her still girlish figure.

"Thanks for coming," Jai could hear Sloan say.

"No, thank you. You throw one hell of a party, Devaroe," the woman replied in an overly friendly and flirtatious tone. "See you at work on Monday," the woman said as she headed down the hall crossing Jai's path, saying hello to her as they passed.

The door closed just seconds before Jai got to it. She stood outside a little confused and knocked hesitantly. She could hear music playing. If Jai was naming that tune correctly it was "Boogie Shoes" by KC and the Sunshine Band. Jai swallowed and knocked harder. Sloan opened the door and when he saw Jai standing there with flowers, Corona, and banana candle in hand, his expression froze.

"Jai," Sloan said surprised, swallowing hard afterward. "What are you doing here?"

"No hello, glad to see you, or nothing?" Jai asked sarcastically. "Looks like I just missed the big party. I imagine you didn't get much work done on those claim files."

"It wasn't really a party," Sloan said nervously. "Just a few friends from work stopped by."

"Oh, so everybody just happen to be in the neighborhood at the same time?" Jai said.

"Come inside so we can talk," Sloan said, opening the door wider. As she walked by him he could smell the sweet scent of Sand and Sable she was wearing. It was sweet just like her, the woman he found himself caring more and more for each day. He closed the door behind her.

Jai looked around, noticing that all the guests were gone. It seems as though the woman in red was the last to leave the party. There were empty wine and champagne bottles sitting out. She walked over to the mostly empty trays of shrimp, veggies, and cheese.

"And how convenient," Jai said, picking up a piece of shrimp and throwing it back down. "You just happened to have had some appetizer trays and bottles of wine laying around to accommodate your surprise guests?"

"It was just people I work with, Jai." Sloan attempted to explain as his voice began to break. "It wasn't anything big. I didn't think you'd want to hang out with them."

"Then you should have allowed me the opportunity to decline," Jai snapped as she turned away from Sloan. She couldn't even look at Sloan right now. She couldn't allow him to see the hurt in her eyes. The first thing that came into Jai's head is that Sloan had invited some other woman, his other girlfriend perhaps.

"Baby," Sloan said softly, trying to rub Jai's arm.

"Don't touch me," Jai said between clinched teeth. "Don't you put your goddamn hands on me."

"Jai," Sloan said, surprised at Jai's harsh reaction toward him.

"No, I don't want to hear it, Sloan. Do you think I'm stupid? Rather than sit here and make up a bunch of excuses and piss me off even more, just tell me the truth and get it over with."

Sloan put his head down in humiliation. "Jai—" he said.

"Say it. Was it another woman, Sloan, or were you just embarrassed, ashamed even?" Jai said, walking up on Sloan. "What is it? You didn't want the people you work with to know about me? Am I not good enough for them to meet? I thought I meant more to you than that, Sloan. I thought that we were more."

Sloan sighed. He didn't even know where to begin his spiel.

"Let me hear you say it." Jai was poking him in the chest with her index finger.

Sloan closed his eyes tight and just began shaking his head in disbelief. He felt awful. There was nothing he could say to Jai that would excuse his behavior. He had been planning the party for months and hadn't said a word to Jai. Hell, when he first started planning it he didn't even know if Jai would still be in the picture by the time the party went down. But she was still in the picture and now she had found out.

Every couple of months or so someone from Sloan's department at work has a brown-nose cocktail party for management. The employees compete to see who can give the best party and leave a greater impression.

With two of his four superiors being women, Sloan hated to admit it, but flirting had become an unwritten part of his job description. He never saw the harm in stroking an ego or two. And the two women loved it. And if Sloan knew one thing about women, it was how jealous they could be of one another. Sloan knew that having Jai on his arm at that party would have definitely changed his working relationship with the female managers.

He didn't have the words to explain this type of situation to Jai. Women never knew how to handle the truth. Not really. So as the date of the party grew near and Jai was still in the picture, he decided to lie by omission and not tell her about the party. He figured if she didn't know about the party in the first place, then he would have no explaining to do.

The situation wasn't looking good to Jai, and no matter what words Sloan dug up to explain it, nothing was going to sit right with her at this point, definitely not the truth. But Sloan had nothing else to offer her.

Sloan had never been with a woman whom he adored as much as he adored Jai. He had never been with a woman whom he wanted to spend all of his time with, let alone take her to a company function. Sloan didn't have the reputation at his company for being a womanizer. And by no means did anyone peg him for being gay. He was just thought of as a decent, hardworking man who wanted to focus and establish a stable career before taking on the responsibility of a family. That's one of the reasons why he had earned so much respect in his workplace. The women, especially, just ate that up about him.

Sloan was uncertain of how he might be looked at in his workplace if they discovered his *dark* secret, that he did enjoy the companionship of the female species just as much as any other man. That he wasn't at home buried in work all of the time. But Sloan didn't want to cause any type of stir just yet. Word was that Sloan's boss, one of the highest-ranking females in the company, would be taking early retirement soon and that Sloan was a possible candidate for the promotion. Sloan had been with the company for years and felt as though he couldn't jeopardize his career with being pegged as a loose and irresponsible man with greater concerns of conquering women than conquering claims.

He knew that if Jai found out about the party, she would have wanted to attend and would take Sloan not wanting her to attend the wrong way. So Sloan's goal was to make it so that she wouldn't find out. Mission failed. If only he could have pulled it off until he got into management. By then most of his coworkers would have been too busy sucking up to him and throwing him parties to even think about being concerned with his personal life.

"I'm sor . . . ," Sloan attempted to say, but anger got the best of Jai as she hauled off and slapped Sloan across his face. She stared at the stunned expression on his face and then she slapped him again, and again before he grabbed her hand in midair. Jai broke down in tears.

"Oh, God this hurts so much," Jai cried. "Rissa warned me."

"The hell with Rissa," Sloan shouted. "It's not like that. If you'd just let me exp—"

"How can you say that, Sloan? Stand here and tell me that you truly wanted me at your little shindig. Why? Is it because I'm black? No, wait a minute. It was another woman wasn't it? You had another bitch on your arm, huh?"

Jai attempted to slap Sloan with her free hand, but he blocked her.

"I know what I did was wrong in your eyes, but you have to look at it from my standpoint. I work for those people. They pay my bills. I care about their perception of me and right now—"

"So does that mean I won't be joining you at the company Christmas party either?" Jai asked sarcastically, cutting Sloan off again, unabling him to complete his explanation. "Thank goodness you were only out with just a couple of guys from the gym and not the people from work the night you saw me."

"I'm sorry, Jai. I never meant to hurt you."

"You never meant for me to find out. You would have had your little party, minus the little *girlfriend*, or whatever you want to call it, and been right back to fucking me tomorrow. Is that all I'm good for, Sloan, sex? I'm okay to fuck with behind closed doors, but that's where you draw the line?" Jai cried.

"It's not like that, Jai. I love you," Sloan said to Jai for the very first time.

"And you know what's funny? For a minute there, I thought you did. And up until I knocked on your apartment door I loved you, too, Sloan. But I can't love someone who I can't trust."

"This is all new to me, Jai. Just give me a chance. I've never seriously dated anyone before. I know I fucked up this time, but I'm learning."

"What a cop-out," Jai replied. "I thought love was supposed to conquer all in the end. I thought the girl always gets the guy and the guy always gets the girl."

"And it does," Sloan said, pleading with Jai.

"Well, who in the hell wrote this fucking script because shit don't seem to be working out that way?"

"I'm not ashamed of you, Jai. I'm not," Sloan said as he hugged her tightly. "I'm not ashamed to have you as a . . . *girlfriend*."

"Oh yeah, then when are you taking me to Columbus to meet your parents?" Jai asked Sloan as she pushed him off of her. "When do I get to meet Mama Mia?"

The room seemed loud with silence as more tears began to run down Jai's face.

"You've visited Columbus eight times since I met you and not once have you invited me to join you."

Sloan was silent for a minute before mumbling, "Sorry, Jai."

"That you didn't have to tell me. I kind of figured out that you were *sorry* on my own," Jai said as she headed for the door.

"No, Jai. Please don't go," Sloan followed behind her. "Let's talk about this. If you'd just give me a chance to say—"

"What you haven't said says it all. You treated me a certain way tonight. Whether you realize it or not. Even though I wasn't here physically, you were treating me in a certain way. A woman doesn't always have to be present to be treated unfairly and disrespectfully by a man."

Sloan looked into Jai's brown eyes that were full of hurt. It pained him to know that he was the cause of it. He could see his reflection slipping out of Jai's eyes and her heart. He felt as though no explanation mattered now.

"You'll never understand just how much you hurt me tonight," Jai said, wiping her eyes. "Good-bye, Sloan." She walked to the door.

"Jai, don't you walk out that fuckin' door," Sloan said, holding back tears of his own. "We can talk about this, Jai. We can work this out."

"Maybe I should have made this clear in the beginning," Jai said. "But I'm looking for love. I'm looking for the kind of love that makes you say fuck the world and everything in it." Jai couldn't help but break down once again.

"And I just wanna love ya," Sloan said with deep sincerity.

"I'm so tired, Sloan. I'm so fucking tired of this shit. You know what I learned tonight?" Jai said as she opened the door. "*Niggaz* is a universal word. *Niggaz* is an action not a person. It's ignorance, egotism, selfishness, and imprudent. And I'm almost one hundred percent convinced that all men are not necessarily dawgs, but they are all niggaz. And yes, Italians, too!"

"Jai, Jai," Sloan said as she opened the door to leave the apartment. KC's timing couldn't have been more perfect as Sloan began to sing along with the 1970s superstar. "I'm gonna miss your lovin' the minute you walk out that door. Please don't go," Sloan sang as if he had recorded the song himself.

But this heart-moving serenade didn't keep Jai from walking down the hall and out of Sloan's life. When she got to her car, she sat behind the wheel and cried her eyes out.

It had been seventeen days, going on seventeen long nights, since Jai had spoken to Sloan. Deep down inside, Rissa couldn't have been more gladdened by the breakup. It killed her hearing about Jai being so happy with Sloan, how good of a catch he was. Rissa couldn't help but be haunted by the thought that it should have been her. Rissa ran down that night in Cream a thousand and one times trying to determine what Jai had that she didn't have that attracted Sloan to her. Rissa hated to admit it, but a white man choosing a black girl over her was a major shoot down.

Rissa found herself in the gym five times a week instead of her normal regimen of three days thinking that maybe she needed more work on her body. She even lightened her hair a little. One can never be too blonde. She even went as far as calling a doctor and making a consultation appointment for breast implants. Now, with Jai and Sloan's breakup, she wasn't constantly reminded of possible flaws with herself. Jai's pain was Rissa's healing. Of course Rissa never let onto this to Jai. She had to be the best friend that she was and be there for Jai during her time of need.

The two had to have gained at least five pounds together over the past couple weeks. They ate out or shared takeout at one another's home, over a good old-fashioned male-bashing session, almost every other day. They had even missed two weeks of Friday evening happy hour at Cream because the place reminded Jai too much of Sloan. It was like pulling hen's teeth when Rissa finally got Jai to go.

The girls hadn't been inside Cream a good half-hour before Sloan and his buddies from the gym walked through the door.

"Don't look now, but the most beautiful man in the world just walked through the door," Rissa said.

Jai turned to see Sloan and those same two guys he was with the night she met him. He didn't notice her and Rissa before taking a seat at a corner booth.

"So how do you feel about seeing him walk through that door?" Rissa asked. "Is your heart racing ninety miles per hour? Are your palms sweaty? Can you hear your heartbeat? Do you have a loss of appetite and words?"

Jai just sat there trying to prevent the tears from rolling down her face. Not being with him hurt. Seeing him hurt.

"Damn, girl, you got it!" Rissa said, putting her hand on Jai's forehead. "You got jungle fever."

The two laughed hysterically. Jai's laughter turned to tears as Rissa handed her a napkin.

"Girl, walk over there and go get your man. Imagine how you would feel if he walked up to some other woman, asked her to dance, and lived happily ever after with her, all because you sat here looking cute, with too much pride to just go over there to him. Imagine that."

Jai looked into Rissa's eyes and could tell that she was speaking from her heart. Rissa didn't want Jai to feel the resentment she herself was feeling inside, but she knew she would get over that completely in time.

When Jai looked at Sloan so much flashed before her eyes. She saw the two of them living in a small cottagelike house with a big backyard, two kids, and a dog. This must have been what Rissa saw the moment she looked at him that night in the club. Before Jai repeated the same mistake she turned to Rissa to get her genuine approval.

"Look, girl, it's been me and you for years and I can live with it just being me and you. But I love him, Rissa. I really do. But, I'm never going to know just how much he really loves me or if we can make this thing work if I don't go over there. But I won't go over there, not if my happiness equals your misery and a dent in our friendship. So tell me how you really feel this time. What do you want me to do?"

Rissa looked over at Sloan who by now was standing up at his table talking to an Asian girl. She was giggling and carrying on, hanging on to Sloan's every word.

"I want you to go over there right now and get your man, because if he takes Suzi Wong onto the dance floor and asks for her number, I'm going to cut my fucking wrist."

Jai and Rissa laughed and hugged before Jai stood up, pulled her shirt down over her tummy, and headed toward Sloan's table. The Asian girl wasn't bad-looking at all. As a matter of fact she was tall and equally as gorgeous as Russell Simmons's wife. Jai was starting to feel a tad inferior, but halfway over to Sloan's table,

Snoop Doggy Dog's "Beautiful" came on and made Jai feel like she was just as lovely as one of the Brazilian women in the video. That song coming on, the song they first danced to, was a sign that she was doing the right thing. Out of all the songs that the DJ could have played he randomly chose that one. It had to be a sign. Jai picked up her pace and strutted over to Sloan's table like a peacock.

"I think they're playing our song," Jai said as she held her hand out to Sloan, separating him and the Asian girl. As her hand hung in midair for what seemed like forever, the consequences of her action ran through Jai's mind. One of two things was about to happen. Sloan was going to humiliate her by declining her invitation to dance and send her back over to her place at the bar with Rissa or he would grab her hand and walk over to the dance floor with her. Fortunately it was the latter of the two.

When Sloan reached for Jai's hand and grabbed it, she closed her eyes and thanked God. As far as Jai and Sloan were concerned, they were the only two people in Cream. Sloan led the way to the center of the dance floor, where it had all began.

"Can we start over?" Jai asked Sloan.

"We can't start over, but we can pick up where we left off and try to fix things," Sloan said.

"I'm game for that."

"I missed you," both Jai and Sloan said at the same time.

"We're different, Jai. You take cream in your coffee and I take mine black. And although we don't see our differences as a distraction to one another, the rest of the world does and we have to learn how to deal with it together."

"Point taken," Jai smiled.

"We can do this, baby. Love does conquer all." Sloan gave Jai a delicious makeup kiss. "Do you have plans for this weekend?"

"No, why?" Jai asked.

"My mom makes one hell of a pasta and tomato sauce," Sloan said, pulling Jai close to him.

"Oh, yeah?" Jai said, smiling and honored to be receiving an invitation to go to Columbus to finally meet Sloan's parents.

"Yeah. And with dessert she makes this Italian bean coffee that's to die for. She makes her own special cream, too. You'll love it," Sloan said, planting a long hard kiss on Jai's lips.

Jai placed her head on Sloan's chest and exhaled.

Sloan looked up at the DJ booth and gave the DJ a thumb up as he lipped the words "thank you." The DJ, in return, gave Sloan a thumb up and lipped the words "thank you" as he held up the twenty dollar bill Sloan had slipped him as persuasion to play his and Jai's song.

NEVER SATISFIED

Kayla Perrin

PROLOGUE

•

"Tell me your fantasy."

Amani Milford shivered at the husky voice, shivered with anticipation as she imagined what would come next. Would it be like she had always dreamed with Aaron? Wild and hot and utterly exciting? Or would he take his time with her, torture her with teasing until she begged him to take her?

She swallowed. Licked her lips. "My fantasy?"

"Whatever you want, I'll do. Anything."

Anything. A nervous breath oozed out of her. Could she be so brazen, tell him exactly what was on her mind?

She forged ahead, not sure where she got her nerve. "I want you to tie me to the bed. With my stockings, once you take them off me."

Reaching for the hem of her skirt, she shimmied out of it, letting the black cotton fall to the carpeted floor. As Aaron's eyes grew wide with appreciation, she couldn't help feeling a surge of power. In fact, she felt so powerful that she pirouetted, giving him a view of her butt, fully exposed as she was wearing only a thong.

"Oh, baby," he growled. "Come here."

Amani slowly strutted toward him. From his seat on the bed, he reached for her, peeling first one stocking down her leg, then the other. With both nylons secured in one hand, he wrapped the other around her waist and pulled her down onto him. Then he rolled them both over so that he pinned her body beneath his while keeping his weight off of her. Amani gasped softly at the delicious force.

"Do you have any idea what I want to do to you?" he whispered.

"Probably exactly what I want to do to you."

Aaron nibbled on her ear before pulling away from her. He moved forward on the bed, taking one of her arms with him. Wrapping the stocking around her wrist, he secured it to the bed head.

"Tighter," Amani told him. She sighed as he yanked harder on the stocking.

Aaron tied her other hand to the bed, then reached for her face. His fingers gently caressed her skin, yet set her body on fire. "Now what? I want to do everything the way you want me to."

"Take my blouse off. Don't be gentle."

He ripped at her silk blouse. Buttons went flying. "And now?"

"Undo my bra. Touch my breasts."

He did, and Amani thought she would go insane with desire. Her entire body throbbed, and she knew she would climax soon. But she didn't want to. Not yet.

"Stop," she managed on a ragged moan.

Instantly, Aaron stopped. But his lust-filled eyes said he didn't want to.

"Take off your clothes," Amani told him.

Moving backward onto his knees, he reached for his shirt. Making her suffer, he took his time undoing every button, allowing her only small glimpses of his magnificent chest before he fully stripped out of it and dropped it onto the floor. Amani held her breath as he reached for the belt. But he carried on with his exquisite torture, slowly unhooking it and sliding it out of his pants.

Amani licked her lips. "Hurry," she whispered.

"Huh?"

The flame burning inside her instantly went out, as surely as if someone had dumped a bucket of water on it.

That was not Aaron's voice!

Awful awareness filled her. The kind that would leave her horribly embarrassed when she opened her eyes and faced the real world.

"Amani!" That was Suzette's voice, an urgent whisper.

Amani didn't want to, but she slowly opened her eyes. Then wanted to die when she saw the curious smile dancing on her best friend's face.

Oh, God.

"What's up with you?" Suzette asked. She leaned across the aisle between the row of desks to be closer to Amani. "Your eyes were closed pretty tight, and you were making these strange little sounds. Like little moans."

"Stop lying." Wanting to bury her head in a dark hole, Amani sat up straight and tried to play it cool. She picked up her pen and focused on her notebook and the task Mr. Hayes had given them—to write a short story about one of the happiest days of their lives. But her body still throbbed, reminding her exactly where her thoughts had just been.

"I'm not lying," Suzette protested. "If you had only seen your face. . . . C'mon, tell me what you were thinking about?"

"I was thinking about the assignment," Amani replied quickly. Perhaps too quickly.

"Then why were you moaning?"

Amani cut her eyes at her friend. "I'm not feeling very well, okay?"

Suzette's grin morphed into a frown. "Oh. Okay. I thought for sure it was something more."

"Well, you thought wrong."

Amani felt a little guilty for lying to her best friend, but she really didn't have any choice. Because there was no way she could admit the truth about what she'd really been thinking.

She would never admit that she had been caught up in an illicit fantasy starring their senior year English teacher, Mr. Aaron Hayes.

1.

"Oh, my God," Amani uttered a moment after the door chimes sounded in Coffee, Tea & Mail.

Suzette Gordon, Amani's longtime best friend and now business partner, looked up at her from the cappuccino machine and asked, "What?"

"Earl," Amani whispered.

"Ah," Suzette crooned as she looked toward the door. "*Earl.*"

Amani spun around, resting her butt against the counter as she scowled at her friend.

"What?" Suzette asked in a mock-innocent tone.

"Don't say his name like that. Like I'm supposed to get all warm and fuzzy inside because he's here."

Suzette held up a hand as if to say Amani didn't have to go on. "I know, I know. It's over with Earl. But hey, at least it lasted a couple months."

Amani resisted the urge to look over her shoulder. "Is he heading toward me? I know he's heading toward me."

"You know he's not coming for me, sugar. You have about three seconds to head to the bathroom. Oops, too late."

"Amani."

Amani squeezed her eyes shut. Then accepted her fate. After all, she couldn't avoid the man forever.

Turning around and grabbing the dishrag on the counter in one fluid movement, Amani planted a smile on her face. "Earl." He was barely an inch taller than she was, and it was always disappointing that she didn't have to look up into his dark eyes. "What a surprise."

"Hey."

"Hey, yourself." She wiped the dishrag over the steel countertop, even though the surface was spotless.

"Haven't heard from you," he said.

"Um. I know. I've been really, really busy." Amani made her way down the counter, wiping with such flair her mother would have been proud.

Following her from the opposite side of the counter, Earl's expression said he didn't believe her. Not that she blamed him. She hadn't returned his calls since she had seen him two weeks ago. Rather, since she had snuck out of his bed while he'd been sleeping.

"So busy that you couldn't return my calls?"

Earl was exactly the reason Amani didn't like to date. What had happened to the days when you could date a guy, no strings attached? Amani had liked Earl. She had been enjoying their companionship. It was certainly a plus not having to wonder who you'd spend a Saturday night with, or if you'd be able to find someone with whom you could go to the movies. Her relationship with Earl had gone from A to B to C, so after a night of drinking and dancing at a downtown club, they had taken the next step. Considering it had been at least eight months since Amani's last sexual encounter, she had been looking forward to it. She hadn't been looking forward to a proclamation of love.

"*I love you.*" Earl had uttered the words *after* he had orgasmed. Had it been during, she would have written the words off as meaningless sex talk. But he'd said the words with a clear head, then kissed her with such passion there was no mistaking their sincerity. She had crept out of his bed two hours later.

He loved her. How ridiculous was that? Good grief. He'd only known her a couple of months.

Not that she could rule that sort of thing out completely. Suzette swore by love at first sight and was happily married now for just over four years. But Amani didn't feel the same way about Earl. In fact, any feelings she'd had for him had fizzled into nothing. The problem was, Earl didn't quite get the hint that she was no longer interested.

"You know we've extended the hours here," Amani pointed out. "I've had to train a couple new workers, which can really exhaust a person."

"If anyone needs a break, it's you," Earl told her.

"I know. But when you're a small business owner, it's not so easy to take one."

Earl nodded, but his expression said he didn't accept her words. "What about this Friday?" he pressed. "Maybe dinner, then a show?"

Earl was attractive, sweet, but Amani knew they didn't have a future—much to Suzette's chagrin, considering she had set them up. And much to her own. She'd had hope that Earl would be the man for her, that they could ride off into the sunset together—which, in Toronto, meant buying a waterfront condo or perhaps an overpriced house in the Beaches. However, after their one intimate night together, Amani had realized that he was not an all night man.

Not a man she wanted to wake up with in the morning.

Maybe she was too picky. Suzette had said as much. Because since her divorce four years earlier—just months after Suzette's grand wedding—she hadn't met a man with whom she felt comfortable waking up beside. Which had led to her taking the walk of shame in the middle of the night more times than she cared to admit.

And even when she'd been married to Carl, she had hated the thought of curling up next to him until the morning came. Which was the first clue that their marriage wouldn't last. Maybe she had suspected what a louse he was from the beginning. No, she had more than suspected, but had married Carl anyway to make her family happy.

That was water under the bridge, as the saying went. She had been there, done that, had the T-shirt to prove it, and didn't particularly want to go there again. She was happy being single. Still, she certainly didn't want to spend the rest of her life alone. The problem was, no one had really thrilled her since she'd been on the market again, and settling would be much worse than being single forever. It wasn't that she was hung up on her ex—she was totally over that cheating bastard—she just hadn't clicked with anyone else.

"I've already called about the tickets," Earl went on.

Inwardly, Amani grimaced. She could avoid Earl every time

he called or came in, but it was pointless. The truth was the best option.

She plopped the dishrag on the counter and fully faced him. "Earl, I just don't think . . ." She blew out a deep, unsatisfying breath. "If I'm completely honest with myself, I guess I have been avoiding you. It's not you," she quickly told him when she saw the look of disappointment in his eyes. "I did some thinking, some soul-searching"—Earl was into soul-searching—"and I realized that I'm at a point in my life where I'm not ready for a relationship."

Earl shoved his hands into the pockets of his slacks. "I see."

"I'm sorry," she said lamely.

"Is this because of your ex? Because you're afraid to trust again?"

Earl was a counselor at a home for troubled teens. He was used to talking feelings. Amani was not. Maybe that was why Carl had taken to talking his feelings in practically every singles chat room on the Internet.

"Maybe," Amani said softly. "I guess that's something I need to work on before I attempt to have any type of relationship. My mother, God rest her soul, always used to say I had issues with trust. I guess because of my father."

Earl waited a beat before asking, "What about your cousin's wedding? Are we still on for that?"

Had he heard anything she'd just said? "I'm not going," she fibbed.

"Oh." Earl's tone was laced with disappointment. "I hope you're not backing out because you're afraid of seeing your ex. Because I'm perfectly willing to be your date."

Suzette, who had disappeared when Amani and Earl had started talking, now approached with a worried expression on her face. "Amani, the customer at cubicle one needs to speak with you right away. Some kind of problem with the computer I can't figure out."

"Oh." *Thank you, Suzette.* To Earl, she said, "I appreciate you coming by, but I've got to run. Duty calls," she added lamely.

"Call me if you change your mind about the wedding."

"Sure thing," Amani said, but she had no intention of ever calling Earl again.

Even if it meant she had to go to her cousin's wedding alone—something she didn't want to do because Carl was going to be there with his new wife, the one he'd married just hours after signing the divorce papers to end *their* marriage. Of course, Carl had been screwing Karen while he'd still been Amani's husband. It had been one ugly mess, and thankfully Amani hadn't seen him in years. It hadn't been her cousin's idea to invite her ex-husband to the wedding, but Rachel's fiancé's. Rohan worked with Carl on the police force.

Karen also worked on the police force. That's where she and Carl had met. It still irked Amani that Karen used to smile to her face while having sex with her husband behind her back.

She really, really didn't want to see either of them. Especially not at an event like a wedding. *Maybe a funeral, with either one of them in the casket,* she thought wickedly.

Oh, get over it, she told herself. Then reminded herself she *was* over it. And she was. But there was also merit to the saying that the best revenge was living well. If she went to the wedding with a date, she would appear to be living well, and Carl would be forced to swallow his hurtful words that she'd never find another man to marry her.

Feeling suddenly desperate over the prospect of not having a date for Rachel's nuptials, Amani looked back at the counter before she reached the first cubicle. Earl was still staring at her. Maybe it wouldn't be a bad thing if he accompanied her to the wedding. As long as she laid out the ground rules ahead of time so there were no misunderstandings.

And found a pair of shoes with an inch or lower heel.

Earl's lips curled into a smile, and Amani quickly averted her gaze.

No, there was no way she could go to Rachel's wedding with him. The man was in love with her. She wasn't in love with him.

Another one bites the dust, she thought wryly, then plastered a grin on her face as she prepared to deal with the customer.

2.

"Finally, a moment to ourselves," Suzette proclaimed in a dramatic tone as she and Amani took a seat at a small table near the back of the café. "Man, I thought this place would never slow down."

The casual observer might look at Amani and Suzette and wonder what they had in common. Amani wore her black hair in a conservatively short do. Suzette had long dreadlocks that she routinely dyed blonde. Amani had a single piercing in each ear. Suzette had several in each ear, one through her eyebrow, one in her nose, and one in her tongue. But despite their mismatched outward appearances, they had a lot in common. They both enjoyed movies and books, fine wine, and karaoke. At any social event, they were the last to leave. They didn't agree on everything, and could argue like sisters, but they loved each other to death and in their own way kept each other sane.

"I think we should fire Mac," Amani said. "This is the third time in two weeks that he's called in sick. We can't afford to have staff we can't rely on. Especially since that article about us ran in the *Toronto Star*, because we're busier than ever."

"Yeah, you're probably right." Suzette wrapped her fingers around the large mug. "Which is gonna suck, because we'll have to hire and train someone else."

Amani looked beyond Suzette's shoulder and out the large window. It was a gray November day. Professional-looking people huddled into their designer blazers, fighting off the chilling wind. Clearly more concerned about fashion, they were hardly dressed for the weather.

"The sooner we do it, the better," Amani said. "Maybe then I can finally take a vacation." It would be so much nicer to look outside a window and see a stretch of white, sandy beach than this dismal scene. "Go somewhere warm, like Jamaica or Hawaii."

"Oooh, now that's an idea. Find yourself some hot island man to bring to Rachel's wedding. That'll show Carl that you can have any man you want."

Amani met Suzette's gaze. "Who was talking about the wedding? I'm talking about a vacation, plain and simple. I haven't taken one since we opened this place five years ago." At the time, with her marriage falling apart, she hadn't wanted to take one. Work had been her saving grace. Now, she was ready.

Suzette sighed softly. "I could use a vacation, too. I hate this time of year."

"Then crank up the fireplace and get cozy with your man. The next one of us to go anywhere will be me. You and Mitch went to Vegas last year. The year before that, Cancun. I went to the Bahamas six years ago when I got married, and I haven't been anywhere since."

A naughty grin formed on Suzette's lips. "Hey, you've got to keep the spice in a marriage."

It was a good thing Suzette was such a great friend, or Amani might be tempted to despise her. From the stories Suzette told, she and Mitch had an amazing sex life. Their attraction to each had been fierce from the first moment they met, and hadn't waned since. On the other end of the spectrum, Amani's marriage to Carl had needed a whole host of spices to add some decent flavor. The sex had become routine and boring once they'd gotten past the first month. On their first year anniversary, when Carl had asked if she would give him a special present—that present being a ménage à trois with the two of them and another woman in the mix—Amani had known that their marriage was doomed.

And now . . . now she had the occasional sprinkling of spice, but nothing she wanted to sample again. Earl had been pretty darn good in bed. If only he hadn't ruined that by falling in love with her.

Amani sipped her tea. "I think I'll plan a trip away. Maybe to coincide with Rachel's wedding. And I'm only half-joking."

"Don't let Carl keep you from going."

"I have no residual feelings for him, but I'm just not comfortable seeing him. After all, we haven't talked since our divorce."

"Oh, wow." Suzette whistled lowly. "Check out *this* one."

"What?" Amani asked. Then seeing that Suzette was staring in the direction of the door, she realized her friend had gone from the discussion about the wedding to checking out some hot man. You'd never know she went home to a man every night, the way she ogled the ones who came into the café.

"What a nice pick-me-up for a bleak Monday afternoon. Now this guy, *he* could be your date. As long as you don't dump him before the two week mark."

"Oh, that was low." And, unfortunately, true for more than one of the guys Amani had dated. But what was the point in prolonging a relationship that wasn't going to work? "I'm done with you setting me up, Suzette. I don't need another Earl."

"Trust me," Suzette said. "Turn around."

Amani sighed wearily. Suzette was always trying to set her up with the hot men who came into the café, which was annoying to the *n*th degree. Just because Suzette had fallen in love at first sight with one of the customers four years earlier didn't mean that Amani would.

"I think . . ." Suzette's eyes narrowed. "He looks familiar."

Curiosity getting the better of her, Amani turned. And when she did, a zap of electricity went through her entire body.

Oh. My. Lord.

"Oh my goodness," Suzette said in a rush. "That's—"

"Aaron Hayes," Amani supplied.

Rather, *Mr.* Aaron Hayes. At least six feet two of drop-dead gorgeous man, she would know him anywhere. She had never forgotten him.

Senior year of high school. English class. She had hung on his every word, and fantasized about him every night.

He still looked as good as he had nine years ago, which was to say he looked pretty damn incredible. He had shaken up Montgomery High School when he'd joined the staff that year, leaving the female teachers and students lusting after him.

But Aaron Hayes had taken it all in stride. He had worn a wedding band, meaning he was off the market. Still, Amani had enjoyed some hot-blooded fantasies about him. Fantasies that would never come true, mostly because she was a student in his class and he would never look at her that way.

He'd made a point of telling her that.

"I think he needs some help," Suzette said.

The sound of Suzette's voice startled her. Amani had forgotten that anyone but she and Mr. Hayes were in this small café. How completely strange that she would feel the same rush of attraction for him, after all this time.

Amani faced her friend. Suzette's pierced eyebrow was arched with mischievous suggestion. "You're drooling," Suzette practically sang.

"I am not!" Nonetheless, Amani wiped the back of her hand across her mouth.

Suzette chuckled as she stood. "Finally, a man who gets a reaction out of you. I was beginning to worry."

Amani was about to ask, "What the hell does that mean?" but she could barely hear her own thoughts over the pounding of her heart. She was more than shocked to see Mr. Hayes, looking as devastatingly sexy as he had nine years ago, standing in her shop.

What was he doing here?

"Go help him out," Suzette instructed her. "Unless you're afraid you'll be tongue-tied because you still have a killer crush on him."

Amani made a fist and shook it at her friend. "Keep that up, and you'll be looking for work."

"You can't fire me, babe."

"Don't remind me."

Amani surreptitiously watched Aaron as she stood up and made a show of collecting the mugs and plates she and Suzette had used. Looking a tad confused, Aaron stepped into a cubicle. It wouldn't be long before he realized that he needed a password to access the computer.

"Put that stuff down." Suzette all but wrestled the mugs from Amani's hands.

"Suzette!"

Suzette curled her fingers around Amani's arm and gave her a firm, but friendly shove. "The man needs help. *Go help him.* And who knows, he could just end up being your date for the wedding."

Aaron lifted his head at that moment and saw her. He smiled a polite smile that said he didn't recognize her. But as Amani walked toward him, something in his expression changed. There was a flash of recognition in his eyes, and the smile changed from polite to pleasantly surprised.

"I know you," he said.

"Mr. Hayes," Amani responded.

"Aaron," he told her. Then he crossed his arms over his brawny chest. "Montgomery High, my first year there, which was ten years ago. You were a senior in my English class. Amani, right?"

"Oh my God." Amani was pleasantly surprised, despite a bit of panic. If he remembered her, did he remember the embarrassing story she had written? "How on earth did you remember that?"

"Some students, you just don't forget."

Her face grew warm, and given her fair complexion, she was sure he noticed the red hues flaming her cheeks. But if he did, he didn't give any signs.

More than nine long years had passed since that embarrassing day in his class, but now she couldn't help wondering if that was why he hadn't forgotten her. After all, how many other teenaged students practically threw themselves at him? That's exactly what Amani had done—in the guise of an erotic story—making a fool of herself in the process.

She had been dreaming about him practically nonstop, and had awoken one day with the ridiculous desire to communicate that to him before she graduated and never saw him again. What better way to do so than in a story, the way she had always communicated her feelings?

Mr. Hayes had been working with his students on a senior class anthology of stories that would be published. Amani had brazenly written a story about an English teacher having an affair with his student. The day after submitting it to him, she had been excited and hopeful when he'd asked her to stay after class to chat. But hope had turned to horror when she'd seen the serious look on his face.

"I'm going to get straight to the point," he'd said. "This story of yours . . ." He held it up. "Is it what I think it is?"

Amani had been too shocked to speak for a moment. But then her brain kicked in. "Um, what . . . what do you think it is?"

"Is this about me? Me and you?"

The way he asked the question made Amani look down in shame.

Mr. Hayes sighed his exasperation. "That's what I was afraid of."

She didn't face him. "I . . . I thought you'd like it."

"Amani, I . . . I think you've misunderstood the attention I've been giving you. It's my fault; I see that now." He looked at her with kindness. "I've been here for you, to help you grieve the loss of your mother. But that's all. Not only am I married, I'm your teacher. We can't be together."

Amani's heart had cracked in two. She had poured all her feelings for him into that story, and he was rejecting her. There was only one thing she could do now: lie. "It's not about you. It's just about a girl."

Mr. Hayes waited a beat. "The story is very explicit. Surely you know I can't publish this in the anthology."

"But it's a good story!"

"It's inappropriate. Besides, if I publish this, people will speculate. If they think we've been involved, I could lose my job."

"How could they do that? We haven't done anything wrong."

"If only things were so simple, Amani." He paused. "The deadline for the anthology has passed, but if you can get your new story to me in a couple days, I can work it in."

"A new story?"

"Either that, or the one you wrote about your mother's death last month."

"No. I don't want anyone to read that." She'd written about her emotions regarding her mother's death for herself—and for Mr. Hayes. It was much too personal to share with the whole school. She hadn't expected him to publish her latest story, but she had hoped he would tell her that he liked her, too.

"I'd like you to be in the anthology. You have until Friday."

Friday came and went. Amani hadn't written another story. In her heart, she doubted she would ever write again. She had been too humiliated.

"Amani?"

Aaron's deep voice brought Amani back from her trip down

memory lane. "Sorry. I'm just so surprised to see you. What brings you by?" May as well keep this conversation as much about business as possible.

"My laptop clunked out, and I need to access the Internet."

"You've certainly come to the right place." As she spoke, Amani's gaze ventured to Aaron's left hand. It was an instinctive action, and she was surprised to see that he no longer sported a wedding band. Did that mean he was divorced?

It doesn't matter. Pivoting on her heel, she started for an empty cubicle. "It's twenty cents a minute, five minute minimum."

"No problem."

She fired up the computer, entered the password, then stepped backward so he could take a seat. "Can I get you a coffee or tea? I've got special flavors, if you like, mild or strong. Anything you want, really." She was babbling.

"Regular coffee. Black."

"Sure thing."

No sooner was Amani at the café counter than Suzette was on her like white on rice. "What's he doing here? Is he still married? Because I didn't see a ring on his finger. Girl, if he's single—"

"My God, Suzette. Do you ever stop? The man wants to check his e-mail. And I'm sure he wants to do so without getting the third degree from me." Although the truth was, Amani was very interested to know all about him.

Not that he'd tell her squat. After all, she had only been one of his students. The best she could expect was respectful conversation.

Suzette didn't know about the story Amani had submitted to Mr. Hayes. She had been too embarrassed to tell her about it.

Pushing the disturbing memory from her mind, Amani

poured a mug of coffee for Aaron, placed it on a saucer and scooped up creamers and sugars. Then she sashayed back to his cubicle, aware that there was an extra pep in her step, an extra sway to her hips.

It was silly, surely, that after all this time, Aaron Hayes could bring about any type of reaction in her at all, but he did. She wished she'd had the foresight to put a fresh coat of lipstick on. Or run a comb through her hair. She suddenly wanted to look her best for him. Again, not that it would matter to him, but it did matter to her. At the very least, he would see that she was no longer the kid in his senior English class that he'd rejected.

He glanced up at her as she reached him, a smile in his dark brown eyes. "Thanks," he said softly.

"If you need any help, just let me know," she told him.

She turned and started her walk away, not daring to look behind her to see if his gaze still followed her movements. But she hoped he was getting an eyeful. How crazy was that?

Entirely, but some things never changed. She had never been able to turn off her raw, sexual attraction for the man. Not even in the nine years that had passed since graduation. Even during her marriage, she had thought of Aaron every now and then, wondering how he was, where he was, what he was doing with his life.

For the next thirty minutes, Amani went through the normal routine of making coffee, serving pastries, and helping customers with their computer queries—all while furtively watching Aaron's back.

She was clearing a table of dirty plates when he stood. Immediately, she lowered the plates and started toward him.

"All done?" she asked, wiping her hands on her apron.

"Yeah."

"Did you log off?"

"Uh huh."

"Good. Your receipt will be printing at the front counter. Minus the coffee."

"That wasn't necessary."

Amani waved a hand. "Oh, no big deal. It was the least I could do. You gave me an A in your English class."

He laughed softly, and Amani felt the stirring of something deep in her gut. Just like that, she had an understanding of what had always attracted her to him. He had a gentle nature, despite his devastatingly handsome looks. It was that gentle nature that had led him to reach out to her in her time of pain after her mother's death. He said he cared with a simple look or touch, and it was wildly intoxicating.

Would he be a quiet lover, Amani wondered, or did his polished exterior hide a wild, untamed side?

"You earned that A," he told her. "Still writing?"

"E-mail." She swallowed, her throat suddenly dry with the direction of her thoughts. "Every day."

"Seriously," Aaron said.

"Once in a while the mood strikes, but I usually end up chucking whatever I've scribbled. I learned long ago that writing wasn't in the cards for me." She shrugged as if to say it was no big deal.

Aaron gave her a long look as he shook his head. "That's exactly what I didn't want to hear."

"It really doesn't matter. I'm much too busy running this shop, anyway."

"And I have no doubt you're doing a great job. But you're an extremely talented writer. It seems like such a waste."

"Mr. Hayes, you're much too kind." Why was he flattering her like this, considering he'd torn her last writing assignment to shreds? "Are you still teaching?"

"Yep. I stayed at Montgomery High for six years. Now I'm at Delta, not too far north of here."

"Right." Amani knew where the high school was.

They fell into silence. Grinning uncomfortably, Amani crossed her arms over her chest. She had no clue what to say to him.

He was the first to speak. "The receipt's at the front?"

"Oh. Right. Let me take care of that."

She hustled to the front of the café. A young man with stringy blond hair beckoned to her, but she held up a finger in his direction, telling him she'd be a second.

At the cash register, she rang up Aaron's total. "Six ninety," she told him.

He handed her a ten, saying, "Keep the change."

She shook her head. "Mr. Hayes."

"No, keep it." He shoved his wallet back into his slacks.

"Thank you," she said softly. Again, there was an awkward silence. Glancing to her left, she saw the young man staring at her, an impatient look on his face. Suzette was busy with someone else, which meant she'd have to deal with him.

"Well, it was good seeing you again," Amani said. "I wish I could hang out and chat, but I've got to get back to work."

"I know." Aaron nodded, his gaze holding hers. He looked away, then back at her. "It was good seeing you, too."

"If you're in the area again—"

"Of course."

Aaron gave her one last grin before slowly making his way to the door. Amani had the distinct feeling that he had wanted to say something else.

3.

"Kiss me."

It wasn't a whispery request. It was an urgent demand. The urgency turned her on.

Before she could step toward him, he circled his arms around her waist and pulled her hard against his chest. Then he smothered her mouth with his, filling her entire body with heat.

"You taste so sweet," he said. "I want to taste all of you."

He tweaked her nipple through her shirt, then moved his hand lower, cupping her feminine mound. Amani softly moaned.

As his lips found their way back to hers, his hands pulled at her clothes. He had her form-fitting top unzipped and off her body in mere seconds. She wasn't wearing a bra—she knew he liked that—and he growled his appreciation.

Less than a minute later, they were both completely naked.

Stepping backward when he reached for her, Amani moved to the bed. Slowly she sat, then lay back, spreading her legs as she did.

"Oh, baby," he said in a gravelly tone. "I can see how moist you are." He walked toward her. "I want to taste you. Will you let me?"

The image of his hot mouth covering her almost brought her to orgasm. "You don't have to ask."

Amani closed her eyes in anticipation. His breath was warm. She knew his tongue would feel glorious.

"Oh, Aaron . . ."

As she moaned loudly, she opened her eyes. Opened them and found no one caressing her naked skin but the satin sheets. Yet her entire body throbbed with sexual tension, as if she'd just been in the middle of an intimate act.

She *had* been. In her dreams.

Sighing softly, Amani's eyelids fluttered shut. She had been dreaming about Aaron. Again.

Her skin was hot and moist, as surely as if she had worked up a sweat with him. And her center was moist. She knew that without having to feel for herself.

She let out a slow breath as she pulled the satin sheet over her breasts. The material skimmed her nipples, and the sensation was as erotic as if Aaron had touched her, only much less fulfilling.

Perhaps there was something wrong with her. What else would explain her inability to fall for available men, and her lingering desire for the one who could never be hers?

Aaron Hayes was off-limits. Or was he?

In high school, he had been off-limits because he was her teacher and he was married. She'd been eighteen when she met him and in her immature mind, that had been old enough because she was legal. She hadn't worried about the fact that he was married when she wrote that erotic story, nor had she considered the ramifications of an actual relationship with her teacher.

But she was no longer his student . . .

"But nothing," she told herself. It had taken nine years to see him again this time, and it would probably be another nine years before their next chance encounter.

Just before noon on Wednesday, Amani was pouring dark-roast coffee grinds into a filter when she heard Suzette say, "My, my, my. Look who it is."

Amani's hands stilled. "Earl?" she whispered, dread settling in her stomach like a dead weight.

"No, not Earl. Someone much, much more intriguing."

Amani dumped the empty coffee package into the trashcan. "Honestly, Suzette, sometimes I think all you do is stand behind the counter all day and check out the men coming in."

Suzette sighed wistfully. "Is there anything better?"

Amani pressed the start button on the coffee machine. "Is it someone I know?"

"Just turn around, dear."

Rolling her eyes, Amani did just that. Then felt like she'd been sucker-punched. Aaron Hayes, looking like he'd stepped off the front page of *GQ* magazine in a black turtleneck, black slacks, and a thigh-long black leather coat, strolled casually toward the deli counter.

"Mr. Hayes." His name escaped on a shaky breath.

"Aaron," he corrected.

"Aaron." She stepped toward the counter, her hands automatically reaching for the tongs outside the pastry display. She lifted them, placed them back down. Looked around for something else to fidget with and finally decided to stick her hands in her pockets. "Your computer still on the fritz?"

"No, it's working again. That's not why I'm here."

"Oh?"

"I wouldn't mind a coffee," he said. "And I'm hoping you have a moment to sit down and share one with me."

"Me?"

He made a joke of looking beyond her shoulder, to where no one stood. "Yeah, you."

"I . . ." Amani glanced to her far right, where Suzette stood. Suzette nodded vigorously. Facing Aaron again, Amani said, "All right. I've got some time."

"Great."

Aaron wanted to sit down and share a coffee with *her*? It was nine years since she'd graduated high school, yet she had that same nervous feeling in her stomach that she used to get when Aaron had wanted to discuss one of her projects with her.

Get a grip, she told herself as she poured two mugs of coffee. *It's not like he can give you a D.*

"Would you like a bagel?" she asked him. "Or a sandwich?"

"If you've got a turkey sandwich, that'll be great. I'm on my lunch break."

"From school?"

"Uh huh."

"So what brings you down here?"

"I'll tell you as soon as we sit."

Butterflies zipped around in Amani's stomach like they were

on speed. She placed the turkey sandwich on a tray, followed by the two mugs of coffee, and a pile of creamers and sugars. Then she made her way around the counter carefully carrying the tray. It wasn't heavy, but she was nervous and didn't want to embarrass herself by tripping.

"Here, let me." Aaron moved toward her and took the tray from her hands.

"Thanks," she said. He was always the gentleman. Even when he'd broken her heart, he'd been a gentleman.

"You want to sit near the fireplace?" he asked.

"Sure."

Aaron led the way to one of the two-seater booths surrounding the gas fireplace. He placed the tray on the table, then gestured for her to sit first.

Lord, she could hardly stand how nice he was. She would never purge him from her erotic dreams unless he became an asshole.

"You have me very curious," she said as she sat. "I can't imagine why you'd come down here to see me on your lunch break."

"I don't have a class right after lunch, so I have some extra time."

Nodding, Amani reached for her coffee. "That still leaves me clueless."

Aaron opened the plastic container that held the turkey sandwich. "This is a great-looking sandwich."

"Aaron!"

Faint laugh lines formed around his eyes as he chuckled softly. "All right," he said. "I'll tell you why I'm here."

"Please do."

Amani held her breath until Aaron spoke again—a good four seconds. "I have a confession to make," he said.

Amani's breath left her in a rush. Had she heard him correctly? "A confession?"

"Yeah."

Oh, man. What could he possibly want to tell her? That he was fiercely attracted to her?

"I didn't come here by chance on Monday."

"You didn't?"

He shook his head. "I knew you owned this place. But I acted like I was surprised to see you when I came in."

Aaron said the words as if he'd just confessed to being a serial killer. He might as well have. Amani was just as surprised.

"I don't understand," she said.

"I saw that article in the paper about you and your business venture. I remembered you right away. Remembered Suzette as well, although her hair is very different. I was proud of your success, but surprised that you were a small business owner. I always thought you'd be a writer."

Amani dragged a hand across the back of her neck. "Oh?"

"Yeah. It's not too often I come across a person whom I sure will make it in the world of publishing. You're one of a few."

Aaron's comment rendered Amani speechless.

"You're that good," Aaron went on.

"A writer? It's a nice dream, Aaron, but this is my life now." She gestured to the café.

"I understand." He took a sip of his coffee. "But I have a proposition for you."

"A proposition?"

"Yeah. And I'm hoping you'll bite."

Proposition. Bite. If he only knew how those words had played out in her fantasies with him.

Then again, maybe he did. Surely he remembered the embarrassing story she had written.

But that was half a lifetime ago. Ancient history.

"I'm all ears." She surprised herself with how calmly she spoke, considering her stomach was in knots. If, by some remote chance, Aaron was here to tell her that he had always loved her and couldn't live without her, then she wanted him to come right out and say that.

His mouth opened. She watched it move. It was a sexy mouth. One she had imagined trailing kisses over every part of her body.

"What do you say?"

Aaron stared at her expectantly, and Amani realized she hadn't heard whatever he'd said. "Um, pardon me?"

His eyes narrowed as he looked at her quizzically. "I said, Delta is doing a Continuing Education program. On Wednesday evenings, I'm teaching a creative writing class. It started a couple weeks ago, but it's not too late for you to join."

Amani blinked, stunned. "You want me to sign up for your writing class?"

"Yes."

"That's why you're here?"

"I figured I'd extend a personal invitation."

"But . . . but . . . but I'm busy. With the shop. It's a small business, and Suzette and I practically run it ourselves."

"Then I'm sure she won't mind scheduling you Wednesday evenings off for a couple months."

"A couple months!"

"Six more weeks, actually. Until the end of December."

Amani frowned. "I don't know. I'm not sure."

"I want you in my class."

Amani's eyes met Aaron's. For several seconds, their gazes were locked. Prickles of anticipation danced along Amani's skin.

She was the first to look away. "Why? Why do you want me in your class?"

"Because in all the years I've been teaching, you were the student with the most potential."

It was a wonderful compliment, and Amani couldn't help feeling a surge of pride. But immediately following the pride was self doubt. She had stopped writing after he had told her he wouldn't publish her story in the senior collection of short stories. She had realized then that she put too much of herself on the line in her writing, and she didn't want to do that again.

"I have a different life now," she said quietly.

"You have a natural-born writing talent. That never dies."

"I'm not so sure."

"I'm sure."

Amani blew out a sigh. "I really don't think I can . . ."

"How about a challenge, then?" Aaron asked, clearly not willing to back down. "A wager of sorts."

"What kind of wager?"

"If you take this course and complete it, you can ask me for anything your heart desires."

Amani's eyebrows shot up at the same time her heart slammed against her ribcage. "Meaning?"

"Whatever you want, I'll do for you."

"Like buy me an all-expense-paid trip to Hawaii?"

Aaron's lips twisted as he contemplated her suggestion. "Maybe not all-expense-paid, but I'm willing to put five hundred into the deal if what you want has a monetary value."

Five hundred dollars!

"But I'm also game to be your housekeeper for a week," he added. "Or your personal chef. Whatever."

"I'm liking this," Amani said in a devious tone.

"But." Aaron wagged a finger. "If you don't complete the course, you have to do something for me."

"The infamous catch. So this is more like a bet."

He nodded as he finally took a bite of his sandwich.

"I don't get why this is important to you," Amani said, eyeing him warily.

He chewed, swallowed. "I told you why."

"I know what you said, but this whole wager thing is pretty serious for a teacher who thinks I have potential. I get the feeling there's something more to why you're here." She paused. "Is there?"

Aaron inhaled and exhaled slowly. "There is," he admitted. "I want to make things right."

Amani frowned. "I don't understand."

"I have a feeling that the reason you stopped writing has to do with me."

The question that popped into Amani's mind was a lame, "What makes you say that?" but Aaron was not just a pretty face. He was a deeply sensitive man, one who had been in tune with his students' feelings. He had reached out to her in a way no other teacher had when he'd learned about her mother's sudden passing.

It made complete sense that he would know, without her telling him, the reason she had decided to put down the pen forever.

Yet she said, "Oh, Mr. Hayes. You shouldn't blame yourself for that."

"I still feel bad about what happened that day. You know it wasn't personal. And please, call me Aaron."

"Aaron." Instinctively, Amani reached across the table and covered his hands with hers. "My not writing has nothing to do with you."

Aaron nodded, seemingly satisfied by her answer. "Good. Then you should have no problem accepting my challenge."

Amani leaned back in her seat. "Oh, goodness. You're not serious about that."

"I am. Name your price."

As much as she had told herself that she would never write another story, excitement now stirred within her at the prospect of letting her creative juices flow once again.

She finally said, "I'll take the course, but there's no need to wager anything."

"Humor me."

He wasn't going to give up. And an idea suddenly struck Amani. A brilliant one. "All right. But what I'm going to ask is really more of a favor than anything else. And you might not want to oblige, considering I'll need this well before the end of the course."

"What?"

"I need a date for a wedding. It's next weekend. Normally, I wouldn't have a problem going alone, but my ex-husband is going to be there, and I'm really not happy about the fact that I have to see him. I'll deal with the night much better if I have lots of alcohol and if I don't have to be alone. You'll probably say no, but there it is, on the table. That's what I'd like."

"This sounds important to you."

"It is."

"Next Saturday?"

"Yes."

Aaron nodded slowly. "All right. I'll go with you."

Amani's shoulders drooped with relief. "Oh, thank you."

"As long as you come to my class tonight."

"Tonight?"

"It's Wednesday. You've missed the first two classes. This is the best time for you to come and register if you're serious about doing it."

There was a part of Amani that knew seeing any more of Aaron would be dangerous. Around him, her heart tended to get involved even if her brain told it not to. But there was another part, the part that hadn't quite died, that was secretly thrilled that he was seeking her out to be in his class. A part that secretly yearned for as much of Aaron Hayes as she could get.

"What time?" she asked.

"The class starts at seven-thirty. Be there around seven, seven-fifteen in order to register and fill out the paperwork."

"All right," Amani agreed. "I'll do it."

Aaron's lips curved in a megawatt smile. Had he actually spent years wondering if she was still writing, and feeling guilty for not publishing her story years ago?

Or was there another reason behind his obvious happiness?

"What else do you want?" he asked. "Provided you complete the course, that is."

"Going to the wedding with me will be payment enough."

He gave her a look that said he wasn't born yesterday. "I need to know you'll be there until the end, so please, choose something else."

"Gosh, you're not going to make this easy."

"No, I'm going to make it right."

She thought for a moment. *What else do I want?* "Okay, here's the deal. If I complete the course, you'll have to dust my entire place."

He raised an eyebrow. Was there a hint of suggestion in his eyes? He asked, "That's all?"

"You haven't seen the dust in my house."

"Good enough," Aaron said. "Now, for my wager. If you don't complete the course—"

"I'll complete it."

"But if you don't, you'll spend a day at Delta with me, talking to my students about how fears can keep a person from pursuing her dreams."

"That's not fair!"

"Which is a moot point, if you won't be losing this challenge." Aaron extended a hand to Amani. "Can we shake on it?"

She accepted his strong hand and shook it firmly. "Get your dust cloth ready," she told him, smirking smugly, "Because you're going to need it."

4.

Aaron tossed his pen down on the desk, leaned back in his leather chair, and stretched his body for a good five seconds. There was no point continuing to mark any more papers before the class started. His stomach was fluttering with nervous anticipation, and he could barely concentrate.

He'd been anxious ever since leaving Coffee, Tea & Mail hours earlier. Anxious at the prospect of Amani really joining his class, although he had practically given her no choice.

Glancing up, Aaron's gaze wandered to the wall clock. It was thirteen minutes after seven. Would Amani show up?

She'd said she would, and he had no reason to doubt her. Unless she decided she wasn't up for his challenge.

He hoped she was. Amani was a brilliant writer. He had known that from the moment he'd read her first words on paper in his class ten years ago. He also knew that the reason she had stopped writing was because of him.

Oh, he couldn't be one hundred percent sure, but his gut told him he was right. When he had told Amani that he couldn't publish her story in the senior class anthology, he had seen the light go out of her eyes. And every day in class after that, the work she had turned in had been substandard. Her last project had been completely void of the emotion and passion of her earlier works. He should have given the project a C, but he'd given her the A he knew she was capable of, partly out of guilt, and partly to boost her morale.

He'd had to reject her subtle come-on, but he hadn't liked hurting her. Even after she had graduated and she was out of his life, he'd thought about her, wondering if she was still hurting. And he'd also thought long and hard about whether or not he had in some way led Amani on.

Not intentionally, but in a way she could have easily misconstrued given her age. He had come to the realization that it was his reaching out to her in her time of grief over the loss of her mother that had ignited her attraction for him. He had been there for her as he had routinely been there for all his students. But he'd been able to connect with Amani on a deeper level because he'd also lost his mother at a young age, and had been able to offer her the kind of comfort she needed at the time.

Right after that, she had started looking at him differently in class. With a doe-eyed expression that said she was infatuated with him.

There had never been any hope for a relationship with them.

He had been ten years her senior *and* her teacher. Besides, he had been married.

But he wasn't married any longer. His wife had left him for a rich man, something he would never be as a teacher.

Aaron blew out a sharp breath as he leaned forward. Why was he even thinking of the fact that he was single?

Because it had been way too long since he'd been with a woman. And there was no doubt that Amani was now a woman, and as such, he could appreciate her beauty and not feel any guilt.

Closing his eyes, he envisioned her the first time he'd seen her at her café. Flawless, light brown skin, and full, luscious lips. And with curves in all the right places, she looked good enough to eat.

Would she like that? he wondered. *A man tasting her nectar?*

Aaron felt the beginning of an erection, and was shocked that his thoughts had led him to this state. After all, he was thinking about Amani, his former student.

Former student and totally gorgeous woman.

So much for changing the direction of his thoughts.

Aaron stood and walked to the window. Resting his butt on the window's ledge, he stared out at the dark night and the string of streetlights that lined the sidewalk. "Think about . . . being castrated."

He actually had to laugh at the ridiculous sentiment, although it did the trick. Thank God. He didn't need an erection when Amani came into the room. Without thinking of her tempting body, he could remember the most important issue. He wanted to see her writing again, which was why he'd come up with this challenge.

She was the one student he had never forgotten, the one he

had influenced the most. And he wanted to right the wrong that had been done.

When he heard the soft rapping on his door, he jumped off the ledge and vaulted forward, colliding with a desk as he did. His heart rate doubled when Amani walked through the door.

Oh, man.

The sight of her literally knocked the breath from his lungs. He knew she was beautiful when he'd seen her at the café, but now she looked stunning. Wearing a hip-length red leather jacket and tight black jeans, she looked good enough to serve up as an entrée at a fine dining establishment.

His groin tightened with the thought. Both the erotic thought and the pull of an erection were surprises, considering he'd chastised himself only moments before for letting his thoughts veer down the wrong road.

But how could he not be affected by Amani? She was a full-fledged woman now. One who liked to dress like a woman, flaunting her magnificent body. His ex-wife, Sandra, had hidden her sexual side.

Why didn't Amani have a boyfriend? She'd mentioned an ex-husband. He wondered what kind of man would leave her other than an idiot.

People had said the same thing to Sandra all the time. *Why would you leave a man like Aaron?* The way she'd painted him out to people in her reply, they thought he was some sort of first-rate asshole. In reality, he had let Sandra have her own way with practically everything in the marriage, up to and including the decision not to have children. He knew her real issue was that he hadn't made enough money for her liking, even though he made a good salary.

Forget Sandra. Shoving his hands in his pockets, he forced a smile. "Amani, hi."

She grinned back at him. "I'm here," she said.

"A little later than I expected, but better late than never. Thank you for keeping your word."

"You didn't give me much choice."

"For your own good, I assure you."

She stripped off her leather jacket. Beneath it, she wore a form-fitting white cotton shirt that hugged her beautiful curves. How long had it been since Aaron had touched curves like that?

"I didn't ask," she said, "but is this class going to cost me anything?"

"Nope."

She started toward him. "What do you need me to sign?"

Not only did she look good, she smelled good. Like roses. The scent was intoxicating.

Aaron lifted a clipboard with a form on it off his desk and handed it to her. "Fill this out. I'll bring it to the office later."

She took a seat at the desk directly in front of his. As she wrote, Aaron watched her. There was something magnetic about her. Something utterly sexy that seemed to come naturally.

"Here," she said after a few minutes.

He took the clipboard, glancing at the form but not really seeing it. "I'm glad you came," he told her. If he inspired her to write again, then this would all be worth it.

"I hope your wife doesn't mind that I borrow you for a few hours next Saturday."

"She won't mind. Since she doesn't exist."

"Oh?"

Amani's tone said she wasn't surprised. No doubt, she had

seen the absence of a ring on his left hand. "I've been divorced for six years. It's a long, ugly story."

"Ah, you have one of those, too."

Aaron simply nodded.

Amani's beautiful lips parted, like she was going to say something else, but the sound of footfalls made her turn instead. As a woman wandered into the classroom, Amani said, "I guess I'd better take a seat. Anywhere okay?"

"I know the last seat on the far right row is available." *But that's so far away . . .*

As Amani gathered her belongings, Aaron couldn't help checking out her incredible form once again. She had certainly rounded out since high school. Her behind was fuller, more womanly. Her breasts were definitely heavier. She had the perfect hourglass figure, and knew she would look magnificent naked.

His eyes lingered on her backside as she bent over the desk to offload her belongings.

Shit, he thought when he felt his growing erection. This time, he wasn't able to make it stop from becoming full and hard. Quickly lowering the clipboard to cover his groin, he made his way behind the desk.

It was going to be a long three hours.

Amani reread what she'd written, then scrunched the three pages into a ball, stuffing the giant wad into her desk.

Why, oh why had she agreed to take this class? Writing was torture. She had known that years ago, and nothing had changed.

Aaron had instructed the class to write about any topic they liked—as long as it was about a deeply personal subject. Like the loss of a pet, he'd suggested. Or the loss of a lover.

Amani had written about Carl, about how his betrayal had devastated her. She had tapped into her deepest emotions and spilled them forth onto the page. The piece was raw, poignant. And surprisingly cathartic.

But much, much too personal.

If there was one thing she'd learned after writing that personal piece about her feelings for Aaron, it was that she didn't want anyone to ever be able to see so far into her soul.

She fiddled with her pen. She could write about . . . about what? About the time her goldfish had died when she was six years old. A smile touched her lips. That would work, and she wouldn't give away too much of herself in the process.

She put her pen to paper, recalling that tragic day so long ago.

At the end of the three-hour class, Aaron stood and announced, "That's it, folks. Time's up."

There were a few groans, and some people didn't stop writing, clearly needing more time to get their thoughts down on paper. Amani, on the other hand, put her name on tops of her pages and numbered them. Then, satisfied with herself, she collected them. She walked up to Aaron and handed him her story.

A shiver of excitement danced down Amani's spine at the grin he gave her, and she knew she would see Aaron again tonight, in her dreams. There was something about him that held her captive, plain and simple.

"There you go," she said.

"Can't wait to read it," he told her.

Other students also made their way to the front of the class, and Aaron gave his attention to them.

Amani wanted to stay, but what would be the point? So she could ogle him and make a fool of herself?

"See you next week," she told him.

"Sure thing," he replied.

Amani lifted her hand in a wave, then went back to her desk. She gathered her belongings and made her way to the door. Before exiting, she glanced over her shoulder.

A sweet sensation passed through her when she saw that Aaron was looking at her.

5.

When Aaron handed the marked assignments back to the class the following week, Amani saw red.

A big red *D*, that is. Circled at the top of her page.

A *D?* Amani stared at the mark with disbelief, sure her eyes were playing some cruel trick on her. But the D didn't morph into an A or a B.

She tucked the story into her binder and slammed it closed. Aaron had the nerve to stroke her ego by telling her how good a writer she was, then reward her with a *D*.

Anger brewing inside her, Amani gathered her belongings in haste. Screw Aaron and screw this course. She didn't have time for this. She needed to hire and train a new person, something she'd be able to do much better if she didn't have the distraction of Aaron and this class hanging over her head.

She was at the classroom door when she heard, "Amani, can you wait a moment? I need to talk to you."

Amani was tempted to charge through the door without looking back, the wedding be damned. She'd go alone, or she'd stay at home and hope her cousin forgave her. The last thing she wanted to do now was go with Aaron. She'd thought that he had humiliated her back in high school with his "You're too young for me" talk, but this D took the cake.

She took another step toward the door, but halted when she heard him call her name again. Sighing with resignation, she slowly turned around.

Other students filed out past her. Slipping into her leather jacket, Amani moved to the wall. She stood there until the last of the students had left.

Aaron's lips twisted in a frown as his gaze met hers from across the room. "Will you come up here, please?"

Scowling, Amani shoved herself off the wall with the heel of her boot. Although she didn't want to, she headed to the front of the class to deal with Aaron. She may as well get this over with as soon as possible.

"Take a seat," he told her.

"Why? So you can tell me how great a writer I am?"

Crossing his arms over his chest, Aaron leaned his butt against his desk. "You can't tell me you're surprised at your mark."

"Oh, God." Amani whirled on her heel.

"Wait."

Aaron's voice stopped her cold. There was a vulnerable tone in his voice, making it all but impossible to walk away from him.

But she steeled her jaw as she faced him again, asking, "Why should I?"

"So we can talk. About your story."

"What's to talk about? You obviously hated it."

Aaron pursed his lips, clearly thinking about what he was going to say. "I think you missed the point of the assignment."

"You said to write about something that was personal. The death of Pinky was very personal to me."

"And that's the key word. *Was.* The death of your goldfish was personal when you were six, but it surely isn't now. Not that it couldn't be, mind you," Aaron added, holding up a hand, "but there wasn't one hint of emotion in your story."

"I don't see why that matters—"

"If you're going to do this—be in my class—don't hide behind a curtain. Show me what you're made of."

"Taking this class wasn't my idea."

"I know. It was mine. But you accepted my challenge."

Amani shook her head. "I thought I was up to it. But maybe I'm not."

Aaron stepped toward her. "No, don't do that. Don't run and hide."

"I'm not as good as you think I am."

"Yes, you are. And you know it."

Amani finally sat. "I've started off with a D. I don't want to take this course if I'll barely pass."

Aaron walked around his desk. Amani's eyes narrowed as she watched him reach into a folder. He withdrew a few sheets of paper that had clearly been crumpled, but were now straight.

She felt a sinking sensation in her gut.

"I didn't count the story you submitted toward your mark. But I did count this one."

Amani swallowed as he walked toward her. She knew what he was going to hand her even before she saw the title, *All That Glitters.*

"H-how did you get this?"

"You left it in your desk."

Damn. He must have seen her shove her wad of paper in there.

"It was garbage," Amani pointed out. "You shouldn't have retrieved it."

"Au contraire. It was exactly what I wanted to see from you. Exactly what I knew you were capable of. And as you see, that story earned you an A+."

Amani's stomach dropped at the memory of what she had written in the story. Feelings of not being attractive enough for her husband, and wondering if that was why he had turned to other women.

"And I understand now why you don't want to go to your cousin's wedding without a date."

Amani shot to her feet. "You had no right."

"Amani, I liked your story."

"I . . . you weren't supposed to read it."

"Then why did you write it?"

Because she had needed to purge herself of the emotions, and writing them down had been the best way.

But she didn't want to tell him that. So she secured her tote and binder under her arm and whirled around, prepared to stomp out of the room.

Before she could, Aaron's fingers wrapped around her upper arm. "What are you doing?"

"Leaving."

"What about the wedding?"

"I don't want to talk about that."

"You're just going to quit, aren't you?"

Amani paused briefly, then said, "Yes."

"Look at me."

"No."

"Please."

If only he wasn't so nice. She could deal with being rude to him if he wasn't such a gentleman.

She angled her head slightly so that her eyes met his.

"You don't need to be ashamed, or embarrassed because I read your first story."

Oh, but she did. She hadn't wanted to admit it to herself, but Carl had dealt a lethal blow to her self-esteem. "I really don't want to have this conversation."

"We all have our issues, Amani. I had a wife who cheated on me with my best man. With me, she was a cold fish, but apparently with him she was insatiable. That didn't leave me feeling very good about myself."

"What are you trying to do—be my shrink?"

Amani watched his muscular chest rise and fall and wondered what it would be like to rest her head against it. She had walked away from her marriage and buried herself in work, but hadn't really given herself time to grieve. Grieving made her vulnerable, and she didn't want to be vulnerable. She had met Carl shortly after Aaron's rejection, and she had no doubt that that relationship had bloomed simply because she had needed someone to help her get over her broken heart.

A relationship that had ultimately eroded her self-esteem.

"Your ex-husband was wrong," Aaron said softly. "You're stunningly beautiful and entirely desirable."

A startled breath escaped Amani's throat. What had Aaron just said?

"You heard me," he told her. "So please, whatever you do, don't question that."

"Why are you talking about this with me?"

Aaron released her arm. Took a few steps backward. "You're a passionate person. I knew that when you submitted that erotic story to me, and the thought that someone has snuffed out that side of you makes me angry."

She was growing hot and moist at his words. "I think . . . think you should . . . stop."

Aaron closed his eyes. "I know." He reopened them. "But for the life of me, I can't. When I'm near you, it's like something comes over me, making me lose all my sense."

Maybe Aaron was on drugs. Yes, that had to be it, because he wasn't making a lick of sense.

"I think I'll just turn around, walk away. Okay?"

Her stomach fluttering with nerves, Amani did just that. She took one step, then another. And felt a mild sense of disappointment that Aaron was going to let her walk away.

But before she could take the third step, she felt his hand on her arm. He whirled her around, drew her close, and planted his mouth firmly down on hers.

Amani was so startled she dropped her tote bag and binder.

The items landed on the floor with a thud. Her mouth opened in surprise. Aaron's hot, moist tongue immediately went into her mouth, tangling with her own.

Amani moaned her pleasure, succumbing to the kiss. Her eyelids slowly closed as she snaked her arms around Aaron's neck. God, did he ever smell good. The spicy scent of his cologne mixed with his natural scent to create an utterly intoxicating aroma. She wanted to sink her teeth into his neck, run her tongue along his flesh, drag her nails down the backs of his thighs.

The kiss was even better than she had always dreamed. Better because it was real.

It was real.

The thought hit her full force. She moaned again and clung tighter to him, not wanting to let him go. As her breasts crushed against his chest, her nipples hardened.

Aaron pulled his lips away from hers and trailed them down the expanse of her neck. Amani arched her head backward, giving him more access to her. His mouth went lower, lower, until he reached the V of her shirt and the roundness of one of her breasts. Then he stilled, but she could feel his warm breath fanning her skin.

Amani made a little noise and jutted her hips, letting him know that he could continue. This was crazy, she knew, but Aaron Hayes had always turned her on in a way she didn't understand. Right now, she didn't want to stop and think about what they were doing. She wanted to keep going, knowing that she would never regret what would happen between them, even if they shared only one night of intimacy.

But Aaron growled in frustration, lifted her to an upright position, and then released her.

Feeling suddenly cold where she had once been warm, Amani simply stared at him.

"I'm sorry," he said.

He had damn near kissed her into a coma. No way in hell was she going to accept an apology from him.

"No, don't say that. Don't say you're sorry."

Aaron dragged a hand over his face. "I don't know what came over me."

"Oh, God. You're going to tell me that this never should have happened."

Amani turned away. But she instantly felt Aaron's presence behind her. Felt it before he placed his hands on her arms.

He leaned his head forward, resting his nose against her hair. The air left his lungs, tickling the back of her head. She wanted to turn around and lose herself in another one of his mind-numbing kisses.

"I should say that," he whispered. "But it would be a lie. I wanted this to happen."

Amani slowly turned in his arms. Every part of her was alive with lustful sensations.

"I suppose I've always found you attractive. Before, you were much too young. Off-limits. But now . . ."

"Now?"

"Please, don't look at me like that. I don't think I'll be able to control myself."

A bolt of electricity zapped her vagina. He really did want her.

Speak now or forever hold your peace. "What if I said I didn't want you to control yourself?"

He swallowed.

"We're both adults now. Both unattached."

"I don't know. I need time to think."

"Think about whether or not you want to take me to bed?"

Aaron put a finger across Amani's lips. "Don't . . . don't make this harder on me than it needs to be."

"I want that, too," she told him.

"But I'm your teacher."

"I don't care about that."

"I want you in this class. I don't want anything to prevent that."

She slipped her arms around his waist. "Nothing will."

Aaron cradled her in his arms, and for the first time in a very long time, Amani felt safe. Cared for. She wanted more of this incredible man.

But then he untangled himself from her and stepped backward. "No."

A pain shot through her heart. "No?"

"Amani, you should be angry with me. I just attacked you like some untamed animal. I showed absolutely no restraint, not to mention no discretion."

"Will you kiss me again?"

Aaron's eyes registered shock. "I don't think you're hearing what I'm saying."

"Just one kiss, then I'll leave." She made the sign of a cross over her heart. "I promise."

Aaron's shoulders drooped as he chuckled softly. "You're too much."

"Thank you."

"I don't know how I got myself into this." His face lit up like a Christmas tree with his smile. Then he moved toward her. He lowered his head as she raised hers.

Their lips met, and Amani swore she saw fireworks.

She ended the kiss after only a few seconds, leaving him wanting more. "Call me before the end of the week. I'll tell you when to get ready for the wedding."

She bent to retrieve her items, and Aaron met her on the floor. He collected the strewn papers and handed them to her.

He rose to his feet in sync with her, his eyes never leaving hers. She read what he was feeling: wariness, shock, exhilaration. She was feeling those emotions, too.

Amani tipped on her toes and gave him another quick kiss. "Call me," she told him. Then she turned and walked out of the classroom, resisting the temptation to look back.

6

Suzette nearly tackled the deliveryman when he entered the café with a bouquet of a dozen roses. Squealing with delight, she pried them from the stunned man's hands.

"Are you Amani Milford?" he asked.

"Amani?" Suzette sounded truly baffled.

"These flowers are for a Miss Amani Milford."

Amani placed the tray she was holding on a table and started walking toward the deliveryman. As she did, warmth was filling her heart. This stunning bouquet was for her?

"These are for me?" she asked.

"If you're Amani Milford."

The guy may as well have been Ed McMahon for how excited she was. "I am."

The deliveryman produced a clipboard. "Sign here, please."

As Amani signed, Suzette sniffed the roses, all the while eyeing her as if she'd just stolen her candy.

"Enjoy," the man said as he handed Amani the bouquet. Then he was off.

As soon as he was out the door, Suzette said, "Who on earth is sending you roses?"

"Don't hate, Suzette. Mitch sends you tons of goodies." And he did. He was always sending her flowers or chocolates, doing his best to keep the romance alive in their marriage.

"I'm about to die of curiosity. Open that card!"

Securing the flowers in one arm, Amani reached for the card with her free hand. Her insides melted when she read it.

Suzette plucked the card from her fingers. "I want to start over and woo you right." Her eyes bulged as she stared at Amani. "Amani! What haven't you told me?"

Amani wanted to lose herself in a dream world, one where Suzette would not intrude. But that would only happen if she'd received this delivery when she'd been home alone.

Besides, seeing this bouquet made it official. What had happened between her and Aaron last night was not a one-time thing. He was attracted to her.

Suzette snapped her fingers in front of Amani's face. "Hello? Anybody home?"

"These are from Aaron," Amani said calmly.

"Aaron as in Mr. Hayes?"

"Uh huh."

"Oh my God." Suzette framed her face with both hands. "Well, I'd say it's obvious he's interested in more than your writing skills."

Amani leaned forward and whispered, "He kissed me last night."

"What?" Suzette screamed. Loud enough that everyone in the café turned and looked at the two of them.

Amani giggled. "I was going to tell you, but . . ."

"But what?" Suzette queried in a lower tone. "You *forgot?*"

"I didn't want to jump the gun. Tell you about it and be all excited if he wasn't interested."

Suzette glanced at the card once again, then the roses. "The man is definitely interested. Woo you?" She bit down hard on her bottom lip. "Girl, that is too sweet."

Amani snatched the card from her friend and held it close to her chest. "You should have seen him. He gave my story a D, then when we were discussing it, he laid on one me."

"A *D?*" Suzette waved a hand. "Forget that. He just kissed you out of the blue?"

"I'll tell you about the story I wrote later. But the short version of what happened between me and Aaron is that I was going to quit the class. Next thing I know, he's kissing me senseless."

"Wow."

"I know."

"How did this happen? I mean, I know *how* so don't give me some smart response. But I mean, why? What am I missing?" Her eyes narrowed on Amani. "Amani, what aren't you telling me?"

Amani's lips curled in a guilty grin. "Well, there *is* something."

"Something like what?" Suzette asked frantically. When Amani didn't answer, Suzette gripped Amani's hands, squeezing hard. "Oh, my goodness. You and Aaron—you two have a history?"

"You could say that."

Suzette gasped. "I thought you were my best friend. How could you not tell me this?"

"Let's talk behind the counter," Amani told her. At least there they'd have more privacy.

Suzette dragged her all the way there. Amani giggled.

"All right," Suzette said. "Out with it. Tell me how you kept an affair with Aaron secret from me, but more importantly, tell me when it happened."

"Girl, don't jump to conclusions. Aaron and I were never intimate. But I did do something really stupid where he's concerned. Nine years ago. Maybe that's why things escalated yesterday. I don't know."

"Keep talking."

"I don't know what I was thinking. The school year was winding to a close. I was feeling very brave—or stupid, however you want to look at it. I've forgiven myself, considering I was only eighteen."

Suzette squeezed her hands harder. "What did you do?"

"I poured my heart out in a story about a girl who falls for her teacher and has a wicked affair with him. I was hoping he'd get that I was writing about him and me, and that maybe we could have some type of affair."

"But he was married!"

"Oh, I had that angle covered in the story. The girl in the story knows he's married and has one night of passion with him."

Suzette's eyes widened. "You wrote that?"

"I was young. Very stupid. And ultimately embarrassed beyond anything I could imagine when he sat me down and told me that our being together was out of the question."

"Ouch."

"Ouch is right. That's why I never had a story in the senior class anthology."

"You told me it was because you'd had writer's block."

"I know what I told you. I didn't want to admit the truth."

Suzette smiled. "Surprise, surprise. But, it looks like you're finally gonna get your man."

"Oh, Suzette. Don't say that. That's *way* too premature."

"Hey, I say go for it."

Last night, that idea had sounded wonderful. Today, Amani had questions. "We barely know each other," she pointed out, her gaze wandering to the brilliant rose bouquet, still standing on a table. "In the way we should, I mean. As friends as opposed to as teacher-student. And you know me and my track record with men."

"Get that crap Carl told you out of your head."

"So far, he's been right."

"Carl is a loser and anyone who doesn't know that can kiss my ass."

Amani hugged Suzette. "You're sweet."

"I just love you. And I want to see you happy. I think Aaron will make you happy." Suzette broke the hug and eyed Amani with a questioning gaze. "Hey, you didn't go home with him . . . did you?"

"No!" When Amani's outburst got curious looks, she smiled sheepishly, then continued in a hushed voice. "No, of course not. He's too much of a gentleman for that. Not that I wasn't tempted."

"Hmm. So next week's wedding night should be extra special—and not just for the bride and groom."

Amani winked. "That's what I'm hoping."

. . .

It was just after three-thirty when Amani answered the café's ringing phone. "Coffee, Tea & Mail," she said.

"Amani, hi."

All the air trickled out of her lungs. *Aaron.*

She was nervous beyond reason, but someone kept her voice cool, calm, and collected. "Hey, you."

"I've been thinking of you practically nonstop since last night."

"Have you, now?"

"Mmm hmm. I couldn't wait until my last class of the day walked through the door so I could give you a call."

Amani's insides turned to mush. The man was too sweet. "I got the roses. Thank you *so* much."

"You're welcome." He paused. "I meant what I said. I want to woo you properly."

Amani's hands were jittery with excitement. "Always a gentleman," she said, for lack of anything more intelligent to say.

"What are you doing tonight?"

"Tonight?"

"Yeah. I was wondering if we could get together."

"Um... I'm supposed to close this place tonight. Suzette's leaving early to spend some time with her husband before he leaves town." *Just my luck!*

"Oh." Aaron sounded disappointed.

"You could always come by and visit me."

"If I come by, I'll want to leave with you."

Just like that, Amani was wet. Lord how she wanted this man.

"I should be out of here by eleven," she told him, a hopeful note in her voice.

"Then you'd keep me up all night, and I *do* have to teach in the morning."

The very thought of spending a very hot night with him had her body tingling with anticipation. "So you just called to tease me, is that it?"

He chuckled. Amani liked the sound of his laugh. It was warm, sensuous.

"I'll try to come by, even if it's just for a few minutes. But I can't make any promises."

"Oh." Amani frowned.

"I know. But I do miss you. And I wanted to give you a call so you'd know I was thinking about you."

She would be relentless with him when she finally got her hands on him. "I'll talk to you later?"

"You bet."

"Wait," Aaron suddenly said. "Don't hang up. Will you be at the café alone tonight?"

"No. A girl named Jennifer will be closing with me."

"Oh, that's good. That makes me feel better."

Amani secured the phone between her ear and shoulder so that she could pinch herself. No, she wasn't dreaming.

"I have a meeting in five minutes with the other English teachers."

"And I need to get back to work. We'll talk later."

"Of course."

Amani replaced the phone's receiver, feeling as if she had died and gone to heaven.

1.

"Jennifer, why don't you head on home?" Amani suggested. It was close to nine-thirty, and the place was dead.

Jennifer stopped sweeping and looked at Amani. "Are you sure?"

Amani approached her and took the broom from her hands. "Yes, I'm sure. I doubt any more customers will be coming in now. You've done such a great job helping me clean up that I'm sure as soon as ten o'clock rolls around, I'll be able to lock up and get out of here."

The young girl was already untying her apron. "Thanks a lot."

Amani watched Jennifer hustle behind the counter. Seconds later, she had her arms through her backpack. "See you Monday," the girl said.

"Take care. Oh, and Jennifer?"

Jennifer halted on her way to the front door. "Yeah?"

"Good luck on your exam tomorrow."

Jennifer smiled widely. "Thanks."

Moments later, the door chimes sounded, and Amani continued sweeping the floor where Jennifer had stopped.

She had been hoping to see Aaron today, but he hadn't shown up after all. Amani would be lying if she said she wasn't disappointed, even though he'd told her he wasn't sure if he could make it. Deep in her heart, she had hoped that he would surprise her.

Maybe tomorrow, she thought, continuing to sweep.

No sooner than the thought came to her mind than the door chimes sounded. Feeling a rush of excitement, Amani looked toward the door. She fully expected to see Aaron, devastatingly sexy, entering the shop.

But her stomach dropped when she saw Earl standing there, not Aaron.

"Earl." Amani gripped the broom tightly.

"Hey, Amani."

He started toward her, and panic spread throughout her body. What was he doing here, just moments after Jennifer had left? Had he been watching her?

Amani swallowed. "What are you doing here?"

"I was just passing by. Saw you in here."

Was he telling the truth, or had he turned into a stalker? "I'm . . . about to close up."

"Did you give any more thought to tomorrow night?"

As Earl approached, Amani took steps backward. But he approached faster than she retreated, and now only a table stood between them. Amani had the feeling it wasn't enough. "Tomorrow night?"

"The dinner and show."

"Oh. I thought I told you I couldn't make it."

"I've been thinking a lot about what you said. About how you're not sure you're ready for a relationship. And I really think this has to do with your ex."

Was this why he had come here? Warning signs went off in her head. Maybe Earl was harmless, or maybe he was a raving lunatic.

"Why are you looking at me like that?" he asked.

"Looking at you like what?"

"Like you're scared."

"I'm not looking at you like that," Amani replied in a rush. But her voice sounded high-strung even to her own ears, and she wasn't sure Earl believed her.

The phone rang, and Amani nearly jumped out of her skin. Then felt like a fool. "Um," she began, flustered. "Give me a second."

She all but ran behind the counter and grabbed the phone. "Hello?"

"Is this Coffee, Tea—"

"Oh." She blew out a relieved breath. "Hey, you."

"Are you all right?" Aaron asked.

"We're still open, but not for much longer. Can you make it here in twenty minutes?"

"Something's wrong," Aaron said, sounding on edge. "Do you need me?"

"Five minutes? Oh, that's perfect."

"I'm on my way."

Aaron disconnected, but Amani continued speaking for Earl's benefit. "Oh, I know how lost you can feel when your computer crashes." She forced a laugh. "Mmm hmm. I can definitely help you with that. Great. I'll be here."

Slowly, she replaced the receiver. Earl's gaze was like a laser, boring into her. "You're sticking around?"

"Yeah. That was a student who comes here a lot. He recently purchased a used laptop, but apparently it crashed, and he needs to print out a paper."

"Oh."

"He should be here in five minutes or so. But it will probably take a while to help him get everything straightened out." Amani planted her hands on her hips. "I'd be happy to get you a coffee or tea, if you want to stick around."

Earl shook his head. "No. I need to be leaving."

"Okay. Well, thanks for dropping in to say hi."

"I'll see you another time." Earl's gaze didn't waver as he began walking backward. He walked until he bumped into a table before finally turning around.

Amani held her breath until he disappeared through the door. She watched him walk out of the view of the windows, then rushed to the front of the store. She turned the lock on the door.

"Oh, man." She buried her face in her hands, feeling frazzled. Perhaps she was overreacting where Earl was concerned, but she was glad he was out of the store.

Merely minutes after she went to the back of the café to put the pastries in the fridge, she heard banging on the window. Startled, she jumped, then relaxed when she saw Aaron's face.

Aaron.

Their eyes connecting, he motioned for her to go to the front door.

Of course. She'd locked it.

Her fear ebbing away, she hustled to the front door and unlocked it. The moment she opened it, Aaron pulled her into his arms. "Are you okay?" he asked, concern lacing his voice.

"I am now," she told him.

His gaze swept the entire café. "What happened?"

"Well . . . nothing, really. Someone I know came in, and I guess . . . I didn't like the vibe I was getting from him. I feel kind of silly now. I overreacted."

"I thought you weren't going to be alone."

"I sent my worker home early."

"Amani." Aaron shook his head. "I don't like the idea of you being here alone. This is a big city. You're right downtown. You need to take precautions to keep safe."

"I know." She slipped her arms around his waist, snuggling against him. "You got here fast."

"I was worried."

"You must not live far."

Aaron pulled back his head to look down at her. "Is that a not-so-subtle way to try and find out where I live?"

She giggled softly. "No."

"I live near Yonge and Bloor." He paused. "Did you drive?"

"The subway's right underneath us, and from here it practically takes me to my door."

"I'll take you home."

"I live in North York."

"So?"

"Bathurst and Wilson area."

"What else do you need to do before leaving?"

"Stick a few more things in the fridge. Do a final count of the cash, which isn't that big of a job because I already got through most of it and left only a small float in the till. But I'll at least be fifteen or so minutes. Too long for me to expect you to wait for me."

"Can I help you?"

"Aaron."

"I'm not going anywhere, unless you're with me."

Inwardly, Amani beamed. She was secretly thrilled at Aaron's protectiveness toward her. "All right. I'll be quick."

The drive to her place had been quiet for the most part, except for the sounds of jazz playing on the stereo and the occasional sprinkling of conversation. Nothing deep. Nothing personal. Amani had gotten the impression that Aaron was tired, or deliberately holding back. After all, he'd joked earlier about her keeping him up all night when he had to work tomorrow.

"This house right here," Amani told him, pointing.

Aaron stopped his late-model Mercedes. The gold-colored car drove like a dream, and Amani almost regretted having to get out of it. Nonetheless, she pulled her purse from the floor onto her lap. "Thanks a lot," she said. "I really appreciate the ride."

"You thank me for everything."

"That's the way my mother raised me."

"Which is fine. I'm not saying that. But I get the impression that you don't expect a lot from a man."

"Meaning?"

"Amani, I care about you. The least I can do is give you a ride home to make sure you're safe."

Amani's shoulders rose and fell in what she hoped was a nonchalant shrug. "I guess I'm just not used to that."

"Tell me your ex would have at least made sure to pick you up if you were scared."

"My ex?" Amani laughed. "Now there's a joke."

"He wouldn't?"

"Carl didn't . . . well, I guess he didn't care. Although I didn't know that at the time."

A beat, then, "I know your mother passed, but what about your father? Is he around?"

"He was never around. He walked away from my mother even before I was born."

"Aw, Amani. I'm sorry."

"Why? It's not your fault."

"I wish you'd had at least one man who treated you right." He reached across the seat and took her hand in his. "I want to treat you right."

From another man's lips, those words could be construed as simply suggestive. But this was Aaron, the man who had held her in his arms as she'd cried about her mother's death. The man who had whispered her words of support when she'd needed them. She knew he cared.

This seemed so right, being with him. When she had fallen for Carl, a part of her had always known that he was a way out of her lonely situation. She had moved in with an eccentric aunt and uncle when her mother's death had left her orphaned, and after a few short months, she'd thought she would go nuts there. Carl had offered a happier future, and Amani hadn't hesitated to take him up on it.

But Aaron had always been the man in her heart.

Amani looked at their joined hands, then lifted her gaze to meet his eyes. "Good night," she murmured.

"No. Not yet." And with those words, Aaron kissed her.

His lips captured hers softly at first in a tender kiss good-bye, but after a few moments, it was clear that neither one of them wanted to pull away. So the kiss deepened, became more urgent, until the sounds of their heavy breathing filled the car.

Aaron's hands went to her face. He sucked the tip of her tongue, her bottom lip. Then opened his mouth wide and delved his tongue into her mouth again, driving Amani insane with lust.

"I don't want to stop," he whispered.

"You don't have to. You can come inside."

The offer itself was a big step for her. Amani never brought a man home. That way, if she didn't want him to stay the night, *she* could be the one to walk away. Like she had done with Earl. She preferred it that way.

But she was engulfed in a fireball of desire, and going anywhere but straight to her bedroom was out of the question.

Aaron trailed his fingers down both sides of her neck, then across her collarbone. Had anyone ever touched her like this?

"I promise, I won't keep you up all night."

Oh, but I want you to, Aaron thought. Twenty minutes or an hour with Amani just wouldn't be enough.

He didn't tell her that, though, because he was still debating her offer. Debating how sensible it was to lose precious hours of sleep, versus finally satisfying his carnal feelings for the utterly desirable Amani Milford.

"Aaron?"

Forget thinking. He reached for his car door and flung it open. By the time he stepped into the cold night, Amani was also out of the car.

Aaron didn't say anything as he made his way around to her. Just reached for her hand, and she gave it to him.

Hand in hand, they walked up the short path to her small brick house.

8

The moment they crossed the threshold into her place, Amani threw her purse to the ground, spun around, and grabbed Aaron by the collar. She drew him to her so fiercely that she even shocked herself.

This wasn't about warm and fuzzy anymore. She wanted to get down and dirty.

She worked her mouth over his, her body growing hotter and wetter by the second. Lord, but the man had an incredible mouth. She could kiss him all day and never grow bored.

Aaron pulled away from her. "Is anyone else here?"

"No. I live alone."

She flicked her tongue over his mouth at the same time her fingers reached for the buttons on his shirt. One button, two. She deepened the kiss. Three buttons. Aaron pulled at her jacket.

Skillfully, Amani maneuvered her arms out of it so that her mouth never left his.

When her jacket hit the floor, she reached for his, urging it off his broad shoulders. The sound of rustling leather mixed with their moaning and panting. Then Aaron's jacket also hit the floor.

His tongue working wonders inside her mouth, he wrapped his arms around her waist and walked forward, forcing Amani to walk backward. She freed his shirt from his pants just before her body hit the wall.

"Oh, baby." Aaron pulled her shirt over her head and tossed it to the ground. "You're beautiful." His hands covered her breasts. "Absolutely beautiful."

Moaning softly, Amani leaned her head back against the wall. She jutted out her large breasts in invitation. She wanted them naked. She wanted Aaron's hot tongue on them.

But clearly he wanted to torture her.

He skimmed the mounds of her breasts with his fingers, the light touch stoking her fire. Then his hands went lower, down her belly to the waistband of her black tights. He dragged the soft material down her thighs. Dragged his fingers back up her legs, stopping them just before he touched her center.

"Can I touch you here?" he asked, his warm breath as erotic on her vagina as any stroke.

"Oh, Aaron, please."

Amani gasped when his finger made contact with her through her thong. Back and forth his thumb went stroking her nub, making it swell.

"I love your scent," Aaron told her. "Oh, baby. I need to taste you."

Amani went perfectly still. She had experienced this in her fantasies, but only in her fantasies. Carl had never wanted to please her this way, and the other men she'd been intimate with had preferred using their fingers to please her rather than their tongues.

Her nub throbbed as Aaron pulled her underwear down. The foyer light was on, giving him a full, X-rated view of her, but Amani surprisingly didn't care the way she had with Carl and the others. Aaron's touch made her feel beautiful, sexy.

"Open your legs for me."

Her knees wobbling, Amani braced herself against the wall for support as she spread her legs.

"That's it. Oh, yeah." He kissed her mound. "You're already wet for me."

Never had Amani been so exposed, yet she felt an incredible thrill. A rapturous moan spilled from her lips when Aaron touched her again. He moved his thumb over her nub in a circular motion, while his other fingers ventured along her folds. The pleasure nearly killed her when he eased a finger inside her.

"Oh yeah, sweetheart. That's it."

Amani writhed around against the pressure of his finger, her body so taut with sexual tension that she wasn't sure she could last much longer.

His thumb still stroking her on the outside, Aaron eased another finger inside her.

"Aaron . . ."

"You want more?" he asked.

"God, yes."

"I want to give you more."

And then Aaron's tongue replaced his thumb. Amani cried

out and slammed her hands against the wall. The sweetest sensation rocked her at her core. His tongue against her was heat on heat, applying delicious friction. How long could she last before she exploded?

Aaron's fingers stroked her from the inside while his tongue stroked her on the outside. Amani could barely manage little gasps for air as the pressure built. And when Aaron took her in his mouth and suckled her, Amani finally vaulted over the edge and into a sea of mind-shattering bliss.

"Aaron . . . oh . . ."

She gripped his head as her orgasm rocked her body, moaning wantonly and thrashing her head from side to side. And still, Aaron didn't stop. He sucked and stroked her until her body was spent from pleasure, until her knees could no longer sustain her weight. They buckled, and she collapsed, falling against him.

Nuzzling her face against his shoulder, Amani held on to Aaron until her breathing calmed from its frantic pace. He held her, too, his strong arm like a security blanket around her. She had never been so vulnerable, never been so satisfied.

"Amani?"

"Hmm?"

"My hand."

Her eyes widened with alarm as she realized that her knee was crushing his fingers. "Oh, gosh," she said, moving herself backward onto her butt. Her pants were like shackles around her ankles, preventing her from doing much else. "I'm sorry."

"No, don't be." He paused. "You okay?"

"Okay?" she asked, her tone resonating with disbelief. "Aaron, I'm more than okay. I've never been this okay in my life."

He stroked her face. "I'm glad."

Amani freed herself of her pants and underwear. Then she got onto her knees and crawled toward Aaron. She wanted to kiss him again.

He indulged her, but only briefly. When he pulled back his head, Amani stared at him in confusion. "What's the matter?"

Aaron glanced at his watch, then back at her. "The time."

"You want to leave me?"

"I don't *want* to leave you, but I think I should. Or trust me, I won't be leaving here for several hours."

His comment made her body throb. He'd given her an explosive orgasm. She wanted to do the same for him.

"You can't leave."

Aaron slowly stood. "Think of this as a promise of what will come."

Amani scrambled to her feet. She threw her arms around Aaron. "Please, no. I want to satisfy you."

"I want that, too . . . but I don't want to rush."

Did he have restraint beyond belief, or could he walk away so easily because he didn't find her attractive? Self-doubt reared its ugly head, making her believe the latter.

She looked down, unable to face him.

"Hey." Aaron gently lifted her head, forcing her to meet his eyes. "What's the matter?"

"I don't know," Amani lied.

Aaron stroked her chin with his thumb. "My leaving now, it's the hardest thing for me to do. You have to know that."

"Then why go?"

"I want to give you something to look forward to tomorrow night."

"Tomorrow night?"

His lips curled in a grin. "Mmm hmm. Tomorrow is Friday. And I don't have to be up early on Saturday."

His words were like a promise, and Amani's body shuddered. If he had given her a whopping orgasm in such a short amount of time, what would an entire night with him be like?

He kissed her, and her eyelids fluttered shut.

"Sweet dreams," he said softly.

Amani had absolutely no doubt that they would be.

"This is a first," Suzette said as she stuffed the sheet of paper into Amani's hand. "Courting by fax?"

"What?" Amani asked.

"Read it."

I'm anxious to see you.
I can hardly wait.
Will you do me the honor
Of being ready by eight?
(Sorry. I'm not much of a poet. If you can't make this date, please call me at the school, 555-6790.)

Amani started laughing, "I can't believe this."

"And I thought Mitch was romantic. That man has clearly got it bad for you."

"I think you're right."

"You *think*? When a man resorts to corny poetry, you know he wants you."

A smile danced on Amani's face, remembering last night. "Can I tell you something?"

Suzette's eyes widened as she drew in a sharp intake of air. "Amani . . ."

"I kinda got lucky last night."

"Oh my God. Where? Here?"

Amani shook her head. She filled Suzette in on Earl's appearance last night and how he'd frightened her, how that had led to Aaron coming by. "Then, he gave me a ride home."

"I'll bet."

"It didn't get that far. But girl, we fooled around for a bit, and I have to tell you, if I never see him again, what we shared last night will be enough to satisfy me forever."

Suzette covered her mouth to quiet her squeal of delight.

At the beginning of this month, Amani would never have imagined that she'd meet up with Aaron again, much less be intimately involved with him. Just when you got used to one hand, life dealt you another one.

"This is so . . . weird," Amani said. "The whole thing seems like a dream. So out of the blue."

"Girl, whatever you're doing, keep doing it. Because it's obviously working. And I know you've always wanted Mr. Too Fine Aaron Hayes."

Amani couldn't deny it. She *had* always wanted him. Was this really her chance to have him?

The kiss in Aaron's classroom had been unexpected for both of them, yet they'd taken their relationship to a new level nonetheless. Tonight, she would discover what it was like to be skin to skin with him, making love for possibly hours. Aaron had promised as much, and Amani knew he would deliver.

She had felt something with him she hadn't felt with anyone else. A comfort level that had surprised her. It had come so naturally, you'd think they had been intimate with each other for years.

Amani was one hundred percent smitten with him, charmed by his sweet nature and old-fashioned charm.

It wasn't the first time she'd felt promise at the onset of a relationship. She had felt hopeful with Earl, but then her feelings had faded. She didn't want that to happen now.

As if! a voice in her brain screamed. *You've only been hot for the man for how long?*

To Suzette, she said, "We'll see how it goes."

"How can you be so flip about this?"

"I don't want to get excited. Jinx myself, you know?"

Suzette rolled her eyes. "How about this. Don't worry about coming in until tomorrow afternoon. Provided we even open at all, considering the weather's supposed to get worse."

Amani looked outside. It was snowing lightly, but the wind had picked up, blowing the flurries around with a vengeance. As a result, snow was piling up outside the door to their café. It looked miserable, but business was booming as a result. People were coming inside to escape the cold.

"Who knows?" Suzette shrugged. "Maybe Mother Nature will be on your side."

"I'll be here by . . . ten."

"Oh yeah, right! You expect me to believe that once you get your hands on the delectable Mr. Hayes, you'll come up for air before the morning?"

What an enticing thought. "Maybe eleven, then."

Suzette flashed Amani a mock-scowl. "Whatever. I won't expect you until one or two. But I suspect the weather's gonna keep you in bed tomorrow, so that won't be an issue. That and at least six feet two of gorgeous black man."

"Shut up, Suzette." Amani playfully whacked her friend on the shoulder.

"Ouch." Suzette rubbed her arm as if she'd been injured. "I don't know why you're beating on me. You know I'm right. Now, what are you gonna wear?"

Amani shook her head. She didn't need Suzette outfitting her in the latest naughty lingerie from Frederick's of Hollywood. "Time to get back to work."

"Oh no you don't. You're not going to dismiss me."

Amani made her way around the counter, wiggling her fingers at Suzette as she did.

"Amani! I can help you with this. You know I can."

Ignoring Suzette, Amani giggled and made her way toward a lost-looking customer.

9

Amani was applying a shape of deep burgundy to her lips when she heard the knock on the bathroom door. "He's here," Suzette said in a sing-song voice.

Amani's heart spasmed. She glanced at her watch. It was ten minutes to eight.

Oh, boy. Aaron was early. Not by much, but early nonetheless. Anxious?

Amani's gaze went back to her reflection. She had gone through the ritual of dolling herself up, even though she hadn't expected Aaron to show. The weather had steadily gotten worse. Not enough to shut the city down, but enough that most people wouldn't want to venture outside unless they had to. Clearly, he wanted to see her.

A long breath oozed out of her as she checked out her appearance. Her short, black hair was slicked back off her face and held in place with gel. Her eyes were enhanced with black liner and mascara, giving her a dramatic look. And she was more than pleased with this burgundy lipstick that she had picked up at The Eaton Centre just last weekend. Her lips looked very kissable, indeed.

A good thing, in case Aaron wanted to kiss her again.

"Just go out there and meet the guy," she told herself sternly.

With that, she dropped her makeup items back into her large tote bag and headed into the café.

His back was turned to her, but even beneath the heavy winter coat, it was easy to see the breadth of his impressive shoulders. Shoulders she had fantasized about more times than she could count.

"All right, Suzette. I'll see you tomorrow."

Suzette came around the counter to hug her. "Night. And hey, do everything I'd do and more."

Amani playfully smacked Suzette's arm as she stepped away from her. And then Aaron turned, taking her breath away with his easy smile.

Swallowing a spate of nervousness, Amani walked toward him. "You really didn't have to come," she told him, "given the weather."

"You didn't call. I told you to call if you couldn't make it."

"I know, but . . ."

"A few snow flurries couldn't keep me from missing this date."

His words were like an aphrodisiac, and she wondered again what it was about Aaron Hayes that made her so easily melt. He could read a grocery list to her and she would find it sexy.

"Well, I appreciate you showing up. Because I've worked up an appetite."

"You like Jamaican food?"

"Oh, yeah. I even know how to make Jerk Chicken."

"So you don't mind if we head to The Real Jerk Pit?"

"Not at all. Are you driving, or do you want me to call for a taxi?"

"My car's outside."

Aaron motioned for Amani to step forward. She did, and he followed her to the door, then opened it for her. A bone-chilling wind immediately swirled around her, and she burrowed into her leather jacket.

"Here. Take my scarf."

Before she could protest, Aaron was wrapping it around her neck. The alluring scent of his musky cologne filled her senses. "You're too kind."

His arm snaked around her waist and he snuggled her close. It wasn't like the wind was going to blow her away, but she didn't point that out. Aaron was, as she'd always known, a gentleman.

He led her to his car across the street from the café. As she knew he would, he opened the passenger door for her and she got in.

"What do you want to hear?" Aaron asked, turning on the radio. "Flow 93.5, jazz?"

"Jazz is nice."

Aaron hit the CD button, and the smooth sounds of jazz filled the airwaves. Amani settled into her seat. They were both quiet on the drive southeast to The Real Jerk Pit. Amani wondered what Aaron was thinking, and she was sure he was wondering the same about her.

She was wondering how they'd gotten to this point. The point of being involved in a relationship. Because there was no doubt about it. They *were* involved. And the relationship didn't have a casual feel to Amani.

She doubted Aaron got involved casually.

She felt a niggling of something in her stomach, an unsettling type of feeling at the prospect of where this relationship might lead. But she pushed the thought out of her mind, forcing herself to concentrate on the here and now.

Aaron found a parking spot on Broadview and pulled into it. They were a stone's throw from the restaurant's front door. Meeting her at her side of the car, Aaron placed his arm around Amani and walked her to the restaurant door. Amani savored the feel of his strong arms around her.

Once inside The Real Jerk Pit, Amani blew out a sigh of relief. It was wonderfully warm and filled with delicious spicy scents. A complete contrast to the dismal atmosphere outside.

Minutes later, they were seated when Aaron reached into his jacket pocket. "I want to give you something."

Amani's breath caught in her throat when she saw Aaron reach into his jacket pocket. *There's no way . . .*

Her eyes watched his hand's every movement. She started breathing again when she saw him withdraw a small card envelope and place it on the table.

"What is this?"

"Open it."

"Is it a card?" she asked.

"Open it and see."

Amani opened the flap and pulled out folded sheets of paper. Lined paper, the kind students used to write on. But instead of being a stark white, it was yellowish.

Amani's heart pounded hard. If this was what she thought it was . . .

"Go on," Aaron urged.

Drawing in a shaky breath, Amani unfolded the papers. Instantly recognizing her penmanship, a wave of embarrassment washed over her. She wished the ground would swallow her whole. The best she could manage was a hand over her eyes. "Oh, gosh. Not this."

A sizzle of warmth spread along her skin when she felt Aaron's strong hand cover hers. He peeled her fingers from her face. "Look at me."

"I can't believe . . ." She opened her eyes and met Aaron's gaze. Her face flamed. "I don't understand. Why would you keep this?"

"You don't have any idea?"

"Other than to embarrass me?"

Aaron's eyes narrowed as he looked at her quizzically. "I hope you don't think I kept it all these years because I was waiting for the perfect opportunity to embarrass you."

No, that didn't make sense. So . . . why *had* he kept it?

"I know you might find this hard to believe, but I always liked your story."

Cringing, Amani covered her face. "Oh, come on."

"I did. I just couldn't tell you that at the time."

Amani slowly lowered her hand. Reality settled over her. Aaron had kept her story. Was it customary for him to do so, and if it was, was it likely that he'd be able to locate her story nine years later? "Aaron." She spoke his name tentatively. "What are you saying?"

The waitress appeared at that moment, interrupting them. Amani was so filled with tension she thought she could explode. She ordered a rum punch, and Aaron did the same.

As soon as the waitress was out of earshot, Amani spoke again. "Aaron . . ."

"I'm not sure why," he said softly. "Maybe because... because it touched me in some way."

This was news to Amani. "My story touched you?"

"I know you put your heart on the line when you wrote it. Put it on the line for me. That's why I kept it." He paused, rolled his eyes. "I don't even want to tell you what my wife said when she found it."

Amani threw a hand over her mouth. "No."

"Oh yeah. She wasn't impressed."

Amani chuckled softly. "Aaron." But her laughter suddenly faded as she caught a glint in his eyes. She stared hard at him, trying to read the emotion in his soul.

"I always thought you were a beautiful woman. And who knows? Maybe if we'd met under different circumstances, we might have explored a relationship."

"My God. I never knew you—"

Amani abruptly stopped when the waitress appeared, planting the drinks on the table before them. "Have you had a chance to look at the menu?" the young woman asked.

"No," Aaron replied. "Give us a few more minutes, will you?"

"No problem."

Amani watched the woman walk away before meeting Aaron's gaze again. Her heart was singing *Hallelujah,* yet her brain told her not to get excited. It was entirely possible that she was completely misconstruing what Aaron was saying.

"I don't know about you," he said, "but I'm suddenly hungry for a very different kind of food."

"I was thinking the same thing."

Aaron's smile was electrifying. "Let's finish our drinks, maybe have some dessert." He raised an eyebrow. "Or take dessert back to my place."

"I say we take it back to your place."

Amani had no doubt that she and Aaron would put it to good use.

Amani followed Aaron into his waterfront condo, then watched as he locked the door behind them. She carried the bag holding their dessert—a warm chocolate brownie, smothered with whipped cream and hot fudge. Thankfully, the drive from the restaurant to Aaron's place was only ten minutes even with all the snow on the road, and the whipped cream shouldn't have melted.

When Aaron and Amani were out of their boots, Aaron turned to her and took her hand. But instead of leading her to the bedroom, he walked her into the living room. Amani looked up at him in surprise.

He kissed her forehead. "Wait here."

Amani placed the dessert on his leather sofa, then stripped out of her coat. She was placing her jacket on the sofa's arm when Aaron returned holding a dark-colored comforter.

"The fudge could get messy," he explained.

"Ah. Of course."

Amani lifted the brown paper bag and pulled out the dessert. The plastic container was still warm. She opened it and dipped her finger into the chocolate. As Aaron watched her, she slowly put her finger in her mouth and sucked the chocolate off.

A flame of desire flickered in his eyes, stoking her own heat for him. Walking toward him where he stood on the comforter, she smothered her finger with more chocolate. As she reached him, he opened his mouth for her. But instead of putting her finger in his mouth, she ran it across his bottom lip.

Aaron flicked his tongue out, but Amani shook her head. Then she lifted herself on her toes, reaching her face to his. Ever so slowly, she licked the chocolate off his mouth.

Aaron wrapped an arm around her, but Amani stepped out of his embrace. "Take off your shirt," she told him.

His eyes never leaving hers, Aaron unbuttoned his white shirt. Amani sampled more chocolate. Only when he tossed his shirt onto the nearby sofa did Amani step toward him again.

She put a dollop of whipped cream on his chest, then slowly lapped it up with her tongue. Next was chocolate on his nipple. Aaron groaned when she licked that off.

He took the dessert from her hand and broke off a piece of the brownie with his fingers. "Open," he told Amani. She did, and he let her lick his fingers clean before putting most of the chunk of dessert into her mouth. The morsel that protruded from her lips he took into his own teeth. Their mouths touching, they chewed and swallowed.

And then Aaron could stand no more. His lips played over Amani's, urging them to open. They did, and he plunged his tongue into her mouth in a burning kiss. He sucked on her tongue; she sucked on his. He simply couldn't get enough of her.

Everything about her turned him on in the most primal way. His free hand roamed her body, cupping her firm butt. He wanted to meld their bodies together.

"I want you naked," he whispered as he trailed his tongue to her ear. He flicked it over the lobe, and Amani moaned and gripped his shoulders.

Reluctantly he stepped away from her. He put down the dessert in order to finish undressing. Now unrestrained, his erection felt some relief. But true relief would come when he lost himself in her softness.

Aaron's penis throbbed with the thought. He kicked his slacks across the carpeted floor. Then he stepped toward Amani, reaching for her underwear before she could. He slowly pulled the wisp of lacy fabric down her legs.

While trailing his fingers up her thighs, he planted a delicate kiss on her mound, inhaling her scent as he did.

He couldn't take any more of this. Gripping her hands, he urged her down. Before she was even on her knees in front of him, he captured her mouth with his. And as their lips mated, he reached for the dessert.

His hand covered with chocolate and whipped cream, he slipped it between their bodies, smothering the sticky sweetness over her breasts. Amani moaned into his mouth.

Her moan was like a surge of power. Lowering his head, he ran his tongue across her firm, beautiful breasts, licking the chocolate and whipped cream off. Her skin was sweet and hot and her moaning was driving him nuts. He slipped his hand between her legs, needing to feel more of her.

Her passionate whimpers sounded like little cries. Aaron met her gaze, concerned. "You're all right?"

She bit down on her bottom lip before replying. "No."

"No?"

Amani's hand curled around his penis. "I need you inside me."

Stroking his shaft, Amani maneuvered herself backward on the comforter. Then she eased her legs apart and lifted her hips. She rubbed his penis across her vagina.

Aaron's erection pulsated in her hand. He had wanted to give her an orgasm with his touch before sinking deep inside her, but he couldn't wait a moment longer. Gently easing himself down on her, he let Amani guide his erection into her warm, wet place.

A groan rumbled deep in his chest. "Oh, sweetheart." He went as deep as he could, until Amani cried out and arched her back. His mouth found her neck, her jaw line, her earlobe. "I could stay like this all night."

"You feel *so* good inside me."

Aaron gyrated against her, penetrating her deeper. "What about that?"

Amani closed her eyes and whimpered. "Oh, yes." She dug her nails into his back when he plunged deep inside her again. "Oooh, Aaron. Yes. Give it to me hard."

Aaron did. He teased and stroked and buried himself deep inside her over and over, bringing her close to the edge of climax several times, then deliberately slowing the pace. He wanted her body so ripe with passion that one touch would make her explode.

"Aaron, please," Amani begged. "I can't take it."

He was close. So close. He thrust deep inside her, pushing deep into her soft place. Amani's breathing grew shallower as her walls tightened around him. It was the tightening sensation that did him in, and he felt the beginning of his own release.

Amani clung to him, calling his name on a rapturous moan. And as he clung to her, as his seed spilled inside her, Aaron's heart filled with warmth.

With love.

10

Amani awoke in the middle of the night. Tentacles of panic gripped her when she realized that she wasn't at home, in her own bed.

It took her another moment to remember exactly where she was.

Aaron's bed.

His arm was draped across her waist as she lay spoon fashion with him. She should have felt secure, but the panic didn't subside.

In the next seconds, the air in the room seemed to grow thick, making it harder for her to breathe. She had to get up. Had to get air.

She reached for Aaron's arm—then felt a rush of sadness. This was Aaron, the man she had dreamed about since she'd first met him ten years ago. This was the man who had treated her with such kindness and respect . . . so why did she feel like running?

The answer didn't come to her, and fighting tears, she lifted his hand off her. He didn't move as she eased her body to the bed's edge.

Looking back at his sleeping form, her heart nearly split in two. They'd spent several hours making sweet passionate love. With Aaron she'd felt cherished, respected. She hadn't felt smothered. Only loved. Yet she still felt like slipping her clothes on and taking the walk of shame out of his apartment.

Amani slowly stood. The mattress didn't make a sound. Maybe if she just walked around, allowed herself to examine her feelings. She tiptoed to the bedroom door.

It squeaked as she opened it, and before she could walk out of the room, Aaron called her name.

She halted in the doorway. "Hmm?"

"Where are you going?"

"I was . . . thirsty. I'm heading to the kitchen for some water."

"Oh." Aaron's voice was thick with sleep. "Come right back, okay?"

"Uh huh."

But Amani didn't. She put on her clothes and quietly snuck out of Aaron's apartment.

"What the hell are you doing here?" Suzette asked the next morning when Amani plodded into the café shortly after ten. When Amani didn't answer, simply walked like a zombie past her to the coat rack, Suzette loudly groaned. "Oh God. Why do you look . . . look like you're coming from a funeral."

Facing Suzette, Amani unwrapped her scarf. "Maybe I did."

"You've got bags under your eyes so you couldn't have gotten much sleep. Which leads me to believe your date with Aaron went as well as expected. You went back to his place, didn't you?"

"Yeah," Amani said glumly.

"Oh, shit. Don't tell me you left in the middle of the night."

Amani slung her scarf on the rack, then put her coat on top of it.

"Oh my God. Why?"

"I don't know why."

"You've decided you don't like him?"

"Of course not. Aaron is like no other man."

"Then why walk away from him?"

"Because . . ." Because what? Because she was deathly afraid that he'd walk away from her first. And then where would she be?

"Amani, you need to call him. I won't let you mess this up."

"I can't."

"Yes you can." Suzette took Amani's hands in hers. "I know your relationship with Carl messed you up. But honestly, Carl being a dog had nothing to do with you. It had to do with his own insecurities."

"Then why is he still happily married to Karen?"

"You don't know that he's happy."

"I'm sure they are. It was me he couldn't live with."

Suzette sighed as she let go of Amani's hands. She reached for the carafe of hot coffee. "Oh, no. I'm not going to let you start with this depressive talk. You know better than that." She poured two mugs. "Thank God there's no one here. We're gonna sit down and have a nice long chat."

Amani made her way around the counter. "I don't want to talk."

"Amani—"

"No, Suzette. I'm serious. At least . . . at least not right now. I need to think."

A moment passed, then Suzette said, "All right. But I'm here if you need me."

"I know."

Days later, Suzette said to Amani, "I'm worried about you. The last time you were sick was when you and Carl split."

Amani sniffled. "I'm fine. It's just a cold."

"You never get colds."

Amani pulled a Kleenex out of her pocket and blew her nose loudly. "It's that time of year."

"You should go home. Get some rest. *Call Aaron.*"

Amani cut her eyes at her friend. "Please, don't start that again."

Amani hadn't heard from Aaron since she'd left his place in the wee hours of Saturday morning. The last four days of her life had been utterly miserable, but at least now she knew the truth. She and Aaron had enjoyed a night of hot sex, but that was all they would ever share. He hadn't called to check up on her. She hadn't called him.

And while part of her yearned to phone him just to hear his voice, she knew that if she did, she'd look like a moron. He had to be thinking the worst about her as it was.

So she couldn't have been more surprised when, not more than an hour later, Aaron walked into the cafe. She'd recognize him anywhere, even bundled under a hat and scarf, wearing sunglasses and a long tweed coat.

"Oh my Lord." Amani's heart thundered in her chest as a surge of warmth shot through her body.

But right after that initial reaction, self-doubt crept over her. Why was he here? To try and convince her to go to tomorrow night's class?

He was looking around, but hadn't yet seen her. That's because she was sitting on a chair in a far corner behind the counter. Suzette was among the customers, offering help, refilling coffee.

Amani watched as Aaron approached Suzette. Then cringed when she saw Suzette point in her direction.

Knowing she could no longer avoid Aaron, Amani stood. Feeling like a fool, she gave him a little wave.

Pulling his knit hat off his head, Aaron sauntered toward her. "Amani."

Not *hi*, just Amani. This was bad.

She wiped her nose with the tissue. "Hello, Aaron."

A beat, then, "My bed was cold after you left. I was hoping to hear from you."

Amani opened her mouth to speak. But the words didn't come, and she cast her gaze to the ground.

"Don't do that, Amani. Don't hide."

She lifted her eyes to his. "I . . . I'm sorry."

"Sorry isn't what I want to hear."

Amani drew in a deep breath. "I don't know what to say to you."

"Really?" Aaron asked, disappointment in his tone. "We shared our bodies in the most intimate way, and you don't know what to say to me?"

"I just thought . . . thought it was best to leave."

"Don't you like me?"

Amani's eyes bulged at the question. "Like you? I lo—" She

caught herself, stopping short of blurting out her true feelings for him.

Aaron didn't seem to notice, thank God. He opened his coat. "Can we sit somewhere and talk?"

Talking was exactly what she didn't want to do. In the early years with Carl, she'd tried talking about how she felt with him. He'd made her feel so nervous that she tripped over her words. Carl would then belittle her, tell her she sounded like a fool and that her feelings were insignificant.

Funny, she hadn't remembered that until just now.

"I'm not good at talking," she told Aaron.

"Then can we sit somewhere and you write your feelings down? I don't care how you express them to me, as long as you tell me what's going through your mind. Don't you think you owe me that much?"

He wasn't raising his voice. Wasn't telling her she was acting like an immature idiot. Instead, she saw a mix of warmth and fear in his eyes.

Fear? Fear that he'd lost her?

Inhaling a shaky breath, Amani walked toward a table near the window. The fireplace was a preferable location, but there were a few people there, and she wanted privacy.

"Let me take your coat," she said to Aaron.

"I'm fine."

He sat at the table, and Amani sat opposite him. She didn't speak though, just avoided his gaze.

"Did I do something wrong?" Aaron finally asked.

Amani looked at him in disbelief. "No. Why would you think that?"

"What else am I supposed to think? You told me you were

coming back to bed, then you took off. Since then, I've waited for your call, not wanting to pressure you. I finally had to come here and see you."

"I don't know why I left. I was just . . . I kinda thought . . ." She could barely get her words out. Frustrated, she slapped a hand against her forehead. "God, I sound like a moron."

"Hey." Aaron's tone was soft, gentle. He reached for her hand. "Why are you acting like this? What are you afraid of?"

"I don't even know how old you are."

Aaron's face twisted with an expression of defeat. "You think I'm too old for you."

He spoke as though he finally understood, but he didn't. "No," Amani said. "That's not what I mean."

"Then what do you mean?"

"We don't really know each other."

"I'm thirty-eight, ten years older than you. Been married once, and that marriage ended in an ugly divorce. I'm an English teacher. I lead a pretty normal life. What else do you want to know?"

"I'm trying to be serious."

"So am I. We got to know each other for a year, Amani. As teacher-student, but also as friends. What's this really about?"

"I'm afraid," Amani whispered.

"Afraid of getting hurt?"

She nodded.

"How do you think I feel right about now?"

"I—" Was he saying that he was afraid of getting hurt? "I don't know."

"No? I thought I wore my heart on my sleeve."

"Every relationship I've had with a man has ended badly, starting with my own father. My mother told me that he came to see me after I was born, but you know what? He walked away and never came back. I was his own flesh and blood, yet he didn't want me."

Aaron stroked his thumb across the top of Amani's hand. How had he not realized that she'd been carrying so much pain? "That's not your fault. It wasn't about you."

"Carl said it was."

"What? Your ex-husband?"

"Uh huh. He told me there was a reason my father didn't want me. Because he looked at me and saw that I was worthless."

"Carl said that?"

A tear fell down Amani's face. She brushed it away. "Yes."

"My God."

"I didn't really remember that until now. I realize, there are a lot of things I don't remember where Carl's concerned. I've had to block them from my mind. He's said so many hurtful things."

"And you internalized them."

"I . . . I didn't think I had."

Aaron gritted his teeth. "You know what? Maybe I can't go to this wedding with you." Amani's eyes widened in alarm. "Because if I see Carl, I'll want to pummel him. And that's no word of a lie." He reached for Amani's face, softly stroked it. "Did he ever hit you?"

"No. Never."

"But he abused you nonetheless. In a more hurtful way. With words."

"I guess. Yes."

"Amani, I would never hurt you."

In her heart, she knew that Aaron was telling the truth. The differences between him and Carl were like night and day. "I know. But..."

"But you're beautiful. Smart. Completely desirable. Any man would be lucky to have you in his life."

"When I was out with Carl, he'd walk two steps ahead of me, like he was embarrassed to be with me. If I reached for his hand, he'd pull it away. And forget about me trying to kiss him. He said he didn't believe in showing affection in public, but I always came away with the feeling that I wasn't desirable."

"*You* not *desirable?*"

"It didn't take long before I started shutting down emotionally. If I didn't feel, I couldn't get hurt. I don't know, Aaron. Maybe I'm just not cut out for long-term intimacy."

"You really believe that?"

"I don't want to. You have no clue—I am so totally hot for you. But there's a part of me, a part that's completely afraid. Afraid to love, afraid to trust."

"Because of your ex. Do you really want to go to this wedding?"

Amani didn't hesitate. "No."

"Then why are you going?"

"Because my cousin is family. I don't want to disappoint her."

"I can understand that, but you need to take care of yourself first. I'll go with you, if you really want to go, but if being in the same room with your ex is going to be too painful, then don't go. It's not like you and he simply broke up and you're taking the coward's way out. This is a guy who manipulated you, abused you. You have a reason to stay away from him."

Aaron made a lot of sense. This wasn't about avoiding Carl. It was about protecting herself.

Everything she'd known on a subconscious level she was filtering into her conscious thoughts. She had felt huge anxiety when her cousin had told her that Carl would be at the wedding. The anxiety had been because of her stark fear over seeing him, over the fear that by seeing him again, she'd take ten steps backward. She had made strides after her marriage, strides toward independence and success. Secretly she feared that seeing Carl again could erode the self-esteem she'd built back up.

"I want you in my life, Amani. And I'm willing to wait for you. Prove to you that you can trust me completely." He paused. "You're deserving of love. And I want to be the one to love you."

"You really . . ." She detected no hint of insincerity in his tone. He was being completely honest. "You really mean that."

"Of course I do."

Joy swelled in Amani's heart, and she didn't try to tamp it down. "I was afraid you'd be too angry with me to even want to talk to me again."

"You can't push me away, sweetheart."

"Oh, God." Amani slapped her hands against her cheeks. "That *is* what I was trying to do, wasn't it?"

"We'll work through this together."

Amani took a wad of napkins from the napkin holder. She blew her nose. How utterly unromantic. "Sorry." Aaron waved a hand, letting her know there was no need to apologize. After a moment passed, Amani asked, "How do you know me so well?"

Aaron shrugged. "I don't know. Your soul connects with mine in a way I can't understand."

"I feel that, too."

Aaron took her hands again, linking his fingers with hers, and Amani's heart melted. She already felt a hundred times better, even with this annoying cold, now that she'd gotten her feelings out. Carl had stolen too much of her and her life. She wouldn't let him take anything more from her.

"I'm going to call my cousin," she said. "If anyone shouldn't go to the wedding, it's Carl, not me. He's the bad guy."

"Hey, that's a great idea."

Amani pulled one of Aaron's hands toward her mouth and kissed it. Would she ever meet a more understanding man than him?

She doubted it.

She had known he was a man of honor and compassion from the time he'd comforted her after her mother's death. That's why she'd fallen in love with him.

The look of kindness in Aaron's eyes made her suddenly feel brave. "Can I tell you something else?"

"Anything."

"I . . ." She took a deep breath. "I've always been in love with you."

Aaron's lips lifted in a radiant smile, one that lit up his eyes and touched her heart. "You have?"

"Oh, yeah. Helplessly."

"That's good. Because I'm in love with you, too, Amani." He nodded when her eyes expressed doubt. "I don't know when it started, but I know that's where I'm at now. What I feel for you, I've never felt for anyone before. Not even my ex-wife."

Long ago, she had envisioned Aaron as her knight in shining armor, and now here he was, being exactly that.

"I think this can work."

"I know it can."

Her eyes bulged. "Did I say that out loud?"

"Uh-huh. And it's okay. I want you to know that you can always talk to me."

Amani leaned across the table. "I do love you."

"I love you, too."

"Will you kiss me? Right here, in front of everyone?"

"I'll kiss you on top of the CN Tower, if that's what you want."

Amani couldn't help smiling as she edged her mouth closer to his. "Oh," she suddenly said. "I shouldn't. I don't want to give you my cold."

"As if a little cold could stop me from kissing those luscious lips."

"Luscious?"

"Oh, yeah. Just like your other lips."

White-hot heat zapped her nub. "Aaron!"

"They are luscious. I can't wait to nibble on them again."

Amani had to shut him up—before she jumped his bones right here. "Come here."

Just before her eyelids fluttered shut, Amani saw Suzette grinning like a fool at her, giving her two enthusiastic thumbs up.

And as her lips finally touched Aaron's, Amani couldn't help thinking that at last she'd snagged Mr. Right.

FANTASY MAN

·

Tamara Sneed

1

Olivia Hawkins watched the small jet taxi to the end of the runway at the private Los Angeles airport. She crossed her arms over her chest and barely resisted the urge to tap her foot in impatience. He was late—of course. It must have been written in the handbook every Hollywood actor secretly received when he hit box office gold—be late at every opportunity. The plane rolled to a stop and the oval-shaped door slowly opened. Olivia held her breath as a sudden wave of uncertainty, nerves, and plain ole lust overwhelmed her.

Olivia could delude herself into thinking that she didn't like Clark Stone, Hollywood's newest action hero and *People* magazine's current Sexiest Man Alive, but she couldn't delude her body into accepting that she wasn't affected by him. He was the original bad boy that mothers told their daughters to stay away from. In his movies—which always opened number one at the box office—he was the cop who barely remained on the right side of the law while hunting down the criminal, and the demanding lover, who expected everything from the women in his bed and gave everything in return. He was every woman's fantasy, and if Olivia's brother, Jack, hadn't brought Clark to the Hawkins' Sunday family dinners for the last five months, Clark would have been her fantasy, too.

Heat and desire flooded Olivia's stomach like a lead ball, when Clark filled the airplane's oval door. It never ceased to amaze Olivia how big he was. His height and broad shoulders also never ceased to arouse her. He stood over six feet three inches, uncommonly tall for an actor. Every rippling muscle on the screen was the result of God-given good genes and a stringent workout regimen. Even the expensive, loose-fitting black outfit he wore couldn't hide his marvelous physique, the broad shoulders, defined chest, or long legs.

Clark lifted the dark, expensive sunglasses he wore, then glanced around the tarmac, his gaze automatically skipping pass Olivia and the black limousine next to her. No surprise. She laughed in disbelief and shook her head. Clark may have been gorgeous and he may have been the star of her nightly fantasies, but as he had proven with his dismissive and disdainful behavior toward her during the dinners at her parents' house, he was also a predictable, arrogant jerk.

Since Jack had first introduced Clark to her and her parents five months ago, Clark had made it obvious that Olivia wasn't worth his time or trouble. While Olivia's parents adored Clark, Olivia saw the truth He was as bad as all the tabloids reported him to be.

Olivia debated on getting back into the limousine and having the driver leave, but then she thought of her brother. She sighed in exasperation then half-heartedly waved at Clark. He looked at her, and even across the tarmac, goose bumps flirted across her skin. She gasped softly as her center pulsated and swelled to life. Just from one look. The ability to produce that much of a reaction in a helpless woman should have been outlawed.

Clark pushed back on his sunglasses then walked down the steps and started toward her. The world went into slow motion and music—Luther or, more like, 50 Cent—pounded in the background. Even if he wasn't hers, he was walking toward her and her body didn't care about the difference. Her nipples tingled under her suit jacket, and Olivia momentarily braced herself against the limousine until she could stand on her own.

Clark stopped in front of her, and she immediately straightened. He didn't smile or take off his sunglasses, he just posed in front of her, as if waiting for her to snap a picture.

Olivia kept her voice neutral as she said, "Good morning, Mr. Stone."

His voice was as deep and sexy as reporters gushed, as he demanded, "Where's Jack?"

Olivia gritted her teeth, then responded calmly, "His wife, Melissa, went into labor this morning, and Jack asked me to accompany you on your appearances this afternoon so that he could be present for the birth of his first child."

He whipped off his sunglasses and his dark eyes bored into her. "You?" Olivia stiffened at the horror she heard in his voice. He asked, almost desperately, "What about your father or your mother?"

Olivia couldn't blame him. She hadn't exactly been kind to him over the last five months. In fact, she had been downright rude to him, including a series of "accidents" that usually involved Clark leaving the dinner table with liquid or food on his expensive, tailored clothes.

Olivia forced a friendly smile then said, in what she hoped was a soothing tone, "My parents would have wanted nothing more than to be by your side today, but they are on a safari in Africa. We won't be able to contact them until next week. You may not know this, but I worked at the agency with Jack and my parents for five years before I went to teach at Cal State Los Angeles. I've represented numerous clients, and I have an extensive background in publicity—"

Clark abruptly interrupted her. "Whatever. Let's just get out of here."

He sat inside the limousine, with a huff of indignation. Olivia glared after him, then forced another smile across her face. She would get through this afternoon if it killed her. Regardless of his unnatural effect on her libido, she could handle this. She pulled a folder from her briefcase then followed Clark into the limousine.

Olivia took a deep breath then began, "First, on the agenda for this afternoon, is taping of the *Ellen DeGeneres Show* then . . ."

Clark pointedly ignored her, while he prayed that the driver would hurry and load his luggage in the trunk. The sooner they were on their way, the sooner he could get rid of Olivia. He cursed Jack for putting him in this position, even as he curled his hands into fists to prevent from grabbing her, laying her on the bench, and tasting that mouth that had kept him awake almost every night for the last five months.

He knew it was insane. He shouldn't have been affected so much by one woman, but Olivia had become an insatiable itch, distracting him at the most inopportune moments, like in the middle of interviews when a reporter inevitably asked, "Anyone special in your life?" Just the thought of her caused him to become undeniably harder, faster than he could ever remember. For five months, Clark had been tortured by this obsession. Other women didn't hold the same appeal, nothing held the same appeal anymore, except watching Olivia move with an understated grace and sexiness, while she ignored him.

Olivia was not the type of woman Clark should have been attracted to. She was cute—from her cinnamon brown shapely, long legs, to her long, graceful neck, the wide dark brown, almost black eyes and the thick black hair that she usually pulled into a ponytail—but not extraordinary. Clark Stone fans expected extraordinary from him—from his movies, to his physique, and to the women he dated. The press may have labeled him as difficult and unpredictable, despite the fact that the same members of the press followed him with their cameras everywhere he went precisely because he was difficult and unpredictable, but the fans loved him. And Clark couldn't disappoint his fans by doing anything ordinary.

He glanced at Olivia from beneath his eyelashes. She must have spent an hour trying to find the most ordinary outfit she could. She wore a dark, severe black suit that covered every inch of her body, except the few inches of leg below her knee, and even the green blouse underneath the suit jacket was buttoned to the top. But, Clark knew that the body underneath that suit was anything but ordinary. His fascination had started with her from the first moment Jack introduced them. She had smiled politely at him and then had returned to the kitchen to help her mother prepare dinner. No fawning, no throwing herself at him. Normally, that would not have made Clark look twice at her—he didn't need to work for women when he had most at his beck-and-call—but before she had turned away, she had smiled at Jack, and Clark had been hooked ever since. He had studied everything about her, from her soft-as-cotton hair, to her long, graceful fingers, and to the magnificent, curvaceous body she tried to hide under conservative, boring clothes.

Clark swallowed a groan as his gaze dropped to the buttons of her suit jacket. It wouldn't take much for him to get her out of the jacket, so that he could finally see and taste her breasts. He would have her open, her petals dripping wet for him, within six seconds, if she didn't protest too much—ten seconds, if she did. He shook his head at the image. Clark Stone did not beg, or cajole, or overpower any woman. He didn't need to, but those images of Olivia still ran through his head. It was the lavender. He had never been this close to her, and he had caught the hint of lavender when she sat in the limousine. It had his senses roaring.

This was all wrong. The last time Clark had seen Olivia, he had nearly exploded in his pants when she leaned over to set a tray of sugar on the table, and had involuntarily given him a shot of cleavage. He had vowed to stay away from her then. He couldn't get involved with a woman like Olivia. She was uptight, conservative, and almost went into spasms if someone ate their entree with the dessert fork. Clark knew because he had done it. Clark was a worldwide star, welcome at any party from Monte Carlo to Milan. She was minivans and oatmeal cookies. Exactly what Clark did not want at this point in his life, no matter how much his body told him that it needed this woman.

Suddenly, Clark realized that he couldn't stay in Los Angeles, even though it was his last day in the states before he flew to Scotland for six weeks of filming. He had debated on going to his best friend's engagement party in his hometown before the plane landed, but he dismissed that idea due to his prior commitments. But, now the engagement party seemed like the perfect way to save himself. He had to get away from Olivia, even if it included leaving the city.

The limousine suddenly purred to life, and Clark sighed in relief. Olivia was still staring at the schedule, so she didn't notice when he pressed the button on the console to lower the privacy shield between the driver and the backseat.

"Hey, man," he said to the driver.

The driver turned around, surprise evident on his young face. It took only one look at the hunger in the young man's green eyes for Clark to know that he was in "the business," too. Clark suddenly noticed the silence in the car and realized that Olivia had stopped staring at the schedule and was now looking at him. He told himself that he should not get hard just because she was looking at him.

"Yes, Mr. Stone?" the driver asked.

"What's your name?" Clark demanded.

"My name? Matt Lawrence. I'm actually a writer, Mr. Stone, and I think you'd be interested in a script—"

"We have a change of plans, Matt Lawrence. I need to get to Red Creek, California, by three o'clock." Clark moved across the large backseat to hand the driver a slip of paper with an address and directions on it.

"What are you doing?" Olivia asked, bewildered.

Clark's entire body stood at attention at the sound of her smooth voice in the close confines of the car. It was the first time he had heard the real Olivia, not the polite publicist, since he walked off the plane. He balled his hands into fists and ignored her for the moment. He had to figure out a way not to attack her before he could speak to her.

Matt scanned the paper, then looked at Clark surprised. "This will take a while—"

"Four hours exactly."

"Four hours?" Olivia repeated, sounding panicked. "You'll miss your interviews and personal appearances."

Clark and Matt both ignored her, while Matt nodded and said, "We can just make it there by three."

Clark forced himself to look at Olivia, then he winced. At least, he wouldn't have to worry about her coming on to him—which had been his secret desire since he had slid into the limousine. Judging from the fire crackling in her eyes, his more pressing worry was her strangling him.

"Ms. Hawkins, where can Matt drop you off?" Clark asked, forcing himself to sound calm.

"Drop me off?" Olivia repeated in disbelief. "Wherever this limousine goes, I go, and this limousine is going to Burbank for a talk show appearance, then to Hollywood for another talk show appearance, and then to a series of other appointments that you don't know about because you weren't listening to me when I was reading your very full schedule."

"I paid for this limousine, and I can pay for another one to take me where I need to go, if you won't leave," he said, with a casual shrug, even as his heart pounded against his chest. He was not normally cruel, especially to women. He *loved* women, but he had to get Olivia out of this limousine. As soon as possible. Her chances of surviving the ride without her legs in the air were not good.

Clark could have sworn the temperature of the limousine

dropped a few degrees as Olivia's eyes narrowed and she glared at Clark. Matt shifted nervously in the front seat.

For several seconds, Olivia and Clark stared at each other then Olivia said calmly and coolly, "Matt, will you excuse us?"

Matt jumped from the car so fast that Clark would have laughed if Olivia hadn't been glaring at him. As soon as the door closed, Olivia said through clenched teeth, "Since you obviously want to be real, Mr. Stone, let's be real—"

"Wait a second," Clark said nervously, recognizing the look in her eyes. He'd seen that look in his mother's eyes a time or two and it always came right before an explosion. Clark had thrown down with the best of them, but nothing was more frightening than a black woman with that look in her eyes.

She continued, unfazed by his interruption. "Your face has been on the cover of every tabloid every day for the last year. You have become a liability to studios and producers due to your bar brawls, bad manners—"

"Bad manners?" Clark interrupted, with a snort of disbelief. "I'm not some little girl. I'm a grown man—"

Her expression was cold fire as she said, "The arrest for drunken misconduct six months ago at that bar in Miami was the final straw—"

"That charge was dismissed," Clark sputtered, half-embarrassed and half-annoyed.

"My brother has been walking a fine line since then. Vista Films wanted to renege on this movie you're about to film in Scotland rather than put out a film with you in it and have it tank because no one wants to spend their hard-earned money to make a spoiled, rich jerk even richer. For the last five months, Jack has been assuring Vista Films that you've reformed, while he's been doing everything in his power to keep you out of trouble, including dragging you to our family dinners.

"The agency that Jack and my parents have worked years to build is riding on you and, since I'm in this car as their representative, it's riding on me. I promised my brother that he would be able to enjoy the birth of his first child, without any problems from Clark Stone for the next twenty-four hours, and I keep my promises. So, you're not going anywhere without me."

Clark stared at her when she finished ranting, and horror seized her. She had just alienated her brother's most lucrative client. Clark would fire her brother, and her brother would lose other clients who would follow Clark out of the door. And, worst of all, Olivia would never see Clark again because he would never come to her parents' house for dinner again.

But Clark did not yell or scream; instead, he sent her a grin that should have set her clothes on fire, as he lazily perused her body, as if taking stock of all the parts he wanted to see and touch. Olivia refused to react to his blatant seduction—too bad her body didn't listen to her. The warmth swirled in her stomach like an approaching tornado, and her center burned, causing her to shift on the seat.

"Fine. If you want to sit in this limo for the next four hours, I'm not going to stop you," he finally said. She tried not to be surprised that he had readily agreed to her presence.

"I'm glad we agreed that you can't stop me," she said dryly, then asked, "What's in Red Creek? Some kind of private orgy retreat for celebrities?"

He laughed then shook his head. "Close. It's my hometown."

"Hometown?" she repeated, confused.

"It's a small ranching community about four hours outside of Los Angeles. Population, thirty thousand—"

"You're missing appearances that have been scheduled for months to go home?" she interrupted, disbelief dripping from her voice.

"Last week, Steve finally got Dominique to agree to marry him. I've known them both since I was five years old, and when we were twelve years old, I predicted they would marry each other. It's only taken Steve about twenty-three years to convince Dominique that I was right. I'm not missing this chance to say I-told-you-so."

"We're going to an engagement party," she said, surprised by the genuine smile on his face. Not the sexy smile she saw on billboards, but a smile that reached his eyes and spoke of connections and love. A different shiver ran through her body. For the first time, Olivia admitted that some of her preconceived notions about Clark may have been wrong. Yes, he was an arrogant, stuck-on-himself actor, but he also apparently could feel love for someone other than himself.

Then Olivia realized that Clark's gaze was directed below her neck, to the middle button on her suit jacket. She hoped that the heavy suit material hid the sudden heaviness she felt in her breasts, the straining nipples. She tried to ignore the heat that radiated from his body and wrapped around her like a warm cocoon, seductive and hot.

Clark smiled at her again, and Olivia began to sweat. He said softly, "This may actually be fun."

2.

It was not fun, it was torture. Clark sat in the limousine, a few inches from Olivia, but he couldn't touch her. As soon as the limousine turned onto the freeway from the airport, Olivia had opened a paperback novel and hadn't said a word since. That had been three hours ago. Clark had been content to stare at her for a while, and then he had closed his eyes and let his imagination run wild. He and Olivia stranded on a deserted island, with no clothes. He and Olivia on a yacht in the middle of the Caribbean. He and Olivia in his bedroom with a bottle of edible massage oil.

Everything about her sang to him, from the conservative ponytail to the downplayed gloss on her mouth. He shifted subtly in his seat, attempting to distract himself from his persistent hardness that was becoming almost painful. This was crazy. He didn't normally find ponytails attractive. What was wrong with him? He cleared his throat and asked casually, "What are you reading?"

"A book," she said stiffly, without looking at him.

"I can see that," he said, hiding his smile.

No woman spoke to him like she did. They usually fawned over him and, sometimes, begged him, but none could put him in his place as neatly and efficiently as Olivia could. And he found that amusing for some reason. He had never thought of himself as a glutton for punishment, but with Olivia, he practically begged for more. He wondered if she would want to be in control in bed, too, and if he would let her. It would be a fight they'd both enjoy, that was for damn certain.

"What is the title?" he said, trying again.

With a long-suffering sigh, she showed him the cover. *Pride and Prejudice* by Jane Austen. She explained, reluctantly, "I teach English literature in the fall, and this will be one of the first novels we study."

"I never could understand why women get so excited about that Darcy character. If that's the key to a woman's heart—indifference and disdain—then it's no wonder that men and women don't understand each other outside the bedroom."

Her eyes widened in surprise. "You've read *Pride and Prejudice*?"

"In college," he said, then asked, curiously, "Can you explain to me the appeal of Darcy? Black women, white women, Asian women . . . I've found all women who read this book fall in love with him."

"Just because I'm a woman doesn't mean that character appeals to me. Just like the fact that a large number of women find your movie characters appealing doesn't mean I do."

He laughed at the less than subtle insult then said dryly, "Hypothetically speaking, if you were one of those women who liked Darcy, what would be his appeal?"

"I have no idea. Why *would* any woman find a character like that appealing? He initially doesn't like the heroine of the novel and insults her because she's below his class level, which was important in eighteenth-century England, but it shouldn't have mattered if he truly loved her."

"You do like him though, don't you?" he asked, then grinned when he saw the truth dancing in her eyes. She had the most expressive eyes. Every thought, every dream was apparent. Clark couldn't help but wonder how her eyes would look when she climaxed.

"I do not like Mr. Darcy," she said, stiffly.

"I could practically hear you sighing while you were reading the book," he teased.

"Well, he does redeem himself at the end of the novel in an attempt to win the heroine's love. He helps the heroine's family, and he shows more honor than any of the other men in the novel . . ." Her voice trailed off and she abruptly laughed. "Okay, I admit it. I love Mr. Darcy! I love this book! Thanks to this character, I'm like every other foolish woman out there who believes that when a man ignores you or insults you, he's secretly in love with you."

Clark watched her smile, and he felt something strange settle in the pit of his stomach. He had not seen such an honest smile in a long time. A sledgehammer of lust hit him and Clark nearly winced from the pain. He had been blindsided, fooled, and tricked. He had been trying so hard to stay away from this woman, when he should have been trying every trick in the book to get closer to her. Maybe if he tasted her once, felt those delicious breasts under his hands—he'd be over her.

Olivia smiled and said, "If you tell anyone about my Mr. Darcy weakness, I'll be forced to hurt you."

Clark grinned at the prospect. He told himself to ignore her for the rest of the limousine ride before he kissed that tempting mouth, except he had an insatiable need to know more about her. "Jack never told me that you once worked at the publicity agency with the rest of the family. Why'd you leave the family business?"

Her smile faded and she said, "Since I was fourteen years old, I've worked in the agency in one form or another. Even though my major was English literature in college, it was a given that I would work at the agency and be a publicist like Jack and my parents."

"You weren't happy there?" he guessed.

"No," she said flatly. "I didn't deal with the clients—that was Jack's and my parents' job. I dealt with the business side. I was a glorified office manager."

"You told me that you had plenty of experience in the business," he reminded her.

"I've heard enough stories about it, but Jack and my parents thought it was best if I was kept away from the clients," she said, while avoiding his eyes. "Something about my lack of tact."

"I don't know what you mean!" he said, feigning surprise.

She laughed, then admitted, "They were right. I never wanted to be in the fancy restaurants making deals or meeting the latest Hollywood-It-Girl. None of that meant anything to me. The whole Hollywood scene has always left a bad taste in my mouth. I started taking classes at night to earn a Ph.D. in English because I was bored and I thought it would be a fun way to spend my empty evenings." Clark's cock twitched because he could think of more fun ways to spend her evenings. Olivia continued, oblivious to his sudden ragged breathing, "After I finished the program, I was offered a temporary position at the community college. I was going to use it as a stepping stone. The first moment I stepped in front of a classroom I knew it was what I had been born to do. Temporary became permanent and I'm still there."

"I bet you're a good teacher," he said sincerely.

Olivia smiled bashfully, and he knew he was right. She met his eyes and said, "If you're doing what you love, other people feel that."

She wasn't talking about anything relating to sex, but that's exactly where his mind went. He'd love making love to her and she'd feel it. He abandoned all pretense of ignoring the sexual tension between them and asked bluntly, "Are you still seeing that man you brought to dinner at your parents' house three weeks ago?"

"You remember him?" she asked, obviously surprised by his abrupt change in the subject.

He had watched every move she had made that night, like some kind of third-rate stalker. But he settled for simply saying, "Yes."

Olivia didn't respond, but instead stared at the book in her hands. She was nervous. It was probably a good thing she was being careful around him, since Clark was scaring himself right now. He had never wanted a woman as much as he wanted her.

She finally answered, "No, but neither Stan nor I would classify our few dates as 'seeing each other'."

Clark grinned, relieved because he had been a little worried about that pencil-neck, uptight fellow professor-type. Clark hadn't liked how the man had looked at Olivia, almost as if the pencil-neck had the right to possess her, to touch her. As far as

Clark was concerned, no man should have that right, except him. He'd worry about what that meant later.

"Why aren't you dating anyone?" he demanded.

Color flushed her brown cheeks and Clark had to grip the edge of the seat to resist the instinct to rip aside her skirt and to drive into her. It was almost sensory overload, her scent, her laughter still fresh in his ears, and the sight of all the luscious brown beauty waiting, wrapped for him.

"The simple answer is that I haven't found the right person."

"And the complicated answer is . . . ?" he prodded, leaning closer to her.

"The complicated answer is . . . I haven't found the right person who is ready to find me," she said, hesitantly, looking at him.

Clark couldn't move as he held her gaze that had suddenly become dark. While every instinct in his body urged him to kiss the lips she had just silently parted, his brain was in sheer self-preservation mode. If he touched her, it would be over. The late-night parties, the spur-of-the-moment trips around the world, the single life that was supposed to love to live. He would lose his life as he knew it.

Olivia suddenly shook her head then turned to the book again. "Ultimately, Mr. Darcy is a fictional character—sheer fantasy—and I don't believe in fantasy men."

His voice was satin smooth as he said, "I fulfill people's fantasies every time I make a movie. Give me a chance to make yours come true."

He almost cringed because he sounded like a straight-to-video corny hero, but he had never been more sincere.

Surprise filled her eyes, then suspicion, before she demanded,

"Why do you suddenly care about my job or who I date, or . . . or my fantasies? You haven't shown any interest in me or my life since my brother introduced us five months ago. In fact, if I remember correctly, the introductions weren't over before you turned away and pulled out a cell phone."

"You haven't exactly been part of the welcoming committee, either," he shot back. "And I know that you did not *accidentally* pour enough salt to start a mine on my plate two weeks ago, either."

He thought he saw a brief spurt of guilt cross her expression before she retorted, "What do you need me for, when you're obviously welcomed by every other woman you've ever come into contact with?"

He was still annoyed, more annoyed than he had a right to be, considering she was right, but his gaze still dropped to her breasts. He licked his lips as he visually traced the lush shape of her breasts—more than a handful, and one hundred percent natural. His hands flexed.

"The tabloids exaggerate, Liv," he said, on a sigh of sheer need, and she visibly went from annoyed to confused within seconds.

The air between the two became thicker. Something shifted and hung between them. Clark wanted to touch her and caress her cheek, but he didn't. Not yet.

"Don't you want me to help your fantasies come true? I have a few of my own that you could help me with," he whispered, his voice husky, as he gently smoothed several strands of hair from her face.

"What . . . what are you doing?" she stuttered, confusion in her eyes as she obviously felt the desire he was no longer able to conceal.

"Something I should have done a long time ago, and then maybe I wouldn't be this desperate or this hard," he murmured then leaned closer, inhaling her scent, inviting the heat of her breath on his mouth. "I want you."

She instantly responded. "No, you don't."

"We can debate that point later," he said, his gaze pinned on her mouth. "I have more important things on my mind right now." The most important thing was to finally discover what she tasted like, so he did. The first taste of her mouth was like a drug, strong and completely toxic. The best kind of toxic because he realized that he couldn't stop kissing her. Not now, not ever.

Olivia should have stopped the kiss, especially when his slick and restless tongue slipped between her lips. This was madness. She was being kissed by Clark Stone, not the actor who everyone loved, but the man who had been in her fantasies for the past five months. It couldn't be real. The man had barely acknowledged her, but now he was clinging to her lips, clinging to her, as if she was a co-star in one of his movies during a love scene.

Her brain shouted at her to stop the kiss, but her body . . . her body was luxuriating in the rush of sensations and emotions that she had never felt before. Not in almost thirty years had she ever felt such intensity, such a rush of heat and such wanting. It was drugging, it was crazy. And she wanted more.

Olivia raked her tongue against his and groaned into his mouth. He answered in a deep moan that reverberated through her throat and traveled down to the core of her body that pleaded with him to fill her. She felt the world tip and then felt the soft leather of the seat under her back. Clark followed her down, laying on top of her, his large, overwhelming body, covering hers. He was so big and so hard that Olivia should have felt intimidated, but instead she wanted to melt into him, accept more of his body.

The bruising kiss continued, as if he couldn't get enough of her mouth, her tongue. His tongue never stopped stroking, his lips never stopped pulling. Olivia was going to drown from the sensations. One of his hands moved between their bodies and touched her breast. She arched underneath him from the jolt of nerve endings he burned with just a simple touch that shouldn't have caused such a riot through her suit jacket, blouse, and bra. She felt a shudder wrack his big body. He gently squeezed her right breast and she whispered his name, and grounded her pelvis into his hardness that rested between her legs. She wanted the jacket off, the blouse off. She wanted everything gone that separated her from feeling Clark's bare touch.

"Liv, you're killing me," he moaned into her mouth.

Olivia took the opportunity to nip his lush bottom lip, then ran her hands along the chiseled length of his arms. She couldn't stop her hips from continuing to move against him, no longer hinting, but demanding what her body wanted.

Clark suddenly cursed and tried to pull from her arms, but she clung to his shirt and ground her mouth against his. He immediately responded, his tongue battling with hers, his lips clashing against hers. She was addicted to his taste and, like a junkie, she didn't know how to stop.

"Uh . . . excuse me, Mr. Stone," came Matt's hesitant voice that was entirely too close and too loud to mean that he was still sitting in the front of the limousine behind the privacy shield. "I tried to tell you that we were here—"

Olivia gasped and tried to push off Clark as she felt the rush of fresh air from the open backseat door, and she realized for the first time that the limousine had stopped moving.

"Close the door," Clark growled.

He didn't move off Olivia, but planted open-mouth kisses on her neck. Olivia never knew that her neck was that sensitive, that the feelings in her neck connected directly to other, more intimate parts of her body. Despite Matt's presence, she moaned from the pleasure.

"Clark," an unfamiliar male voice said, sounding amused and concerned.

Clark froze, then quickly moved off her. He smoothed down her suit, his movements efficient and impersonal, then he climbed out of the limousine. Olivia felt her entire face flush, for a reason that had nothing to do with lust or hot kisses. She had never been so embarrassed, so out of control. But, when Clark touched her, she had no idea who she was.

"Olivia," Clark called her name from outside the limousine.

Olivia forced herself to get out the car. For a moment, she forgot about her embarrassment, forgot about the still lingering sparks in her body from Clark's kisses, because she was looking at paradise. The limousine had stopped in front of a white spilt-level ranch house, with a wraparound porch, that was surrounded by rolling, green hills and towering redwoods. The air even smelled more fresh, more crisp than any air she had smelled before. Olivia had never been a "nature person." She got the shakes if she didn't have a Starbucks coffee in her hand by nine o'clock every morning, but she knew that she was looking at heaven.

Olivia turned from the view and the embarrassment returned as an older man, who stood next to Clark, stared at her. He wore faded jeans, scuffed cowboy boots, and a plaid shirt. He even wore a much-creased and obviously much-used cowboy hat. He looked like an older black version of the Marlboro man, tall, rugged, and unfazed by anything.

"Jarod, this is Olivia Hawkins," Clark introduced her, as if the two hadn't been clawing each other only moments earlier. "Liv, this is my father, Jarod Danforth."

"Nice to meet you," Olivia said, shaking the man's offered hand. His grip was strong and callused. Jack had mentioned that Clark and his stepfather were close, and Olivia could tell by Clark's easy smile at Jarod.

"You, too," Jarod murmured, examining her, with a set of unspoken questions in his dark eyes, no doubt wondering where his Hollywood-perfect stepson had found her.

Olivia was saved by a high-pitched shriek and then an older woman ran from the house toward Clark. Olivia couldn't help but smile as the woman threw her arms around Clark, the love evident on her lined dark brown face. She looked like Clark, dark chocolate, perfect, and beautiful. Even with silver threaded through her black, short hair, with her thin, athletic figure, she could have given the twenty-one-year-old women on the cover of magazines a run for their money.

"Mom, you look great," Clark said, while planting a kiss on her forehead.

Clarice Danforth smiled, then hugged him again. "I'm so happy to see you, baby. I wish Jarod and I didn't have dinner plans with the Brosnans tonight. . . . If you had told us sooner that you were coming. Maybe we should cancel—"

"Don't worry about it, Mom," he said, gently, as he brushed strands of hair from Clarice's eyes. "Besides, I'll be at Steve and Dominique's for most of the night, and I have to leave early in the morning for Scotland."

Olivia's heart pounded at the gentle tone in his voice. Clark was apparently capable of gentleness. Olivia swallowed the sudden lump of arousal and embarrassment in her throat because she realized that she had just experienced a different form of Clark's gentleness in the backseat of the limousine.

"How was the drive?" Clarice asked her son.

"Very interesting," Clark responded, as his gaze drifted to Olivia. She averted her gaze in embarrassment when his mother turned to her.

"This is Olivia Hawkins," Jarod performed the introductions since Clark was unwilling or unable to, as his eyes silently kissed her still swollen and tingling lips.

"Hello, Olivia," Clarice said, with an open smile.

"I work for Clark," Olivia blurted out. When Clarice and Jarod glanced at each other, Olivia shook her head in dismay and said quickly, "I mean, I don't work for him *like that*, I don't work for him at all. . . . My brother, Jack, is a publicist, and I'm here in his place in a strictly professional, business capacity."

Clarice's eyes crinkled at the corners, like Clark's, as she smiled and asked, "Would you like homemade brownies and milk in a strictly professional, business capacity?"

Olivia smiled sheepishly then relaxed and said, "That sounds good."

Clarice linked an arm through Olivia's arm and led her toward the kitchen. Olivia glanced over her shoulder to see Jarod leading Clark in the opposite direction. She tried not to feel disappointed. She told herself that she could handle being away from Clark, despite his ability to make a woman want to holler.

3

Olivia stared at her reflection in the full-length mirror and frowned at the too-tight jeans she had been forced to wear. Clarice had offered Olivia jeans, a T-shirt, and boots so that Olivia could change from her suit, which didn't exactly fit the horse-and-straw surroundings of Red Creek. Olivia hadn't wanted to change. Her suit was like her armor and had been the only reason she hadn't been caught in the backseat of the limousine with Clark in between her legs, rather than just on top of her. But, it had been difficult for Olivia to refuse the older woman, another trait Clarice shared with Clark.

Olivia sucked in her stomach then managed to snap the jeans closed. She vowed to start her diet immediately . . . although, it would have to be tomorrow, since she had eaten three of Clarice's caramel fudge brownies earlier. She shook her head and immediately reached for the button to wrestle the jeans off. There was no way she could leave the room, looking like this. The tightest clothes that Olivia owned were exercise clothes and she only wore those to clean the house. Just as she started to unbutton the pants, there was a knock on the door.

Olivia's throat clogged as she froze. Clarice and Jarod had already reluctantly left for their friends' house, so Olivia knew it wasn't either one of them on the other side of the door. She hadn't seen Clark in a couple of hours, and she had assumed—or, maybe, hoped—that he had already gone to his friends' party without her. But, the truth was that Clark was outside the door, and he was going to finish what they started in the limousine. She knew it, how a woman always knew when a man planned to finish the unfinished. Olivia was scared of Clark, of his mastery over her body. A few minutes in the limousine and she had changed from a respectable, conservative college professor into a woman who begged. No man should have that much power over her, especially a man she would probably never see again after today. And because she was powerless, she found herself walking to the door and opening it.

Olivia gasped when she saw him. He had changed, too, and now wore worn blue jeans, a long-sleeved shirt, boots, and a black cowboy hat. He should have looked comical, like a Hollywood star playing dress-up, but this was the real Clark Stone. Every unbelievable sexy inch of him.

Clark barely shot a glance in her direction before he looked around the room and whistled. Clarice had placed Olivia in Clark's boyhood bedroom, which included all of his old football trophies and awards, posters of athletes and Janet Jackson, and the military camouflage bedspread.

"I can't believe Mom hasn't changed this room since I was

eighteen years old," Clark said, walking into the bedroom. "I haven't really looked in here since Mom started putting me in the guest bedroom downstairs."

Olivia closed the door behind him, and the room grew smaller, until she felt there was no inch of the room not filled with Clark.

"You played football? Football jocks and drama geeks don't eat at the same lunch table in school. How did you get involved with acting?" she croaked, attempting to be normal around him. Just because her body was overheated with need for him and honey dripped from her body at the sight of him didn't mean that she couldn't attempt to have a normal conversation.

"For the first twenty years of my life, I breathed, ate, drank, and slept football," he said, his gaze still roaming around the bedroom. "I had a football scholarship, and things were going great, until I injured my knee junior year. Before the injury though, I needed a few extra credits and a drama class fit my schedule—I didn't have to wake up too early or stay too late—and it fit, like football never had . . . hey, I thought I had lost this."

He walked across the room in a daze, then grabbed a stuffed animal that rested on a built-in shelf. Olivia laughed at the amazement and joy on his face. He turned to her, clutching the toy, then his smile faded. His whole expression faded and the toy fell forgotten from his hand. Clark's gaze grew as hot as a blazing forest fire as he stared from her feet to her mouth, taking in the too-tight clothes. He became so still that Olivia wondered if he still breathed.

He drawled softly, "You make one hell of a cowboy."

Olivia couldn't help but smile, as emotions flooded her stomach then drained directly to ache between her legs like a radar-guided missile. "That's the best compliment I think I've ever received."

Clark laughed softly and moved toward her. For the first time that day, Olivia had no intention of going anywhere. She was exactly where she wanted to be. This whole day had been a fantasy, one day where she wasn't Olivia, the conservative English literature professor, but she was a woman who was wanted by a man. A man, who happened to be Clark Stone, but more importantly, a man she was in love with. Olivia took a deep breath when she realized it was the truth. She was in love with Clark. She probably had been since two months ago when she accidentally spilled red punch on the front of his white shirt during dinner. He hadn't gotten mad. In fact, he had pretended to be bleeding and proceeded to die spectacularly in front of her small cousins, much to their disturbing delight. As twisted as it was, that was the moment she had fallen.

He caressed her right cheek, and the touch shot through her body like a bolt of lighting. Her body had always known she was in love with him. She had just refused to accept it. His voice was husky, as he said, "Liv—"

"I know," she whispered. She closed the distance between them and pressed herself against his chest, her hands wrapping around his thick, strong neck.

Clark immediately stopped the strange thoughts coursing through his mind about possession—because he didn't believe in possession. He liked no-strings-attached, no expectations. But, then he nipped her lips. It was sweet and entirely too short, and possession became desire and something else that curled around his body and filled his groin. Her gaze searched his face before she licked his bottom lip. Clark framed her face with his hands because he had tasted perfection and nothing on earth would stop him from tasting her again.

His tongue dipped into her open mouth, searching the sweetness and reveling in the slick warmth. His hands moved down her back to cup her behind through the hard, thick denim. She moaned in pleasure and it was a sign for him to move closer, to slant his head, and to plunge his tongue deeper into her mouth.

Her hands moved to curl around his neck, the soft pillow of her breasts pressing against his hard chest. The kiss deepened, became carnal and erotic, and became its own show, not just the precursor to the main event. Then she subtly moved her hips against his, her heat drawing his hardness. He couldn't get enough of her mouth.

Clark slowly removed his hands from the softness of her body, slowly pulled his mouth from hers, even as his tongue reached for one last dip in her mouth. Olivia stared at him, her hand moving to cover her mouth, over her swollen lips, which was a blessing in disguise because Clark couldn't stare at her lips and not want to taste them.

Her hands dropped hesitantly from her mouth, and she whispered, "Clark—"

Clark kissed her again because he couldn't not kiss her again. She gasped in his mouth as her hands grasped his shirt and pulled him close. His hands went to the hem of her T-shirt. He needed to feel her skin. He felt like a primitive hunter with one, primal thought dominating all else. Her. He had thought about her too long, he had wanted her for too long, even though he hadn't known it. He lifted the hem and when his hands touched the soft skin of her stomach, he shuddered in awe. Her skin was like rose petals, soft and gentle.

Her mouth ravaged his. He didn't know when he lost control of the kiss, but he did. She had taken control. Her hands roamed over his head, her mouth plundered his. Her hands were everywhere, sliding over his skin, holding him tight. And he smiled into her mouth, right before she devoured him again.

His hands traveled under the T-shirt. He found himself hesitating, even though he never hesitated when it came to getting what he wanted. One of her knees moved in between his legs and that was a green light he was unable to resist. His hand touched one lace-covered breast and the softness made him mutter a curse. His other hand moved to the bare, soft round skin above her waistband. He tried to squeeze a finger under the waistband, but the fit was too tight, and it made him think of other tight spots. He almost exploded on the spot.

She moaned into his mouth, and his hands continued their erotic perusal. Skimming and squeezing and caressing the pliant flesh of her breast and her stomach. His mouth accepted her sweet assault, while his hands moved closer and closer to the source of her heat. He had never been this taut, this ready. And then through the heavy denim he felt her, her heat, her wetness soaking the material. She shuddered against him and her hips bucked.

Her knee stopped moving and settled—almost painfully—on his hardness. It was as if there were no clothes between them, he felt every touch, every scratch, as if he was nude. He groaned from the need to bury himself inside of her. He was on the edge of no return. He wanted to be gentle and sweet, but he was breathing too hard and shaking too much.

"Liv, if you don't want this, we should stop. Now. I don't want to hurt you," Clark whispered, his voice harsh.

Olivia moved onto the bed and stared at him. She stretched, drawing his attention to her breasts, to her legs, to the area between her legs.

"Then don't hurt me," she whispered, finally, then stretched out her arms to him.

Her soft words tore a hole through the sensual fog that had blocked out all other thoughts since he had seen her in those jeans. What was he doing? He was almost between her legs, and he hadn't even had the Clark-Stone presex talk. He never forgot "the talk," where he explained to a woman that he was not the forever-type or even the second-date type. "The talk" left him blameless in the face of any hurt feelings because he could always say that the woman had known the score. Of course, some women hadn't exactly bought that defense the next morning, and there had been a few unpleasant incidents that he preferred not to think about, but Clark felt it worked more often than not. He had "the talk" down to a science, but staring into Olivia's eyes, the words suddenly failed him.

"What is it?" Olivia asked, her arms falling to her sides, obviously noting his hesitation.

Clark said automatically, "I'm a busy man. I travel a lot for work. Making movies is the most important thing in my life right now and everything else—and everyone else—comes a distant second."

"What are you saying, Clark?" she asked, sounding confused, and Clark didn't blame her. He was confused himself.

He ran a hand over his hair then met her gaze. Something sharp stabbed into his heart at the trust he saw in her eyes. She trusted him. Of course, she trusted him. A woman like Olivia wouldn't have opened the bedroom door for him if she didn't trust him.

Clark coughed to force out the air trapped in his lungs, then said, "I don't want to mislead you. Tonight is all I have to give."

An unrecognizable emotion flashed across her eyes then she said simply, "I know."

He stared at her amazed, not truly believing what he had heard. "You know what?" he asked, hesitantly.

Olivia sounded amused as she said, "I know who and what you are. You're all about fantasy, and fantasy is a one-night thing. It's hard to keep the fantasy alive in the face of mortgages, broken water heaters, indigestion, and all those other things that make up day-to-day life. I don't want to think about that other stuff tonight. Tonight, I just want you."

Clark stiffened because he could deal with reality just as much as the next guy. Or at least he thought he could. It had been so long since he had been forced to a small part of him wondered if Olivia was right.

"But, what about a relationship?" he sputtered.

"A relationship," she said, sounding as if she had never heard of the word.

"Don't women like you require a relationship?" he sputtered.

She laughed and murmured, "If I didn't think you meant that as a compliment, I would be seriously insulted right now."

"Olivia—"

She held out her arms again and said softly, "Clark, we only have tonight."

Clark would have been a fool to resist that plea, and he was many things, but he wasn't a fool. He pushed aside his hesitation.

"The talk" had gone better than expected, and he had nothing to worry about. So why was he still standing across the room while Olivia laid on the bed?

He was almost frozen by indecision, just by the sight of her on the bed, laid out how he had dreamed. He wanted to start by tasting her breasts, but he also wanted to start by exploring her beautiful mouth. Finally, he moved onto the bed, hovering above her, staring at her slightly swollen, glistening lips and her hot eyes.

Olivia apparently grew tired of his inability to make a decision and pulled him to her. Her mouth ravaged his, as her fingers wildly flew to the buttons of his shirt. He didn't know when he lost control of his fantasy, but Olivia had taken control and made him her fantasy. Her hands roamed over his close-shaven dark hair, her fingernails raking through the silky stubble, making him moan into her mouth. Her mouth plundered his. Her hands were everywhere, sliding over his skin, holding him tight. She paused for a moment to pull his shirt off his shoulders and throw it to the floor. He smiled at the admiring look she gave his chest, right before she devoured him again.

She whispered his name, and something else incomprehensible, and Clark struggled with the buttons on her pants. He heard her soft laughter as she watched his hands. He finally got the jeans and the clinging underwear off her, and they both sighed when he touched her soft and wet curls. Heat and arousal steamed through his body, causing him to curse against her mouth.

He explored her wetness with one long finger, pumping in and out of her, swearing as her body greedily clung to his finger. Her whispers of pleasure drove him on and on. He groaned with the need to bury himself inside of her, and he inhaled her unique female scent that sent him into a high fever. He couldn't slow down anymore, he couldn't be thoughtful, no matter how much he wanted.

Olivia could feel the tremble in Clark's hands as he moved slowly against her, mimicking how their love-making would be. She had never felt such lust, such a need to be filled by one man. Her hands fumbled with his pants, and he mumbled "no," as his hands dug into the bed sheets on either side of her head.

"Stop, baby," he groaned, as her hand reached into his pants, underneath his briefs.

Her eyes slid closed of their own accord when she felt his hardness. It wasn't just a dream. He wanted her, almost as much as she wanted him. She ran her hand down the length and released a deep moan of need when she felt the shape of him. He mumbled her name, as a needy plea, and his eyes closed.

"Wait," he pleaded, as Olivia guided him inside of her to the spot that ached for him.

The fit was tight and almost painful, but both sighed in relief that the excruciating wait was over. Olivia bit her bottom lip, her teeth sinking into the sensitive flesh, and squeezed her eyelids shut. For a moment, Clark didn't move. His hot, moist breath washed over her face as he balanced himself on his elbows above her, every muscle in his body quivering with strain. Then he moved. Testing. Olivia sighed his name and squeezed his bare, slick shoulders. It was heaven, it was hell, it was like nothing she had ever known.

He began to move—slow then faster. And faster. The pleasure stabbed Olivia in the pit of her stomach, as he plunged into her. Her body gripped him. Her legs quivered as she spread her thighs wider to accommodate him. He was thick and hot, and filled her like she hadn't known she wanted to be filled. Then Clark shuddered and collapsed on top of her. Olivia smiled and pressed a kiss on his damp forehead.

"I'm sorry, baby," he croaked, his voice hoarse. "I'll make it up to you."

She smiled, then nuzzled her face into his neck. Almost with Clark Stone was better than all-the-way with anyone else.

Clark splashed water on his face then looked at his reflection in the mirror above the sink. He was staring at a drowning man. He had known that it would be good with Olivia, but he hadn't known how good, how magical, as corny as it sounded.

Clark cursed then wiped his face with a towel and walked out the bathroom across the hall from his old bedroom. He closed the bedroom door behind him, just as Olivia was attempting to pull on the too-tight jeans, her body wriggling to a seductive tune in order to get them up over her hips. Her bra and T-shirt already covered her addictive brown skin, and Clark realized he hadn't explored her breasts nearly enough.

"Where are you going?" he demanded, as he unzipped his own pants that he had slipped on when he had walked to the bathroom.

Olivia turned to face him, her gaze instantly dropping to his manhood that was doing a valiant job of coming back to the land of the living. Her gaze instantly flew back to his eyes. He could see her visibly gather her composure before she said, "I thought you were leaving to go to your friends' party."

Maybe it was the almost dismissive note in her tone, or his own confusion about the feelings bubbling in his chest, but his jaw clenched in anger as he growled, "I'm not nearly done with you, Liv."

She held his gaze for a moment, before she looked away and said, "This shouldn't—"

"You regret what we just did?" he demanded.

"I don't regret anything that happened," she said, sounding just as angry as he felt. "Do you?" He immediately shook his head in response, but otherwise remained silent because he didn't know what he would say. She took a deep breath then said quietly, "I haven't been in this situation before—"

"Good," he snapped.

Her eyes narrowed as she looked at him, but she continued, "I don't know how I'm supposed to act after what we just did. You've been the perfect fantasy man, better than I could have dreamed myself."

"And?" he prodded, his anger increasing with each word.

"And as soon as we leave Red Creek, the fantasy will be over. You'll go back to your life, and I'll go back to mine."

He clenched his jaw in anger. He should have told her the truth right then—that he had dreamed about her since the first moment he saw her and that even after making love, he wanted her even more, but he was too angry. He was also too scared because a small part of him wondered if Olivia wanted the fantasy of Clark Stone, but not the reality. She wouldn't have been the first woman to tell him that.

Clark stalked across the room and grabbed her around the waist. Her eyes widened, as he gently, but forcefully, pushed her onto the bed. He was on her in an instant. He should have left the room because he was out of control, but he couldn't leave her right now if his life depended on it.

He grabbed her wrists and raised them above her head, trapping her hands against the sheets. She watched him, a mixture of confusion and surprise in her eyes.

"What are you doing?" she asked, breathlessly.

"Your fantasies may be over, but mine have just started," he told her, then ground his mouth against hers. He thought kissing her would relieve the unquenchable need to taste her, but it didn't. If anything, it drove him more insane. His hands tightened around her wrists and she winced, but that didn't stop him from drinking from her mouth, drawing the sweet essence of Olivia from her.

"This is insane, Clark," she whispered, attempting to turn her head away from his mouth.

"What's insane? Me, wanting you until I can't think straight? Or, you, wanting me just as much?" he asked, as he transferred both of her wrists to one hand and used his other hand to rip open the T-shirt, like one of the out-of-control men in his movies that he hunted down like animals. He pushed the cups of her bra under her breasts, and she began to struggle. His hardness roared back to life and poked into her soft stomach.

Her abrupt struggles only made her breasts jiggle invitingly. He bent over and drew one beaded nipple into his mouth, licking the salty sweetness of her skin. When she was moaning and wriggling under his tongue, he moved to the other breast. He didn't have nearly enough patience to be this close to her breasts, so he easily flipped her onto her stomach. He couldn't form words anymore as he stared at her smooth, unblemished back and the behind that had held his attention across the dining room. He pulled down the jeans and when she wriggled her hips, he knew she was just as crazy as he was.

He touched the twin globes then squeezed. His body twitched to be inside of her, and Clark pulled off her panties. He pulled a condom from his wallet and quickly sheathed himself, while she rubbed her thighs together on the bed. He gripped her hips and pulled her to her knees and hands on the bed. He bent over and nuzzled the curls and lips between her legs, inhaling her scent, becoming nearly giddy with it. Her struggles ceased as she moaned into a pillow near her face and her hands gripped the bed sheets.

Clark couldn't wait any longer. He gritted his teeth as he eased into her. She was still wet and hot, still willing. She moved around his body like a second skin, squeezing him hard, drinking from him. He heard her whimpers of pleasure as he began, deep and forceful. He thrust into her, using her, like he had never used any other woman. One hand reached around to play with her nipples, while the other hand moved to the bud of nerves between her legs that was tight and erect for him. He caught the bud and moved his fingers around it, gently squeezing and pulling. Olivia screamed his name as her hips moved in opposition to his, drawing him tighter and closer.

She grew tighter and hotter around him. Clark's hand at her breast grew almost abusive, rough and demanding, but Olivia seemed too involved in the pleasure to notice. He felt her contract around him before she screamed his name hoarsely. Clark rammed home a few more times before he strained soundlessly and lowered her to the bed, laying on top of her, still connected.

Silence, besides the sound of the leaves rustling in the wind outside the open bedroom windows, settled in the room as Clark rolled off her. Olivia tried not to cry out from the loss. Every nerve in her body was sensitive at that moment, every muscle screamed in pleasure and demanded to know what had taken her so long to find this. Clark left the bed and she heard him walk out the bedroom to the bathroom across the hall. Olivia kept her eyes trained on the ceiling because she hadn't even noticed when he put on protection, but she remembered not giving him time to do so the first time they made love. He returned a few moments later and crawled back into bed.

She glanced at him and found him watching her. She quickly clapped her hands over her head, realizing that her neat ponytail had come loose and her hair looked like . . . looked like she had been rolling around in a bed, having the time of her life. At least, she didn't have to worry about any makeup smearing, since she had sworn off the stuff, except for lip gloss and mascara, after a disastrous incident with eye shadow and blush in high school.

"You look beautiful," Clark said, quietly, moving her hands from her head.

"You're beautiful," she corrected him. "I'm average."

"Who told you that?" he asked, outraged.

"No one, but I'm a realist."

"Then let's be real, Liv, you're gorgeous," he said, as his hand rested on her right hip under the sheet. This time his touch was comforting and soothing.

"I've seen the women you date, Clark," she said, with a dry laugh. "I can't go to a grocery store without seeing your face on the cover of a magazine, with a beautiful woman draped around you. They're these specimens of perfection, which is why half the men in America are jealous of you. You have to admit that the average woman you date is . . . she's nothing like me."

"You're right," he said, softly. "You have a smile that would have driven Michangelo or Da Vinci crazy because they never would have been able to capture it on canvas. And your eyes, I've never seen such light and fire dance in anyone's eyes like they do yours. When you come, I see paradise in your eyes."

Olivia averted her eyes. If she didn't know that this was just a one night fantasy, she would have believed that Clark meant every word.

His voice lowered as he said softly, "I think that's why I was so out of control." His eyes were dark and troubled, as if he couldn't believe his own behavior. His gaze moved to her shoulders then her breasts and regret ravaged his face at the visible marks from his hands. "I'm sorry if I was too rough."

"You weren't," she said, with a slight smile.

He sounded uncertain as he said, "I've never lost it like that before. I've never been that selfish before." His hand dropped from her face as he whispered, "I'm sorry, baby, but you drive me crazy."

She smiled gently. "Somehow, I never imagined that when you told me I drive you crazy it would be in bed."

Clark sent her a lopsided grin, and Olivia's heart dipped.

"Are you talking dirty to me?" he teased.

"No," she said, firmly.

"You could in the future, you know," he murmured, his hand squeezing her hip. She stared at him, speechless. He glanced at the fading sunlight streaming into the windows and cursed. "We're going to be late."

Olivia attempted to speak, but her mind was still stuck on the words "future" and "we," as if they were a couple. Clark couldn't have meant it. This was fantasy; he had said exactly that before their first kiss. There was no "future," no "we," no matter how much her heart clung to the idea.

When Clark turned to her, Olivia said, "I'm going to take a shower."

"Is that an invitation?" he asked, eagerly.

Olivia laughed, but shook her head. She needed to be alone for a few minutes. She needed to give herself another reality check. She was falling for the fantasy, believing there was more than one night between them. She didn't want one night or, even, one month, she wanted the rest of her life. Her heart wouldn't settle for anything less, and her heart wouldn't survive anything less.

"I just thought that since I planned on taking a shower, too . . ." He pouted when she shook her head again. He begrudgingly nodded then said, "There are clean towels on the rack. We need to leave in half an hour."

Olivia grabbed one of the voluminous sheets and wrapped it snugly and securely around herself before she moved from the bed.

Clark openly watched her, his gaze glued to the knot at the top of the sheet. "If you're not letting me in the shower, at least, flash some skin."

"You've seen enough skin for now," she said, with a smile.

Clark grinned in response, and, if possible, Olivia fell in love a little more.

4

"I'd recognize that ugly mug anywhere," came the lazy, familiar drawl as Clark walked into the large yard behind the Tate two-story, rambling house.

The pronouncement was followed by a round of cheers and cowboy yells that made Clark grin. Steve Tate, Clark's best friend since kindergarten, pushed his way through the crowd of men and women and threw his arms around Clark.

Clark accepted the tight embrace from Steve and slapped him on the back. After the two had tried college for three years, he had convinced Steve to move to Los Angeles. Clark had begun the arduous task of trying to find work as a black male actor in Hollywood, while Steve had worked in construction and missed Dominique Gilbert. Steve and Dominique had pretended since the three were children that they were just friends, but once Steve left Red Creek and Dominique called him crying six months later, Steve had returned, and the two had moved in together, taking over Steve's parents' ranch, when the elder Tates retired to Oregon.

"Ladies and gentlemen," Steve shouted over the country music blasting from the stereo inside the house. The crowd of familiar faces quieted, and Steve clamped an arm on Clark's shoulder. "I present to you, Clark Stone, the ugliest thing to ever be grown in Red Creek."

Clark laughed then shook his head at Steve, who grinned and almost made Clark believe they were sixteen years old again, cruising Main Street on Saturday night and complaining that there was nothing to do. Then Clark looked at Olivia, who was standing at the back of the crowd, laughing at the reunion. Images of her hot, sweaty, and panting beneath him burned his eyes. There definitely hadn't been nights like that when he had been sixteen years old.

Clark pushed aside thoughts of Olivia and tangled sheets and accepted handshakes and embraces from the people he had known his whole life.

"Clark!" Dominique called, splitting the crowd with her scream. She threw her arms around him and he bent over to pick her up. She was petite, barely reaching the middle of his chest, but she had always been the one who had Clark and Steve jumping to do whatever she wanted. He set her down and grinned at her.

"All right, get back to your drinks and dancing," Steve ordered, waving people away from Clark. "Y'all act like you've never seen a world-famous actor before!"

There was more laughter, but the press of the crowd dissipated as people returned to the various picnic tables distributed around the yard, inside the house, or to the makeshift dance floor. Clark grabbed Olivia as she tried to follow the crowd. He wanted her with him. He was feeling predatory tonight, especially after noticing a few looks in her direction from other men in the crowd, who obviously sensed fresh meat. She sent him a questioning look, but before he could respond, Steve clapped him on the back.

"We're so glad you came, Clark," Dominique said, her hazel eyes twinkling with delight.

Clark looked at the beaming couple. Steve and Dominique had been together for so long that they were beginning to look alike. Same vanilla-colored skin, dark, curly hair, and hazel eyes. Steve was taller than Clark, but more thin, which prompted the nickname "Urkel" in high school; whereas, Dominique was petite and voluptuous, like a very short, very pretty version of Jessica Rabbit. Clark had never been jealous of Steve—Steve was the closest thing to a brother that Clark had ever had—but once in a while when Clark saw Dominique look at Steve like a woman looked at only one man in her life, Clark acknowledged the jealousy. Clark was surprised when he found himself glancing at Olivia and wondering—maybe, hoping—if she would ever look at him like that.

"I thought you couldn't make it," Steve said to Clark.

"I had to be here," Clark said, grinning at the couple. "It wouldn't give me the same unbridled joy to say I-told-you-so over the telephone."

Steve rolled his eyes in exasperation, while Dominique laughed. Steve said dryly, "You made a lucky guess twenty-plus years ago, and now I have to hear about it once a week."

"Lucky guess," Clark repeated, shaking his head, amused. "Any idiot with two eyes could see what was in store for you two."

"And any idiot with two eyes did see the truth," Steve muttered to Dominique, but loud enough for Clark and Olivia to hear. Olivia laughed, while Clark pretended to glower at Steve. Clark could act like a "Hollywood big-shot" outside of Red Creek, but when he returned home, there was no room for a big head.

"Hi," Dominique said, turning to Olivia, with a bright smile. Clark didn't miss the quizzical glance she shot at him, before she stuck out her hand to Olivia. "I'm Dominique Gilbert and this is my fiancé, Steve. If you want any dirt on Clark, just let us know. We're happy to dish."

Clark knew he had been rude in not introducing her, but the moment he said her name, his friends would know and then Clark would have to admit the truth—Olivia was more than one night.

Olivia shook her hand and said, "Nice to meet you both. I'm Olivia Hawkins, I'm a . . . friend of Clark's."

Steve embraced her, and Olivia visibly stiffened before she smiled and wrapped her arms around him. Clark frowned when Steve sent him a knowing wink, as if Steve knew exactly what he was thinking.

Steve reluctantly released Olivia and said, "Welcome to our soon-to-be home."

"You two have been living together for the last ten years," Clark said, laughing.

"Yeah, but now we're getting married," Dominique responded, as if that made the difference.

"How did he finally wear you down?" Clark asked, curiously.

Dominique shrugged then said, with a feigned sigh of exasperation, "When a man asks you the same question every night for a year, you finally either give in or move out."

"Good thing I'm persistent," Steve added then said to Dominique, "Why don't you show Liv some of those embarrassing pictures of Clark from junior high school."

Clark started to protest, but Dominique laughed gleefully and grabbed Olivia's hand. She said sweetly, "Steve and I only ask for thirty percent of any price you get for them from the tabloids."

Clark watched helplessly as Dominique dragged Olivia into the house. Olivia sent him a smile over her shoulder and Clark would have gone after her, half-dazed by arousal, but a strong hand clamped down on his shoulder. He shook his head in confusion then realized that Steve still stood next to him.

"You look like you could use a beer," Steve said, cheerfully.

Clark nodded then followed him across the yard, half-heartedly smiling at the friends who yelled to him. Steve grabbed two bottles of beer from a bucket filled with ice and bottles of beer and soda, then kept walking across the dirt field to the large red and white barn behind the house.

Clark accepted a bottle from Steve as he walked into the coolness of the barn, smelling of hay and horses. He stopped at the first stall and ran a hand down the nose of the large, softly whining horse. In the barn, the sounds of the party were far away, which meant that Olivia was far away.

"I remember when your father caught Dominique and me in here when we were fifteen," Clark murmured. "You were supposed to be lookout."

"I called him over and told him you two were in here," Steve said.

Clark laughed and stared at his best friend, amazed. "You did what? You claimed you didn't like her. You said you didn't care if I made out with her."

"I cared," he responded, simply, then added with a smile, "And I never left you alone with her again."

Clark shook his head in amusement, then turned from the horse and opened the bottle of beer. He took a long swig before he asked, "How's the ranch going?"

"It's tough work," he responded, his expression grave and almost worried. "We're getting by."

Clark had offered before, and had been turned down, but he still said, "If you need money—"

"I appreciate that the offer is there, man, but we're good," Steve quickly interrupted him, but sent Clark a grateful smile.

Clark nodded in understanding. If the tables had been turned, he wouldn't have accepted anything from Steve either. Red Creek men may have been poor, but they were proud. Clark changed the awkward subject and said sincerely, "You have a good life here."

Steve stared at him, surprised. "I should be saying that to you. You have the life that every man dreams about. Dominique showed me a magazine that had a picture of some actress you were dating. Man . . ." His voice trailed off as he shook his head in admiration.

Clark forced a smile, but didn't respond and continued to run his hand down the horse's snout. Steve asked, concerned, "What's wrong?"

"It's her."

"Olivia," Steve said instantly. When Clark looked at him surprised, Steve grinned. "You've never brought anyone back to Red Creek, and you've never—in all the years I've known you—looked like you were about to throw a temper tantrum because a woman walked away from you."

"It's that obvious?"

"It's kind of pathetic, isn't it? One day, you're a man, living your life, thinking you have some control. The next day... you're like a calf, stumbling around the range, bawling for his mama."

"Something like that," Clark murmured, trying not laugh at Steve's musings.

"You love her, don't you?" Steve asked, studying Clark carefully.

"This is not a good time," he responded, avoiding the question. "I'm doing good at the box office, but I can do better. I'm on the verge of breaking into the same leagues as the white actors—Tom Cruise, Arnold, Harrison Ford. I can be the best, but I can't be side-tracked or railroaded or tied down. Olivia would expect that, y'know. She'd expect me home with her... although, she'd understand better than anyone what I'd need to do to reach the top since her family has been in the industry for years. Her contacts could be an asset. She does make me feel like a normal man, and not like a freak. She's funny and smart... but, then there are the women. I'm supposed to give up all those women for her?"

"Who would want to give up one-night stands and fun times with some of the most beautiful women in the world for every night with one woman you can trust and depend on?" Steve agreed.

Clark was not amused as he glared at Steve, who tried to look innocent. Clark muttered, annoyed, "She teaches English at a community college in Los Angeles."

Clark laughed, as Steve said, appalled, "She's an English professor? You almost flunked English in high school."

"And I wouldn't be surprised if she had never seen one of my movies," he muttered, then drained the rest of his beer and tossed the empty bottle in a bin near the door. "Even the president of the United States has seen my movies."

"Someone who hasn't seen your movies?" Steve's disbelief was so energetic and dramatic that Clark almost didn't believe him.

"Yes, I'm in love with her. Satisfied?" Clark muttered, which prompted Steve to burst into hysterical laughter. "It's not that funny, Steve."

"You're right. What would be truly funny is seeing you up to your elbows in dirty diapers. Now, that's a picture I would pay to see on the cover of *People* magazine."

"You know, there are some people who would pay to be my friend and wouldn't give me half the problems you do," Clark shot back.

Steve laughed, then opened his beer. "Now, use those acting skills, paste a smile on your face, come eat some barbeque and get back to your woman. There are a lot of single men in Red Creek."

"I need to think," Clark said, shaking his head. Steve's smile faded, as if he finally took Clark's angst seriously, then he nodded and left the barn.

Clark's feelings were too raw and too foreign for him to be around Olivia right now. He would probably start sprouting poetry or vowing to give up his wild ways. Then he realized that he had given up his wild ways. He hadn't been in the tabloids in five months because of her, not because Jack had been babysitting him. The truth was that Clark didn't think about anything anymore, except Olivia. Going out didn't hold the same allure. He would sit in the bars for a few painful hours and then he would leave disgusted with himself and disgusted with the bar. He had finally stopped going a few months ago. His life had been minivans and oatmeal cookies for a long time, and he hadn't even realized it.

"Clark," came Olivia's soft voice behind him.

Clark whirled around and as soon as he saw her, he cursed Steve, who had no doubt sent her to the barn. He still wasn't prepared to face her, except there was nowhere else in the world he'd rather be than standing with her in this hay-strewn, dusty barn, with the musty horses around them, singing to them. As far as Clark was concerned, it was better than any candlelit, five-star hotel room.

"I've never been inside a barn before," she said, glancing around the dark interior, lit by the moonlight through the open doors and open windows. She turned to Clark and he instantly looked away from her. She mused, "Seeing you around your family and friends . . . you're nothing like I thought you were."

"How did you think I would be?" At her guilty look, he laughed and said, "I guess I don't want to know. Is that why you always avoided me? You thought I was as bad as the tabloids paint me out to be."

"I didn't avoid you," she protested.

"Yes, you did—"

"That is not true, Clark," she said, laughing in disbelief. "I couldn't avoid you because you never looked at me. You never spoke to me, and if we were alone in a room together, you would leave."

He became still, and his eyes glinted dangerously, causing Olivia to soundlessly gasp. Would she ever stop wanting this man? He said softly, "I wanted you even then, Liv."

"What?" she sputtered, shocked.

Olivia searched his face for any sign of his usual teasing, but all she saw was sincerity. He was an actor, Olivia knew he could fake any emotion, but she refused to believe that he could fake this. She noticed the gleam in his eyes that he tried to hide, as his gaze dropped to her breasts. It was lust, she told herself. Plain and simple. She refused to believe anything else.

Clark was suddenly a frenzy of motion as he moved toward her, setting off the whinnying of the horses in their various stalls, as if the animals sensed there was a dangerous man in their midst. Olivia took several defensive steps from him, then found herself backed against a stall door, a horse nudging her shoulder toward Clark, who had stopped in front of her, his hardness a tent in the front of his jeans, the only part of him that touched her.

His intense gaze bored into her as he said, "We have a few hours left before I have to leave."

Olivia tried not to react visibly to the pain that slammed into her. Nothing had changed in the last few hours, no matter how much she had hoped. She had fallen more in love with Clark since entering Red Creek, and he was still living in the fantasy. Olivia knew that he felt something for her, she could feel it in his touch and see it in his eyes, but he had made it clear from the beginning that this was a one-night deal. One all-night fantasy. And whatever Clark felt for her was obviously not enough to change that, no matter how much she loved him.

Because she had the right for tonight, Olivia touched his warm, rough cheek. Clark's nostrils flared as if her touch literally took his breath. Olivia sighed in acceptance. She would dwell on her stupidity tomorrow. Now, she would allow herself to make memories to keep her warm for the next sixty years. And when they were done making love, she would get away from him as soon as possible; otherwise, she would beg Clark to give her a chance and Olivia didn't want to see the pity in his beautiful eyes as he explained to her once more that his life could never include her.

Olivia inhaled deeply then murmured, "If we only have a few hours left, why are we still talking?"

He didn't respond, but instead grabbed a thick plaid blanket off a nearby tack then motioned toward a ladder that led to the hayloft.

"Have you ever made love in a hayloft?" he asked, with a devilish gleam in his eyes.

Olivia grinned as she shook her head. She should have never come to the barn. She was still tender, still worn out from their previous exertions, but in a day, he had become as important to her as oxygen. She wasn't complete unless he was near her or inside of her.

"No, I haven't," she said, softly.

"Me either," he said, then began to climb the ladder. Olivia took a deep breath, then followed him. He stepped onto the loft and then grabbed her hands and pulled her past the last four rungs of the ladder, until she stood on the loft.

Clark eagerly spread out the blanket then laid on it, propping on his elbows to watch her. For a moment, Olivia was nervous, wondering what would happen tomorrow in the light of day, or if any of the partygoers would come to the barn. But, then Clark held out his hand. Olivia was helpless to resist him. Ever. She slowly straddled him. He felt right underneath her, and he was hers, if only for tonight.

Since he seemed content to simply hold her, Olivia moved first, ravaging his mouth, reacquainting herself with the taste of him. Then his hands were on her, touching her over and under her clothes, branding her. Olivia should have been ashamed of her body's reaction to Clark, of how quickly he could arouse her—with a look, a touch, a movement, but she couldn't feel the shame. Maybe tomorrow, but tonight her hands just went to his shirt. She averted her eyes from his direct gaze and unbuttoned his shirt, one button at a time, to reveal his soft skin over hard muscle that women across the world sighed over in dark movie theatres.

With a reverence that Olivia only showed to rare books, she gently pushed his shirt off his shoulders and allowed it to pool to the ground as her hands ran across the smooth hardness of his chest. He was still, his eyes watching her. If she hadn't felt the slight tremor pass underneath her hands each time her fingertips brushed across his nipples, she would have thought he felt nothing. Then she met his dark eyes. There was lust and a pleasure-pain that awed her with the proof of her effect on him, not to mention the bulge in his jeans that made her mouth dry.

Clark abruptly took her hands in his, when her hands touched the button to his jeans. "You can't do this to me again, Liv. I don't want to rush this."

"What do you want to do?" she whispered, meeting his gaze.

The soft smile on his face faded as he said huskily, "You."

"Oh."

He grinned and she wondered if that was the right thing to say or the wrong thing to say. He torturously and slowly drew the T-shirt over her head. Next, his hands moved to the waistband of the jeans. His gaze held hers as he slowly pushed the pants down, an expert at removing the tight denim now, as if he had all the time in the world. And maybe they did because for all Olivia knew the rest of the world had ceased to exist. She already had lost track of time, of anything outside them and the hayloft. His fingers skimmed across her skin as he pulled the jeans down her legs, then rose to his knees to yank them from around her ankles.

Olivia suddenly felt self-conscious as Clark openly stared at her body. He was perfect, hours obviously spent working out. A six-pack did not come naturally. Olivia exercised only when forced and had her share of a thirty-year-old woman's physical imperfections. She hadn't had time to be self-conscious earlier because Clark hadn't given her time; he had torn at her clothes and been inside of her before she could form a coherent thought. But, now he was going slow, taking his time, and she didn't know if she could survive scrutiny from a man with one of the best bodies she had ever seen—in the movies or in real life.

Then Clark licked his lips and Olivia realized that he didn't care anything about her cellulite because he was too busy worshipping her smooth skin. Olivia suddenly felt a different type of insecurity. Probably how most women felt when they stared at a big man who had set his sights on her, and she realized there was nothing she could do about it.

"The magic of haylofts has been greatly underreported," he whispered, his eyes trained on the triangle that her panties covered.

Olivia smiled as she pressed her thighs together, covering what Clark stared at so hard.

His gaze moved to her face as he said with a slight smile, "You aren't getting shy on me now, are you, Liv? Not after everything we did earlier."

"No," she retorted, sounding entirely too stiff to be laying on a blanket in the middle of a pile of straw nearly nude. "What are you staring at?"

Her nerves must have been apparent because Clark paused in unbuttoning his pants and moved over her until they were face to face. In the moonlight streaming through the small, square windows in the hayloft, she saw how gentle his gaze was, and how honest it was.

"You," he said quietly, as he trailed one finger from her bottom lip, down her neck and to the spot in between her breasts where the clasp of her bra was. A path of butterflies followed his finger, causing her to unconsciously arch her back in response. His hand hovered above the bra clasp for a moment and he licked his lips again, as if she was a buffet he couldn't wait to dig in to. "You're beautiful, Liv, I should have told you that earlier. Beautiful, sexy, and so smart that you could embarrass a brother if he's not careful."

At her sigh of surrender, he unclasped her bra and her breasts spilled free. As if the sight of her breasts alone was the magic key to unlocking his reserve, Clark suddenly covered her, his big legs on either side of her body, the maleness of him hard and insistent against her bare thigh as his mouth covered hers. It was all she needed to forget her shyness, her fear that she wouldn't compare to his models. Instead, she felt beautiful and loved. His mouth raked across hers, alternating between soft nibbles and hard, bruising kisses that made her grasp his shoulders and silently beg for more. His lips pulled on hers, bathed hers, and massaged hers.

Her legs opened underneath his and he instantly settled in the space, as if he belonged there. While his mouth occupied hers in those hard, thorough kisses that made her shiver in need and lust, one of his hands snaked down her body. Goosebumps raised in the aftermath of his progress and she tensed in anticipation to the end of his journey. Through damp cotton, he rubbed the heart of her and she bucked against the movement of his slender and clever fingers.

"So soft," he whispered, against her mouth. He sounded almost wicked as he added in a deeper tone, "So wet."

Olivia whimpered again and tried to move one of her hands to touch him in return, but she ran into denim and moaned in protest.

"I want to touch you," she whispered into the darkness.

"Not yet," he said then took one breast into her mouth.

Olivia screamed his name into the night. His tongue was hot and wet and insistent as he suckled her nipple. His other hand moved aside the strip of panties in the way. The rush of cool air caused Olivia to lift her hips in ecstasy, partially to rid herself of the panties and partially to silently beg him to fill her. In partial response, his fingers began to trace the length of her swollen and wet nether lips.

His mouth moved to her other nipple, causing another involuntary buck of her hips, as one of his fingers slowly worked its way into her depths. Her eyes slid closed and her mouth dropped open in wordless pleasure at the feel of his long finger inside of her. He took that opportunity to kiss her again and his tongue began to thrust into her mouth, exactly like his finger.

A second finger joined the first and Olivia couldn't control the wild contortions of her body in response to the carnal feelings. She was going insane and if this was insanity, then she would gladly be a card-carrying member.

"Liv," Clark whispered, in a voice too deep to be real, as his fingers continued to confine her in a sensual prison. "I want to taste you," he whispered, the words barely piercing through the haze of sensual need and delirium. He kissed her once more, drugging her with his tongue and the fingers still working inside of her.

Olivia stared at him, wondering how she was supposed to have the power to respond. Her body no longer felt like her own—over the last twenty-four hours, she had ceded all power of it to him. He planted a kiss in the middle of her round belly then moved farther down.

She wriggled against the blanket, and his hands massaged her thighs, as if to calm her down, but that was impossible because he then gently pushed her legs wider apart. Olivia opened her eyes in time to see his head move between her thighs. She bit her bottom lip to hold in her scream at the first expert swipe of his tongue. It was followed by a longer, slower lick then a shorter one, and he continued to alternate his pace, never giving her a rest from the attack of sensations. Her body was now completely out of her control as the emotions built and intensified precisely where his tongue struck. His fingers moved inside of her again. His skillful tongue and his touch were all designed to drive her crazy, to make her lose whatever shred of control she thought she had left. It would have been humiliating, if it wasn't so wonderful.

Olivia couldn't stop her body. She wanted him, needed him. Her body gripped for him, not just his fingers.

"Clark, please," she gasped hoarsely.

He groaned deep in his throat. "You taste and feel so good," he murmured. "I could play with you down here all night."

"Clark, please," she said, more insistently.

He grinned, and she actually had the energy left to grin back at him as a shudder wracked her body. He stood, with a liquid-controlled grace that amazed her, and unbuttoned his pants. She was momentarily awed by the sight of him. He stood tall and proud and all-male. Dark, muscular, and arrogant as hell.

Clark pulled a condom from his wallet in the pocket of his pants, then crawled back onto the blanket. He was moving too slow, and after waiting too long, Olivia couldn't wait anymore. She grabbed his picture-perfect behind and squeezed.

That was apparently all the encouragement Clark needed. He closed his eyes and joined them with an unnerving precision. Olivia gasped in relief and pleasure as he filled her. She screamed as the emotions slammed into her center at the same time that he did. He was buried to the hilt and she drew up her knees to feel him deeper. It was a mistake on her part because then it all hit her like a cosmic force as Clark began to move, slowly and expertly, as if he had been loving her like this since the beginning of time.

It was as if they hadn't been with each other that morning, the passion and the desire was so new and too intense. They moved in sync, perfectly and erotically. Olivia moved her hands across his broad back to hold on to his shoulders. Her eyes opened briefly as the feel of his hardness, the feel of his warm, sweet breath on her face, combined with her feelings of love. Right before she gasped his name in completion, she saw something in his expression as he stared at her that made her wonder if this was about more than one night, if there were expectations. Then all thoughts fled her mind and her entire body tensed in the outpouring of pleasure. After a few more fluid thrusts, Clark froze above her, then whispered her name in a husky croak of reverence before he lay on top of her.

No words were needed. Olivia didn't need to be held or need to hear soft words of encouragement. She had felt and heard everything she needed.

5

"Mr. Stone? Mr. Stone, are you in here?"

Clark opened his eyes, momentarily disoriented, as he stared at the unfamiliar barn roof lit by bright sunlight and felt the unmistakable sting of straw pricking him in the bare ass. He wondered if it had been a dream, but it couldn't have been a dream because the last twenty-four hours with Olivia by his side had been better than anything he could have imagined. It had been better than signing his last multimillion dollar contract. Even though he had never won an Oscar, he knew it was better than winning an Oscar could ever be.

He had kissed Olivia and touched her because he *needed* to, not just to pass the time or because he was expected to. Being inside of her, kissing her, tasting her, it had been more than he had been prepared to handle and now he couldn't imagine another day without her. Even after a full night of loving her, the taste of her lingered on his lips and made him hard again. He instantly turned to Olivia, and he was surprised to find her space of the blanket empty.

"Mr. Stone?" came the voice again.

Clark cursed, recognizing Matt's voice. He frantically searched for his pants and slipped into them before he leaned over the edge of the loft. Matt stood in the middle of the barn, peering at the horses around him, very carefully. Clark snorted in amusement. City folk.

"Matt, where is Olivia?" Clark demanded.

Matt flinched in fear, before he realized that Clark was above him. "Mr. Stone, we have to get moving. Your flight for Scotland leaves—"

He repeated, his tone more demanding, "Where is Olivia?"

Matt was hesitant as he said, "She called me twenty minutes ago, and I took her to the train station. She's waiting for the nine o'clock train back to Los Angeles—"

"She left?" he asked, in disbelief. Had last night meant nothing to her? Was he going to have to accept just one night with her?

"Yes, sir."

Clark grabbed his shirt and half-climbed, half-fell down the ladder. As straw poked the bottom of his feet, he realized that he had left his boots above. He didn't stop, but grabbed Matt's shirt and said, "Take me to the train station right now!"

Matt hesitantly shook his head. "Ms. Hawkins told me to get you out of Red Creek and to the airport as soon as possible. Somehow, the paparazzi found out you were here. A whole herd of them are outside the gates of this ranch right now. If a bunch of your friends weren't standing around the gates, blocking the way, they'd all be in here right now—"

"I love that woman and you're going to take me to the train station right now so I can tell her."

Matt stared at him for a moment then nodded. Clark sighed in relief then started to run out the barn, but Matt grabbed his arm and said with a smile, "Could you, at least, put on your shirt? I would hate to have to explain to my mom back in Kansas City why there was a picture of me on the cover of *The Star* with a half-nude Clark Stone."

Clark nodded absently, put his shirt on backward, then raced out the barn barefoot toward the black limousine parked at the entrance.

Olivia heard the commotion outside the one-room Red Creek train station before she saw Clark tearing into the station, with a pack of reporters hot on his heels. His bare heels, she noted confused. She stared at him, horrified, uncertain how to feel, how to react.

Clark spotted her sitting in the corner of the train station, and he ran toward her. Lights flashed in her eyes as cameras went off around her. Clark appeared oblivious to the fifteen extra people and the cameras behind him, as he focused on her.

"Were you really going to leave me?" Clark demanded, the moment he reached her.

Olivia stared uncertainly at the large camera lenses, but Clark gently turned her chin until she met his eyes. For the first time, she allowed herself to see the love in his eyes. It was time for her to believe in herself and their love. The feelings between them were too powerful and all-consuming to be anything but once-in-a-lifetime love.

"They don't matter," he said softly. "No one else matters, except you and me. Why'd you leave?"

"You told me that it was a fantasy. I thought that you didn't want anything more than one night."

"When did I say that?" he croaked, in disbelief.

"In the limousine before we kissed, and in your old bedroom, in the barn—"

He interrupted her impatiently, "In the barn, I was too crazed with wanting you, but I meant to tell you then—I should have told you at the airport—I've been in love with you since the first moment I saw you, Liv."

"Really?" she whispered, as tears filled her eyes. The crowd of reporters pressed closer, sensing a cover story.

"I still remember it. You were wearing a gray dress and eyeglasses. Your hair was in a funny, little bun. You looked like a librarian," he said, with a soft laugh. "I didn't know it was love, I didn't know what it was, I just tried to ignore you and hoped that the feeling would go away. But, now, for the first time in months, I know exactly what I've been feeling. I'm in love with you, Liv."

She stared at him, her mouth open in surprise. She forgot the cameras, forgot the excited reporters, and the gaping train station employees. She forgot everyone, except Clark. There was so much love flooding her throat that she couldn't speak.

Clark mistook her silence for hesitation. His expression fell, and he gripped her hands and urged, "Yesterday, you gave me a taste of what it would be like to have you in my life, and I can't go back to how it was without you. I'll break my water heater if you want, and I always have indigestion. I can be real for you. Just give me a chance. Tell me you want me, too, Liv. I know you hate the industry, but not everything about it is bad. I'll cut back on the number of films I do, I've always wanted to do independent films. . . . We can make it work, just tell me what to do, and I'll do it—"

"I love you, Clark," she blurted out then laughed at the wide smile that crossed his face. "I don't want to change anything about you. Not one arrogant inch."

He laughed, then framed her face with his hands and rained kisses on her cheeks and forehead. She wrapped her arms around his neck and the two kissed, prompting a round of applause and hoots from the crowd. As soon as they parted, the reporters proceeded to shout incomprehensible questions at them. It was madness and Olivia loved every second of it because she was with Clark.

"Come with me to Scotland," he pleaded, as if the two stood alone in the room. His arms moved around her waist like a clamp, as if she had any intention of ever leaving him. "I heard it's beautiful. It can be our honeymoon. You can return to the states, in time to start fall classes at the college."

"Honeymoon?" She giggled in absolute glee and happiness.

"Marry me, Liv. Let's live in this fantasy for the rest of our lives."

Olivia laughed then bobbed her head up and down in response, too overwhelmed by emotion to speak. She would have never thought that after spending twenty-four hours with a man she thought she despised, all of her dreams would come true. Dreams that she hadn't even realized she had. Clark whooped like a true Red Creek cowboy, which prompted the other Red Creek citizens—friends and neighbors who had heard about the drama and poured into the station—to follow his lead. The station filled with the sounds of flashing cameras, cowboys yelling, and laughter.

Olivia laughed at the mayhem, then whispered into Clark's ear, "Somehow, I doubt this is what my brother had in mind when he told me to make certain that you keep a low profile this weekend."

Clark laughed and kissed her again, just to make certain that all the cameras got the shot.